RAVEN

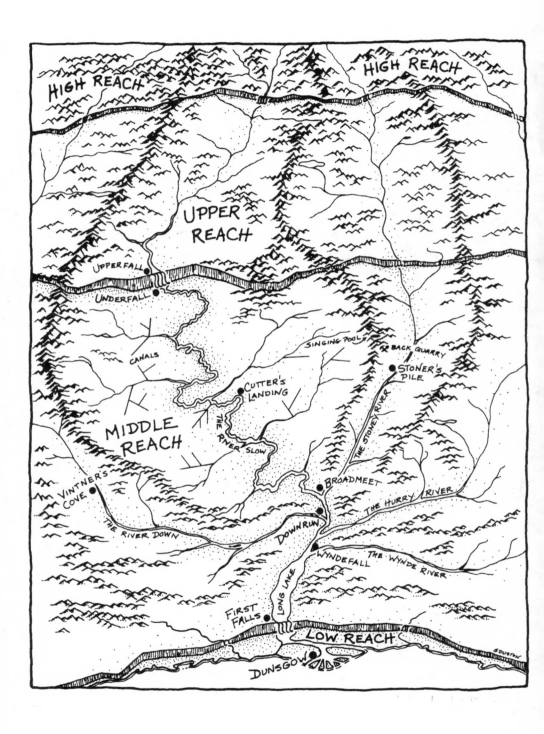

RAVEN

by Dean Whitlock

Clarion Books * New York

Clarion Books
a Houghton Mifflin Company imprint
215 Park Avenue South, New York, NY 10003
Copyright © 2007 by Dean Whitlock
Map copyright © 2007 by Sally Duston Whitlock

The text was set in 11-point Meridien Roman.

www.clarionbooks.com

Printed in the U.S.A.

Library of Congress Cataloging-in-Publication Data

Whitlock, Dean.
Raven / Dean Whitlock.
        p. cm.
Summary: Raven, a shape-shifting mage, is determined to save her baby
half sister Sarita from the evil Steward and his son, who are equally
determined to get rid of the baby and take her inheritance for themselves.
ISBN-13: 978-0-618-70224-4
ISBN-10: 0-618-70224-5
[1. Birds—Fiction. 2. Magic—Fiction. 3. Fantasy.]   I. Title.
PZ7.W59167Rav 2007   [Fic]—dc22
2006027348

MP 10 9 8 7 6 5 4 3 2

For Trina

A great mage, and the first to ask for Raven's story

One

A light sea breeze sped Raven out of the grimy haze that cloaked Dunsgow. With a croak of relief, she left the city's spewing chimneys behind, winging quickly above the broad river toward the immense cliff that marked the inland boundary of the low reach. Flattening her black wings, she soared effortlessly up and up the sheer drop, just outside the curtain of mist that billowed from the great crush of waterfall plunging into the pool at the bottom. Finally, she topped the lip and could see the middle reach again after so many months. Long Lake stretched its sixteen blue leagues toward the mountains. Sails and steamboats dotted the water. Wavelets rolled in the breeze. With a joyful dip of her tail, she turned a somersault and flew on.

Soon the lake narrowed into the Big River. It was still several leagues wide at this point, but rugged hills crowded its banks. With her sharp eyes, Raven could see the upriver ridge lines growing wider and taller, till they vanished into the unseeable distance. Beyond them, she knew, stood another towering cliff, then the length of the upper reach, then the final cliff and, finally, the rugged high reach at the base of the mountains. A place where magic was strong, a very part of river and stone. She soared above the western ridge line and flew steadily onward. Raven felt strong herself, and full of life. The brisk, clear air was a joy to fly through, a gift to breathe. She'd been cooped up far too long in crowded, filthy Dunsgow.

Cities are for pigeons, she thought. A raven needs country, mountains, big rivers, a bigger sky.

Raven spotted Wyndefall ahead, where the ridge branched

into a second valley and the Wynde River flowed into the Big. As she flew past, she heard the squabbling of a council of crows. She turned and followed the racket and found them clustered around a half-eaten deer carcass in a little clearing.

Just like the council of humans in Dunsgow, she thought scornfully. Since last fall, Raven had played messenger for Paskovek, the council moderator, and she was sick of such pecking and posing. As far as she was concerned, anyone who wanted to be a councilor was the last person you could trust with the job: corrupt, power hungry, or simply self-centered. The worst of them treated her like an errand girl, with no more respect than they'd show to a homing pigeon. She had one last message to deliver, but never again! And afterward, who knew? She could follow the ridge line all the way to the highest peak on the high reach if it suited her fancy. Maybe there she could finally master her talent, and find work more suitable for a bird mage.

Raven calmed the crows with just a few words of command and joined them. Yes, using her talent was easier here, just one reach higher than Dunsgow. Even the food was better: The first bite of raw venison tasted every bit as good as the fresh air. She ate her fill, flew to a nearby stream to drink, and sat a few minutes preening in the top of a budding ash tree before heading upriver again.

Raven could fly fifty leagues in a day if she needed to. She was in no real hurry now, but she pressed on, sailing tirelessly on the currents of wind that swirled above the ridge. It branched again as she passed the junction of the Hurry River on the right, and again at the River Down on the left. Here the river was called the Stoney-Slow. It was still broad and steady, for all that it lacked the inflow from three of its five tributaries. Boats of every kind carved its surface, heading upriver and down. At midday, she reached Broadmeet, an ugly burgh straddling the final branching of the ridge line, the great Y where the Stoney River and the River Slow came together. Traveling upstream was like flying backward through time, seeing the great river divide into its five parts, watching a tree return to its roots.

Raven gave a wide berth to the pall of chimney smoke that hung above Broadmeet, and then she was over the River Slow. Baron Cutter's river.

And he can have it, she thought.

The widest and broadest of the five rivers, the Slow curved back and forth in great sweeping oxbows through swathes of pasture and hay field for Baron Cutter's herds of cattle. The wide valley was brown and bare now; hints of green showed only in the sunniest spots. The spring thaw was young here, and the swollen river sprawled muddy along the lower fields.

Raven could admire the sweep of the valley, but it gave her no joy to return. She had run away from Baron Cutter four years earlier. She'd been back only once, and forced to flee again, helping two friends escape. But she had promised one of them, Fireboy, that she would carry a message to his family. That meant flying through the heart of the valley, right to Cutter's estate. She'd been a servant there, a bondservant, working to pay off a debt that was three generations old. Every hour of labor went toward paying that bond, but it never seemed to do any good. Wagehands actually saw a few coins; bondservants saw nothing but more debt. Not that it made much difference to Cutter. He cared more for his cattle than he did for any worker.

"Kah!" Raven clacked her beak. She hated the man, and hated her memories of this valley. She almost wished she hadn't promised to deliver the message. Except that her mother was here.

Raven hadn't seen her mother in four years, and still wasn't sure she wanted to now. But there were questions she wanted answered, questions for her mother. If Raven could bring herself to ask them. She felt a burst of anger whenever she remembered her final night at the manor, the night she ran away. It was still that hard to think about.

Raven flexed her wings and let herself stall. She fell a hundred feet, then twisted up and out in a hard backward roll, burning off uncertainty in a flurry of loops and dives. Feeling a little better, she leveled off and continued upriver.

She spent the night on an island where the river had cut an oxbow so deep that it met itself on the return loop. The next day she flew over scores of farms and several villages. Men and women worked at the boat landings and in the fields and kitchen gardens. And everywhere there were cattle, in pastures, pens, and barns. Dull eyed and skinny after the long winter, the leftovers from last fall's slaughter, they chewed calmly at the stubble.

"Eat slowly," Raven called. "The sooner you fatten, the sooner you die!" She dove at a placid steer. "Stay stringy! Make the bloated Baron chew! And that goes for you and your auntie, too, Flat Face!" she added to a startled farmhand.

The steer snorted indignantly, then went back to chewing. The farmhand gaped. Raven soared away, chortling.

She reached Cutter's Landing in midafternoon. She spotted the meat house first, sprawling along the riverbank a league downstream of the manor house and farm. It was as big as some of the villages she'd passed, with its feedlots, smokehouses, pickling sheds, and lodgings. Swirling flocks of starlings, crows, and cowbirds gorged themselves at the offal pits behind a screen of trees inland. Raven hurried past, to the Landing proper, where a tree-lined road led from the wharf through plowed fields to the walled manor. The sight of the house brought an unexpected thickness to her throat. She had spent most of her life in the back wing of this gray T-shaped stone mansion. From the air, it looked small and uninviting, but it had been home. She spotted a groom she knew in the shadow of the open stable, and recognized one of the three scullions turning a spit on the outside fire. And there in the side yard, where a cluster of dwarf cedars ringed a white gravel path and a circle of grass, was a woman seated on a stone bench.

Raven faltered. The woman wore clothing that was much too rich for a bondservant, but she was grayfolk and small and held her head at a proud, familiar angle. Raven looped back and looked again. At that moment, the woman turned toward the house. The sun flashed on bright eyes, a sharp nose, a pointed chin. It was her mother, Roxaine.

Raven looked away, flew toward the farm. Then she hesitated, stalled, spiraled uncertainly. Finally, she flapped heavily to one of the cedars and settled into the top branches. Her mother was watching the manor with an odd, expectant look. Her face was just the same, but she was so well dressed. Raven was afraid she knew why.

Go down and ask her, Chicken Heart, she told herself. You'll never have a better chance.

Right, she answered. Right.

She dropped to the ground behind the trees. Showing up as a bird might not be the best way to start. Or would it? Raven agonized a moment, then decided against it. She closed her eyes and reversed the spell that made her a raven. In moments, her sleek black feathers began to fuse into flesh, and she lengthened into a slender fifteen-year-old grayfolk girl with thick black hair and charcoal skin. Her eyes changed the least; girl or raven, they were black, bright, and very sharp.

Raven shivered in her thin shift, glad to see it had changed properly. She had only just learned the skill of spelling clothes along with her body. The light shift was all she could manage. As she looked down at it, she hesitated again. Did she want to show up for the first time in four years half naked? Better to shock Mam as a bird; much better, in fact. Raven was proud of her mage talent, even if she hadn't fully mastered it. It was special. Rare. She was the only bird mage in the world, as far as she knew. She took a deep breath and made her raven spell. Her skin tingled as the feathers re-formed, engulfing skin and fabric both. Her joints ached for a few moments as the bones and muscles shifted and changed and shrank. Her eyesight sharpened; sounds displayed edges she could never hear as a human. Scent almost disappeared. She stretched her wings. Faster than it took to tell, she was a raven.

Right! Now fly out there and face her.

Still she hesitated. Then an older woman came out of the manor. Raven lowered her half-raised wings. Roxaine rose and took a step toward the newcomer, face shining with happiness. The woman held out something; her mother took it. A baby. Raven went numb. Roxaine cradled it in her arms, greeting it with childlike words. She brushed her hand over its soft hair, then sat, undid the front of her gown, and pressed the baby to her breast. It took the nipple with a hungry mew.

"Eat well, little daughter," Roxaine said.

Daughter? But who was the father? Raven shied from the most likely answer. It was only a guess; she didn't know; she would wait, and ask, and not lose her temper until she knew for sure. Not even then, if she could help it. She would just leave, and that would be that.

Raven swallowed a knot that suddenly threatened to choke her. She stared at the tiny girl at her mother's breast. The thought sank in: This was her sister. Half of her wanted to fly right over and touch the silky hair. The other half was so jealous, she wanted to curse.

Raven fretted beneath the cedars while Roxaine fed the little girl, then carried her back into the manor. She watched through the windows until they reappeared in one of the rooms on the top floor. She lifted off then and flapped to the gable above the window. She could hear her mother humming. She recognized the lullaby and fought down another lump in her throat. The baby made a burbling sound, then sighed. Her mother hummed a while longer, while Raven tried to crane her neck low enough to peek in. Finally, the humming stopped.

"Sleep well, Sarita," Roxaine whispered.

There were footsteps. The door closed.

Raven dropped to the windowsill and peered through the small wavy panes. There was a high-sided bed in the far corner but no sign of people. Raven pushed her heavy beak between the window and the jamb. The sash swung inward a little, then stuck. Raven kept pushing, but the hinges were too stiff. Muttering a curse, she looked down. The parts of the yard she could see were empty. Balancing carefully, she reversed her spell. She began to change and almost tipped off the windowsill. She focused on her wings, scrabbling for a purchase as feathers shrank and fingers grew and she could finally grasp the sash. She teetered for a moment as the rest of her changed, then pushed the sash inward and tumbled into the room.

"Blazing mages!" she muttered, half wrapped in the drapes that had framed the window. The rod pulled loose, whacked her on the head, and clattered to the floor. She tripped and stumbled against the bed.

The baby woke, stared at her an instant with unfocused eyes, and started to cry.

"Hush!" Raven hissed. She scurried to the head of the bed, waving her hands and whispering inanely. "Come, chick, be quiet. Good girl. Good Sarita. It's me, see? Your big sister." She hummed a few notes of the lullaby. She tried making a sweet smile.

The baby clenched the sheet with two tiny fists and let out another wail.

Sweet sun on the River, Raven thought. Did I sound like that? Desperate, she picked up the baby, sheet and all, and jiggled her against her chest. Fumbling a hand free, she shoved her pinky into the noisy mouth. The wailing stuttered to a halt.

Raven and the baby sighed together in relief.

Silent, her sister was a lot easier to take. Even pretty, Raven thought, as they studied each other. Prettier than me. She felt another twinge of jealousy, then smiled. The little girl was only a few months old; who knew what she'd look like grown up? At this age, all babies looked like grubs. Pretty grubs, maybe, but still—

The door flew open and the older woman bustled into the room. She spotted Raven and froze, wide-eyed. The baby made a pleased little gurgle, and Raven felt her left hand go warm and wet.

At that moment, her mother stormed in.

"Louella! What is the matter with—" She stared at Raven.

Feelings flashed rapidly across her face: recognition, shock, joy.

"Penelope!" she cried.

Something like fear struck Raven in the chest. She couldn't say a single word, to ask or accuse. Her mother came forward, arms outstretched. Raven held up her sister like a shield between them.

"The baby," she croaked. "She's wet."

Louella snatched Sarita from Raven's grasp and hurried her over to a table on the far wall, crooning like a broody dove.

Roxaine's smile stiffened. She dropped her arms, rubbed her hands. "Well, Pigeon," she said. "I had given up hoping you'd . . . But I suppose you heard about your sister and came to see for yourself." She tried a fresh smile. "I've missed you."

Raven crossed her arms. "Who?" she asked. Her throat was too dry. Don't be such a coward! she chided herself. Ask! She swallowed and tried again. "Who is the father?"

Roxaine turned quickly and went to shut the door. When she turned back, her face was composed, but she studied Raven with guarded eyes. Something glimmered behind them: sadness? anger? Maybe it was just fatigue. Up close, she looked disheveled, despite the fine embroidered dress. Her eyes were red and puffy, as though she'd been rubbing them.

The silence stretched. Raven felt more and more awkward, more and more angry. "Well?" she demanded.

"Darvin," Roxaine said. "Darvin is her father."

"Darvin?" Raven asked, though she knew she'd heard the name before.

"Cutter," Roxaine said impatiently. "Yes, him, the Baron."

"Darvin Cutter?" Raven couldn't quite believe the Baron had a first name. As if he were a person, someone you could like.

Roxaine raised her head and brushed back her hair. "That's right, my daughter's father is Baron Cutter. Is that so hard to believe? Am I so ugly?"

"Of course not!" Raven snapped. "You're— Blazing mages, he's the Baron! The bondholder! The man we ran away from!" Raven tried to control her voice. She glared, and was surprised to find she was actually looking down a little to meet her mother's eyes. "The man *I* ran away from," she said. "I guess you decided you had a better reason to stay."

Her mother frowned back. "It's not that simple, Pigeon." Her voice was stilted, as though Raven were still just a child.

Raven gritted her teeth. "What's not simple? Being whipped for sneaking a biscuit? Locked up for tearing a sheet? Having Steward steal a month's worth of bond wage just because you dropped the lady's chamber pot?"

"It's not like that anymore!" Roxaine said. "You can say whatever you like about that brute Steward, but Darvin has changed. He's raised wages, including the bond wage. He's told the foremen to stop using the whip. He's become a different man, Darvin. He's been very good to me. And he'll be good to you, too, if you give him half a chance."

"What chance? I'm . . . I *was* a bondservant. You still are."

Roxaine smiled. "Not any longer. Darvin wrote off my bond."

"In exchange for what?" Raven demanded. "An heir?"

"In exchange for my love."

"So you're his mistress."

Roxaine's smile chilled. "I just said we're in love. I am his fiancée."

"But not his wife?"

Now she looked troubled. "Not yet. There have been . . . complications."

"He doesn't like children after all?"

Roxaine frowned. "Darvin is sick," she said. "It came on so suddenly."

Raven nodded, sure she understood. "He's dying, isn't he? You didn't force the question soon enough."

Now Roxaine glared. "He proposed months ago," she snapped. "Without any prompting from me. I tell you, we are in love. And that has changed him. Both of us."

"I can just see you two," Raven said. "Regular birds of a feather, cooing together while he orders the help around. I bet you really like it when he tells you to wash his breeches." Roxaine's eyes flared. The words sounded cruel to her own ears, but Raven couldn't stop herself. "Oh, yes, I forgot: Darvin wrote off your bond, didn't he? Now you can order everyone around yourself. And all it cost was one daughter."

Roxaine slapped her.

Raven fought for control, dumbfounded. Her mother had never hit her before. She blinked violently, refusing her own tears. She clenched her fists at her side so she wouldn't hit back. Words—she could always strike back with words. Only none came.

The door jerked open, cutting through the shock. A tall, bulky man strode in, blond, ruddy, pale eyed. Raven knew him immediately: Jan Steward, Cutter's right-hand man.

"What is going on here, Roxaine?" he demanded. "We can hear you all over the house!"

"This is none of your business, Steward," Roxaine snapped.

"Cutter's health is my business," he said. "You of all people should know how ill he is. If you can't find a quieter way to manage your nurse, at least do it in the—"

Roxaine turned on him. "I know exactly how ill he is! Who spends every night sitting by his bed while you're snoring?"

But Steward was staring at Raven. He glanced quickly to her mother's face and back. His eyes narrowed. "The other daughter," he murmured. "The little runaway."

"Get that look off your face! I told you this was none—"

"Loyal!" he shouted, head half turned toward the open door. "Bring the shackles!" He grabbed for Raven's arm.

She spun and ran to the window, then realized how high it was. She could never change in time. He followed her. She kicked. He grunted and bent double. The baby's cry rose to a shrill wail. Raven ducked under Steward's groping hand and fled.

oyal Steward was in his father's office on the ground floor when he heard the shout. He jumped up so quickly, the desk chair flew back against the bookcase, jarring loose a heavy account book. It tumbled off, nearly hitting him on his head as he grabbed the shackles his father always kept on a hook by the door. Loyal kicked the book, cursing whoever had shelved it so carelessly, and charged into the hallway.

He reached the stairs in two long strides and took them at a run. He pounded up the first two flights, threw himself around the turn at the landing, and collided headlong with someone coming down. They cracked heads. A knee struck him in the chest, and he tumbled backward, slamming onto the wooden landing. The shackles flew out of his hand. He had scattered glimpses of a dark, startled face. A furious girl. She stepped on his stomach and pelted down the stairs. Gasping, Loyal lurched to his feet and staggered in pursuit.

By the time he reached the ground floor, she was already out the door. Loyal raced after her, calling for help. "Hunter! Gardener! To me! A runaway!"

The girl flew across the yard, but Loyal had his wind back now. His long legs were eating up her lead. And when he caught her . . .

Gardener appeared around the corner of the house, a spade in his hand.

"Cut her off!" Loyal yelled.

The girl veered, making for a break in the holly hedge at the other side of the yard. Loyal eased his pace. She was fleeing toward the perfect trap: The holly surrounded a maze. The thick, thorny hedge made it impossible to escape. All he had to do was herd her along. The girl disappeared through the gap. Loyal smiled.

"Block the exit!" he ordered Gardener. He stopped at the gap and took a moment to catch his breath. Ostler appeared in Gardener's wake, followed by Hunter and his boy. Ostler had a coach whip and a length of rope; Hunter and the boy carried firearms. Loyal took the rope and sent Ostler to keep watch with Gardener.

"Set aside your firearms," he ordered Hunter and the boy. "It's one girl."

"A girl with fists, if that eye is any indication," Hunter remarked dryly.

Loyal touched his swelling eyebrow and flushed. Hunter would never dare speak to his father like that. "We want her in one piece," he said. "A dead worker's no use to us."

"Even a runaway?" the huntsboy drawled.

Loyal sneered. "She'll break soon enough at the prison farm."

Hunter leaned his firearm against the hedge. The boy copied him sullenly. He was seventeen, Loyal's own age, though not nearly as tall. In Loyal's opinion, he was too stupid and surly to ever be huntmaster.

"You and I will go in after her," Loyal told Hunter. "We'll either catch her or drive her out to Gardener and Ostler. You," he added sharply to the boy, "watch this entrance in case she manages to slip by us."

The boy's frown deepened. Loyal let him stew. He might be the huntsboy, but he needed a lesson in manners. Besides, Loyal had to be the one who caught the girl; his father would expect it. He started in.

Just then, the boy snatched up his firearm and aimed at something above the hedge. Loyal swung his arm and knocked the barrel; the shot went wild. A large black bird swooped over the manor wall and dipped out of sight.

"I told you, no shooting!" Loyal snarled.

The boy, already reloading, lowered the weapon with a guilty frown. "It was only a blasted crow," he muttered.

"It looked more like a raven, young Steward," Hunter remarked. His expression implied some importance that eluded Loyal.

"Raven, crow, it's no matter! We're hunting a runaway girl, not field vermin." Loyal glared at them a moment longer, then led the way into the maze.

He and Hunter searched from one end to the other but found only Ostler and Gardener at the exit, empty-handed. They went back through and then forward again, double-checking every angle and dead end. Somehow the girl had escaped.

Seething, Loyal threw down the rope. "Check the hedge all along," he ordered. "There must be a hole."

"Unless she went over the top," Hunter said.

"She'd have been torn to shreds," Loyal snapped. "Gardener, find that hole and fix it. Hunter, you and your boy look for some sign. Use the dogs if you have to. Ostler, back to work."

He turned and strode stiffly toward the manor house. Slackers! he thought. He should have docked them all a day's pay. That's what his father would have done. Without Jan Steward, the entire estate would crumble into chaos around their ears. Of course, he was the one who had to tell his father the girl had escaped, while they went off and took a break as soon as his back was turned.

Loyal found his father on the second floor, outside the Baron's bedroom. By then, his anger had turned to dread. He had a speech all rehearsed, but the Baron's conniving mistress was there, along with the herb witch and the healer. They were in the midst of a half-whispered argument, hissing at each other in tones that would have woken anyone well enough to wake. They broke off, all turning to glare at Loyal as though he were the cause of the argument. The healer, a pale young mage only recently brought in by his father, stared at Loyal's puffy eye. Loyal glared back.

"Ah, your, uh, eye could use some treatment," the healer said, glancing away.

"And what would you propose?" the herb witch asked. "Bleeding? A lancet in the eye?"

"Hush!" Jan Steward commanded. He turned to Loyal. "I heard a shot. What happened?"

"H-Huntsboy fired against my order," Loyal stammered. "At a crow."

Roxaine let out an audible breath. "What about the girl?" she demanded.

Loyal replied to his father. "She escaped," he said. "There was a hole in the hedge."

A slight smile touched Roxaine's lips. His father's frown deepened.

"Gardener's fault, of course," Loyal hurried on. "I set Hunter and the boy to find her trail. I think we should dock—"

"Tell them to use the dogs if they have to," his father ordered.

"Yes, sir, I did," Loyal said, but his father had already turned his glare back to Roxaine. Jan Steward was an imposing man, over a fathom tall, broad in girth and manner. His gaze had been hardened by a life spent enforcing Baron Cutter's will. But Roxaine, as small and dark as he was tall and blond, glared back unflinchingly.

"Make no mistake," his father said. "We will catch her."

"Don't waste Hunter's time, Steward. She is no longer your bondmaid."

"No one I know has paid off her bond."

Roxaine's black eyes flashed. "She is my daughter! Her bond was written off with mine, and you know it!"

Her daughter . . . Now Loyal realized why the girl had looked familiar.

His father's face reddened. "She ran away long before there was any mention of bonds being written off. She is criminal before the fact."

Roxaine stepped right up to him, fists clenched. "The Baron—"

His father cut her off, voice raised. "The Baron is too ill to support your claim, one way or the other." He dropped back to a harsh whisper. "And that is what we are supposed to be discussing here. Our master is ill. *Your* herb witch has not cured him. *My* mage—"

Now Roxaine cut him off. "Mage? He's more tick than mage! Darvin can't eat? Bleed him! Can't sleep? Bleed him! Too hot? Bleed him! Too cold? Bleed him! Bleed, bleed, bleed!"

The healer puffed up. "You have no concept of healing. The, uh, the blood is necessary for the healing spells. Ah—"

"Spells?" Roxaine countered. "All we've had so far is a constant stream of hand waving and gibber. I've heard more magic from a cage of monkeys."

"Ah, uh . . ."

"We've seen no better from this hag," Steward said. "The Baron has swallowed her noisome potions till they run from his pores, and to what effect? None! Look in there—he sleeps like he's dead."

"Which he will be if this leech doesn't stop bleeding him!"

"Ah, blood carries the, uh, aural ethers."

"Nonsense!" The herb witch snorted, her gray lips pursed. "Blood bears the sanguinary humors and lubricates the spleen."

Loyal listened with growing anger as they threw jargon and counter-jargon around the hallway. Neither the hag nor the mage was worth the price of a bushel of beets, as far as he could tell. Fakes, like all the rest.

"By the River, enough!" His father's order brought them to silence. In the tense hush, the Baron's labored breathing sounded clearly from behind the door. For a space of moments, it stopped. Roxaine blanched. She reached for the doorknob. Then it started again, slow and thick. Wearily, she dropped her hand.

"You've had your turn," Steward said to the herb witch. "Go."

The mage settled his robe and smiled, but Steward turned on him.

"You have one chance. Do what you need to make your magic. It had better work."

"Ah, of course. Right away. Ah . . ." He waved his lancet weakly and fumbled for the doorknob.

Roxaine made to follow, but Steward stopped her. "Let him do his work."

"He may need help," she said.

"Then he will call for it."

She bridled anew. "Darvin is my husband."

Loyal couldn't take her any longer. "Not yet!" he snapped.

His father silenced him with a glare. Loyal looked away.

"You are Cutter's present consort," his father told Roxaine. "Nothing more. And I am not so lonely and easy to charm as our Baron."

"Ah, lady," the mage said, "it really would be better for the Baron if I, uh, made my spells in, uh, private. You, uh . . . distractions, concentration . . . ah, I'm sure you, uh, understand?"

Roxaine seemed about to spit, but she gave in. "I will wait right here."

The mage nodded quickly and slipped through the doorway.

Steward glared at the two women one last time, then turned on his heel. He gave Loyal a glance that was hardly less severe. "Come with me," he ordered, striding down the hall.

As soon as they were on the stairs, he eyed Loyal coldly. "How could you let her escape?"

"Through the hedge, Father. It was Gardener—"

"Are you lame? She should never have reached the hedge."

Loyal flushed. "She caught me by surprise," he muttered.

His father's lips thinned. "I want her found, oaf. Get to it!"

Loyal watched his father's back disappear around the landing, then punched the wall twice. Why couldn't he ever do what his father wanted? He found the fallen shackles a few steps farther down and scooped them up, rattling the chain in silent rage at the scurvy runaway girl. The little harridan! he fumed. Worse than her mother! What was her name? Something inane, like . . . Pigeon. No, that was just her mother's silly nickname for her. He used to tease her with it.

Raven would have been more like it, he thought, remembering her sharp tongue.

Loyal stopped dead. Hunter had said the bird looked like a raven. Said it in an odd tone, as if he'd expected Loyal to take some meaning from it. What was it about a raven?

Then Loyal remembered: Barely a year ago, a young fireboy had run off with a stranger. They'd stolen a steamboat. Loyal had been on the chase boat, along with Hunter and his boy and a handful of baronsmen. They had chased the runaways downriver for a full day, only to lose them that night. The thieves had had the nerve to blow up the steamboat as a diversion. But there had been more than the two boys; there'd been a big black bird with them. A raven. It had attacked the wharfmaster. Croaked out insults.

Blast that Hunter! Loyal raged. He had made the connection; why didn't he just come out and say it?

Loyal stopped himself and took a deep breath. Roxaine's daughter a mage? It was too far-fetched. You could count real mages on the fingers of one hand. And a raven mage to boot? He'd never heard of such a thing. Certainly, there were a few real mages, but they were seers or truthsayers: men of arcane power. Like that weather mage last fall who had exposed the Duke as a puppet of his own mage brother.

Again Loyal stopped short. The weather mage had been helped by a bemagicked girl who took the shape of a raven.

He pounded the railing, then raced downstairs and out the door, yelling for Hunter.

Three

Raven flew at ground level until she was in the shelter of the nearest windbreak. Her heart was pounding. She cursed Loyal Steward. Father's little toady! Trust him to shoot at her.

She'd had enough run-ins with him when she'd lived at the manor. He loved to play the little steward, repeating his father's orders, counting the spoons after every meal, weighing the salt. Otherwise, he completely ignored you, sharp nose up, as if you didn't exist. Unless you broke one of their asinine house rules. Then he knew exactly who you were, the bossy, dung-eating little starling!

"Kah!" She clacked her beak and spent a few minutes preening, but as soon as her mind left Steward, it went to her mother. Raven felt both anger and an ache that she couldn't ignore. The Baron's mistress! And worse: She had borne his child, a wailing little baron.

No, it's not Sarita's fault, Raven told herself. Babies can't choose their parents. Poor little grub, what hope did she have to grow up normal, with parents like that? At least she wouldn't have to take any orders from Steward or his stiff-nosed son. She'd be bossing them around.

"Kah! I never should have come back!" Raven croaked.

But she still had a message to deliver. She would find Fireboy's father, and then she was off to the high reach or just the nearest ridge. Anywhere but here. She took wing, keeping well behind the trees as she made her way toward the barns.

Raven had never met Fireboy's father, but she knew who the breedmaster was. She had seen him many times at the spring fair and the Riverfest each harvest season, two of the few times that house staff had a spare moment to mingle freely with workers from the farm and meat house. He led the parade of bulls and judged the ox-pulling contests. His name was Phillipe, and he worked in the breeding barn. Raven hoped she could catch him before he left for dinner.

Cutter's barns covered several acres near the farmhands' lodgings. There were hay barns, granaries, cattle sheds, a small dairy—a dozen large wood-and-stone buildings in all. At the center of the complex stood the stone breeding barn, where Cutter kept the prize bulls and cows and bred his cash crop. Raven flew through the square loading door into the loft, gliding between stacked bales of hay to land in the loose straw beside a trapdoor. A flock of pigeons roosting in the rafters took one look at her and exploded toward the exit in a mutter of wings. She ignored them, focusing on the spell to turn back to her girl self.

Girl self. The thought irked her. Seeing her mother—and Steward and his bully boy—had made her feel like a little girl again. Only she wasn't, and hadn't been since she'd run away. She knew things few adults knew, had done things most couldn't imagine, even if she still had a lot to learn. That nasty Loyal could play at being steward, but she was nearly a master mage.

She shivered, and wished again she already was a master and could transform thicker clothing. She had been an apprentice for three years, but her mistress had been jealous of her talent and withheld many important skills, and then died suddenly a year ago. Raven had been practicing her magic diligently all winter. Some things were easy: She had always been able to calm and command other birds, and now she could change herself to other birds than raven, though it was more difficult. But there was so much she still couldn't do well. Or at all. Warm clothes were just one frustration.

Raven rubbed her shoulders. Warmth drifted up through the trapdoor from the stalls below. She could smell the cows, generating dung and heat. She peered through the opening to see how many people were down there as well.

"You're a mage!"

Raven spun, searching for the one who had spoken, and almost toppled through the trapdoor. Small hands grabbed at her. She sprawled kicking in the loose hay. Her assailant retreated onto a bale, staring at her with wide eyes. She glared back. It was a young boy, grayfolk, curly haired, with a very round face that looked a little familiar.

"I saw you change!" he said in an awed whisper. "You're a mage!"

"And you're a—" She realized why he looked so familiar and swallowed the insult. "You're Fireboy's brother." She'd never met him, either—she'd only met Fireboy himself a year ago, for that matter—but she vaguely remembered seeing this little brother riding on one of his father's bulls.

His eyes went even wider. "Fireboy? You mean Sam? You know Sam?"

"Is that his name? Everyone calls him Fireboy now. He sent me to find you."

"Where is he?"

"In Dunsgow."

He came close. "How come he left? How come he didn't come back? Was he caught? Is he hurt?"

"Hush, chick!" Raven warned. She took his shoulders and set him back a pace. "He's fine. He's even got his own boat."

"His own boat? He's a boatman?" He looked utterly surprised.

Raven laughed. "That's right. Not just a coal shoveler anymore. What's your name?"

The boy stood to his full height, which wasn't that tall, and puffed out his chest. "Leo," he said, "but everyone calls me Hero."

Raven stifled another laugh. He wore the name like a hat two sizes too large: a small boy—no more than ten, she guessed—with enough young pride to believe his nickname.

"Lucky me," she said. "I may need a hero to help me find your father and then get out of here without being spotted."

"I'll help," he said, as though the job were already done. "What's your name? I bet it's Raven!" He grinned when she nodded, and was the spitting image of his brother. "Will you change me?"

"Right now I need to find your father."

"After?"

"I could give it a try, but I can't stay long: Young Steward's trying to shoot me."

Leo grew fierce, or as fierce as his wide face and wild curls could manage. "I'll keep them away," he declared.

"Let's hope you don't have to, my little Hero." Raven stepped toward the ladder. "Come on, help me find your father."

Hero scooted ahead of her to lead the way.

The ladder came down in the center of the barn. Slate-floored aisles stretched right and left between the stalls. The posts and rails were neatly chamfered. Yellow light filtered in through small glazed windows. Cutter kept his breeding stock in better lodgings than his workers.

A shovel scraped somewhere to the right. Hero held a finger to his lips and led on. They hadn't gone more than two steps before the door at the end of the aisle started to slide open. Raven glimpsed pale hair and a sharp nose. Loyal Steward!

Immediately, Hero threw open the gate to the nearest stall and shoved her through.

"Wait here!" he whispered.

"But—"

He closed the gate in her face, then latched it and scurried away.

Raven heard footsteps approaching and backed away from the gate. Hot breath blew down her neck. She turned slowly to face a massive, wet nose. An iron ring spanned the huge nostrils. She lifted her gaze to face fist-sized brown eyes with no hint of kindness.

The bull snuffed at her, glowering. Raven glowered back. The bull was not impressed. He tossed his head, and the tips of his horns flashed. Raven yielded. She thought her spell, then stopped. She didn't dare become a raven here. The footsteps were nearly at the stall. The last bird she wanted to be was a drab, dirty pigeon, but it was the only bird likely to be in a barn. She altered a few words of her spell and forced herself through the change. Her eye level sank toward the floor as her body contracted. Her head seemed to squeeze against her eyeballs. She felt as if she'd been stuffed into clothes that were eight years too small.

Frantically, she dodged the bull's tossing horns and flapped to the ledge above the stall window. Steward, Hunter, and the hunts-boy came into view. The boy glanced in, eyes narrowed against the window's glare. The bull let out a mean, grunting bellow and stamped. The planks shook. The boy jumped.

"You want to watch old Mangle," someone said. "He's temperamental." It was a short, broad-faced grayfolk: Fireboy's father, Phillipe.

"Get back!" Loyal ordered curtly. "We don't need him roused." He pointed to the ladder that led to the loft. "You two look up there. I'll check the rest of the stalls."

"I'm sure Borly or Kurl would have seen any bird that big if it flew in here," Phillipe said in a soft, easy voice. "They're right down there mucking out. The others are at dinner."

Suddenly, a high shout from behind made them all turn. Hero ran up, his face full of excitement.

"Father! Father!" He pulled at Phillipe's hand. "Come see the big crow! Steward, sir! Come look! It's the biggest crow I've ever seen, big as an eagle! Big as me!"

"Where?" Loyal demanded, already striding toward the door.

Hero ran after him, followed quickly by the others. "It flew out of the loft," he said. "Up to the roof of the near barn. It sat there staring at me like . . . like it knew me!"

His voice faded as they hurried away. Raven heard the door

slide shut. The little chick was clever; maybe he deserved his nickname after all. Then she caught herself nodding stupidly, just like a blasted pigeon. Cooing in disgust, she forced herself to stay where she was, as a pigeon, just in case Hero got caught in his lie.

In a few minutes, she heard the door open and shut again. Footsteps hurried up the aisle, and Hero and his father came into view.

"She's in here," Hero was saying. "With old Mangle." He peered through the gate, then came right in. Old Mangle snorted nastily, but Hero reached up a small hand and patted the huge nose.

"Go gentle," he said, and amazingly the bull did, nuzzling the boy's head so fondly, he almost fell over. For an instant, Raven felt a slight tingle on her face, like the puff of a faint breeze. Then it was gone, before she could be sure she'd really felt it at all. She shivered, then flew out of the stall, landed, and reversed her spell.

"What in the five rivers did you have in mind, putting me in there with that blood-hungry beast?" she exclaimed.

"You're a beast mage," Hero said. "Old Mangle wouldn't harm you."

"I'm a bird mage," Raven corrected. "He'd just as soon gore me as smell me."

Hero looked skeptical. "Why would he do that?" he asked, reaching up to stroke Mangle's huge nose. The big bull moaned pleasurably.

Phillipe flashed a proud smile. "He's been taming the bulls and cows all his life; barn cats, too. He forgets others can't. Seeing you change like that . . . well, to some people like me, it might look pretty odd. A bit frightful, even. To him, it just means you ken the way of animals." To Hero, he said, "Birds and beasts don't think like each other, Son. One has an air spirit, the other a land spirit."

"But the ox-picker—" Hero protested.

"I don't pick ticks!" Raven snapped. "Beasts and I don't speak the same language."

Hero thought about it, then shrugged. "What other birds can you be?"

"Not now, Son," Phillipe said patiently. "Come out and close the gate." Then he called up the aisle. "Borly, Kurl, come here." The sounds of scraping stopped, and a man and woman appeared from the end stalls. They eyed Raven suspiciously. "She's all right," Phillipe told them. "She has word from my boy Sam. You keep watch. Let me know if you see anyone coming."

Their faces cleared and they nodded; then each went to one of the doors.

Phillipe turned back to Raven. "Who are you, mistress mage? How do you know my Sam?"

"I was with him when he ran away," Raven replied.

His eyebrows rose. "I recognize you now. You're Roxaine's first daughter. You ran off years ago."

"Yes," Raven replied, "but that's a different story." She told him about her adventures with Fireboy and their friend Carver: their flight downriver on the stolen steamboat, their arrival in Dunsgow, their battle with the great mage Krimm. Phillipe listened quietly, asking a question here and there. He had a gentleness about him that matched his soft voice. When she finished, he shook his head in amazement.

"My Sam really did all that?"

"He did."

"We'd heard about the Duke and the great mage." He chuckled. "What we heard was even more fantastical, but nobody said it was my boy in the middle of it. So he's the one they call Fireboy. And he's all right now? Got his own boat?"

"He does, for helping defeat Krimm. That doesn't mean much here in Cutter's valley, but in Dunsgow he's his own man, making a good wage. You didn't get any of his letters?"

A hint of anger showed in the set of Phillipe's wide mouth. "Not a one."

"That swine Steward's doing, I'll warrant," Raven muttered.

"Well, the important thing is that Fireboy is making money to pay off your bond. Yours, too, Bull Brain," she added to Hero. "But he's going to pay off for his mother first—your wife. She being at Miner's now and no family with her."

Phillipe was nodding. "That boy, he's thinking right."

"He figures that, together, the two of them can pay off your bond twice as fast."

Phillipe shook his head, anger once more in the line of his mouth. "Gonna take a long, long time for that," he said. "You tell him just pay off Leo here. No sense wasting work on me."

"What do you mean?" Raven asked. "Your bond can't be any more than your wife's."

"Oh, it can," Phillipe said bitterly. "When Sam ran off with that boat, Steward put it on my bond."

"What?" Raven exclaimed.

"You heard. Said he's my son, it's my cost."

"He was 'prenticed out to that oaf boatman Bozer," Raven said. "If anything, the cost should have gone on him."

Phillipe shrugged. "Maybe, maybe not. Fact is, it's on me."

"But you're the breedmaster."

"That made no difference to Steward." Phillipe gave a humorless chuckle. "And being master means more work, not more money, not for a bondservant. Oh, a little more," he relented. "Enough so I won't slack off, I suppose. They know talent needs some reward. But not enough to buy a steamboat. Not in my lifetime."

"You could run away, too," Raven said. "Come with me now."

"No, I've got Leo here." Phillipe smiled at the younger boy, who had been listening carefully, stroking old Mangle's nose through the slats in the gate. "I can't leave him alone, and I can't risk him getting caught."

"I'll go," Hero said. "I'm quick as a cat. The baronsmen won't catch me."

"I know the country," Raven said. "I have the eyes of every bird to spy the way. I can keep you safe all the way to Dunsgow."

"No," Phillipe said firmly. "I won't risk the boy to the prison farm. Better he waits here till his brother can pay his bond."

"But—" Hero protested.

"No," Phillipe repeated, with a parent's no-nonsense tone. Hero subsided unhappily. "We have to stay here," Phillipe said to Raven. "You go back and tell Sam."

Raven would have argued longer, but Kurl called out from her doorway. "Breeder! It's young Steward! With Hunter and the boy!"

"I'll go stop him!" Hero cried, starting toward the door.

Phillipe grabbed his shoulder. "You've been hero enough today," he said.

Raven was already changing back into a pigeon. "I'll tell Fireboy you're being bullheaded," she said, her voice rising as her throat changed, "but don't think he'll let you rot here like this."

"You just tell him to worry about his little brother."

"Kooh!"

The barn door started to open as Raven leaped into the air. With a word of command, she sent the other pigeons into a flurry of alarm and joined them in a mad rush out the loft window. Hunter's boy was watching in the dooryard, his short, ugly firearm half raised. Raven resisted the temptation to spatter him. Instead, she flew around with the flock until the barn roof hid her from view. Then she beat a hasty retreat toward the trees. Pigeons were small, stupid, and sloppy, but at least they were fast.

Four

Raven sped away till she was well out of sight of the buildings, then landed in a woodlot. She quickly changed to human, then raven, then took wing again. She seethed with anger. That grasping Steward had charged the stolen steamboat to Fireboy's father! It was just like him, the egg-stealing shrike. And his prig of a son, going after her with Hunter and his dunghill of a boy. And her mother . . .

She shied from the thought. She was done with her mother. But Phillipe and little Hero—blazing mages, they should have run off with her! It would take years for Fireboy to earn enough to pay off Hero's bond. Steward was always raising the price of clothing and food and every little thing you wore out or broke. He'd probably add the steamboat to Hero's bond, too.

Raven remembered her mother's constant anger at every charge. Roxaine's own mother had been a farmer's wife, working a small vineyard on the River Down. Roxaine's father had died; then the vines had withered under some pestilence. Her mother had two children already and was pregnant with a third. Desperate, she'd appealed to Baron Vintner for help. He'd agreed to pay off her debts and give her work, in exchange for her bond. Hers and the children's. It was a common-enough story: She never paid off the bond, and neither had her children. Whether you pledged yourself or were sent by a judge, once in bond to a Baron, you never went anywhere. Unless you went on your own, as Raven had. She knew Phillipe was only trying to protect Hero, but that kind of protection was prison. Look at her mother: still stuck on the estate. She'd had her chance four years ago. She could have escaped, too. They'd planned it together, hadn't they? Blazing mages, it had been her mother's idea in the first place!

Raven had never known her father; he had died soon after she was born. He'd been a bondservant for Baron Vintner, too, but Vintner had sold her mother's bond to Cutter, who needed a new maid for his ailing wife. Roxaine was pregnant, but that didn't matter to the blasted Barons; the unborn child was part of the deal. As she grew, Raven was trained to clean and sew, fetch and carry; and she hated it. At night, Roxaine told tales of mages and magic. She embellished the stories with exciting escapes and brave runaways who fled to the secrecy and safety of the high reach. They whispered together of making a new life upriver. Finally, Raven did run away. Alone. Because at the last minute her mother backed out.

Raven still ached every time she remembered. Squeezing into the pantry cupboard, hardly able to breathe, neck twisted, muscles growing more and more cramped as she waited for darkness and her mother to come. Starting at every noise. Staring through the crack between the hinges. Dry mouth, beating heart, mind set on one dream: escape. Night fell. The manor stilled, but her mother didn't come. Finally, Raven couldn't wait any longer. She crept painfully from the cupboard, determined to sneak upstairs and find her. She'd almost been caught then. Steward had appeared suddenly, snooping about the house with a hooded lantern.

Raven had dodged into the dining room and under the table just ahead of Steward's light. He paused; then some noise distracted him and he went down the back hallway. She waited, heart pounding, and sure enough, he came back and began searching the kitchen. She slipped through the sitting room into the front hall and tiptoed toward the stairs. As far as the Baron's parlor.

Raven froze right in front of the doorway. Inside, a single candle flickered on the mantel. The dim light outlined two people: Baron Cutter slumped in a chair, her mother standing beside him.

Her right hand rested on his shoulder. The other rested in his hand. As she watched, he lifted her mother's hand and pressed it to his cheek. Then he kissed it. Raven could only stand and stare, mind blank.

Then Steward reappeared. He charged from the sitting room, unhooding his light, shouting. Raven fled down the hall. The only door was the stairway, but there was no escape up there. She jerked open the little window at the end of the hall, scrambled through, raced for the back gate. The window was too small for Steward. Thwarted by his own bulk, he bellowed for Hunter and the dogs. Raven had fled across the fields. Alone.

Now, distracted by her memories, Raven landed wearily in the top of a tall pine.

Why? That was the question she still couldn't answer. Why had her mother stayed with Cutter? How could she love that man? What had she been doing there in the parlor in the first place? Raven chided herself for losing her temper earlier, losing the chance to ask, the chance to tell her mother how it made her feel, to tell her off.

She clacked her beak angrily. Oh, Mam had made out all right for herself. The Baron's consort didn't have to shovel manure, and neither did her daughter. Sarita, that is, the Baron's daughter. She was his only heir. When she grew up, she would hold the bond on every one of Cutter's servants. What would she think then of her older sister, the runaway?

The thought dulled Raven's anger. She would have liked a sister. She'd had no close friends growing up, only her mother, and look how that had turned out. But her mother had always said that something good could come from everything. Would Sarita be the one good thing that came from all this? Or would she grow up just like her father, an overbearing Baron? Raven hoped not; not that sweet little baby.

It was growing dark. She peered ahead, thinking she should probably try to cover a few more leagues before nightfall. If she flew high enough, she might even be able to make out the high wall of the upper reach, even in the twilight. She would have been there already, if only . . .

It doesn't matter, she told herself. You had to speak to Phillipe anyway. You're done here. Go.

But night was falling fast, and the upper reach didn't seem to matter much either. Nothing did. She could go wherever she wanted, do anything she liked; nobody cared but her. Right now, even she didn't care. She could hear a mouse rustling through the fallen needles below but couldn't summon the energy to catch it. She'd flown too far that day, bespelled herself too many times, seen too many old faces. She tucked her head under a wing and fell into a fitful doze.

Hours later, a faint sound dragged her from a clinging dream: She and her mother were flying—both winged, though her mother had her human face—flying from something awful, something slow and implacable that was gaining on them no matter how hard they flew. Raven tried to call out, but she couldn't open her mouth. She saw her mother's mouth move but couldn't hear the words, only a dull ringing, like a failing heartbeat. Her mother fell behind, into blinding walls of cloud. Raven turned, hovered, tried to fly back toward her mother. The air was too thick. She couldn't move. Her mother faded into the clouds, till only her mouth was left, moving without words.

Raven came awake, but the heartbeat continued. Finally, she recognized it as a bell, tolling a slow, hollow dirge from the distant manor. Raven shivered and forced away the last unsettling image, but the sense of the dream remained. She had to go back, to see what the bell meant. Her heart was still cold as she took off and flew downriver through the thin moonlight.

Soon she made out the lights of the estate. There were far too many of them for this time of night, lamps burning in the manor, in the workers' lodgings, on the wharf, even in some of the barns. As she flew nearer, the tolling grew louder. Someone was ringing the bell in the cupola above the front gatehouse, the steady knell of mourning.

Raven flew to the breeding barn, setting off the pigeons again. She swooped straight down through the trapdoor to land on the railing of Mangle's stall. The big bull had thrust his head over the gate and was staring down the aisle. A trio of lanterns glowed at another stall there, and Phillipe's two helpers, Borly and Kurl, watched at the doorway. Inside, a cow gave out a long, low groan that subsided into quick, uneven panting. Raven flew over and landed on the railing. Borly and Kurl looked up in surprise. Borly raised his hands as if to shoo her away.

"Don't!" It was Hero, inside the stall with his father. They were both tending to a cow only a little smaller than old Mangle. "It's just Raven."

"I was here this afternoon," Raven croaked. "The girl with the message."

Borly's mouth fell open. Kurl gasped.

"It's all right," Phillipe said. "She's a mage."

Then another lowing groan drew everyone's attention to the cow. Hero stroked her snout and whispered into her huge velvety ear. She lowed again, sides heaving. Her head jerked, lifting Hero right off his feet. He never let up his crooning. Phillipe moved directly behind the cow. Then, to Raven's amazement, he thrust his arm inside her, right up to his shoulder.

"Turned all wrong," he grunted. Sweat poured from his round face as he reached and shifted. He squinted his eyes, as though he were trying to see through his fingertips. "Got her now. . . ." The cow groaned again. Phillipe grunted again and twisted something inside. There was a gush of liquid, a wet *squelch,* and a calf slid out, all wet and shiny. Phillipe staggered back and sat in the hay, the newborn calf in his lap. There was a moment of surprise, then all of them laughed in relief. Even the cow's lowing sounded relieved. Borly went in quickly with rags to wipe down the calf. Kurl took the cow's head, and Hero went to help his father up. They were all chattering like magpies.

"Does that happen every time?" Raven asked, eyeing the slimy calf with a mix of wonder and disgust.

Phillipe came over, wiping his arm on a rag. "Just now and again," he said. He sounded tired but satisfied. "Sometimes they need a little direction from outside."

"Kah! You were almost inside."

Phillipe chuckled. "You do what you have to, to get 'em out alive. Can't just let 'em die. These girls in here, they're all the Baron's special breed." He stopped then and listened to the faint tolling of the bell. His smile faded. "They're beyond his worry now."

"So it was the Baron," Raven said.

Phillipe nodded. "Birth and death. Can't have one without the other."

"He got sick, then he got sicker, now he's died," Borly said. He made an odd face, as if he'd just realized he was speaking with a raven. Then he shrugged. "Nothing the herb witch or that healer mage could do, I guess. Must have been his time."

Raven didn't like to think death was as simple as all that, but she wasn't sad to see Cutter go. Except for what it might mean for her new sister.

"What about . . . ? Who'll be the Baron now?"

"Well, little Sarita's his heir," Phillipe said, "but she's too young." He sighed. "I guess Steward will be in charge till she's grown."

"Steward?" Raven echoed. "That squeezing, bloody-minded shrike?"

"Who else is going to do it?"

"What about my—her mother?"

"Roxaine? The Baron didn't marry her," Kurl said. She came over and leaned against the railing. The cow was licking the calf lovingly.

"That's right," Borly said, wadding up the messy rags. "And even if he had, Steward'd never stand for it. That Roxaine, he hates her head to toe. All the changes Cutter's made since they fell in love? The wages? The food? I wager more'n half were her doing, and Steward knows it."

"He can't forget she was just a house servant," Kurl said.

"A bondservant, at that," Borly agreed. "No offense, Breeder," he added quickly.

"None taken," Phillipe said, with a gentle smile.

"It's just that Steward," Borly went on, "he treats me and Kurl as low as you. Wagehand or bondservant, he likes to play duke at you. But bondservants . . ." He shook his head. "He never did like it when the Baron put a bondservant over a wagehand, like you here. Then to have a bondservant rise up from the Baron's bed? No doubt about it, soon as the Baron's buried, he'll find some way to get rid of Roxaine."

"Send her to the prison farm right now, if he could," Kurl said. "Or worse."

"That's right." Borly nodded sagely. "Banish her, he would."

"Or worse," Kurl repeated. "The both of them."

"That's right. The baby, too."

Five

L oyal paused outside the door to the Baron's parlor to rub his weary eyes. It had been a long night, sitting up with his mother and father, keeping deathwatch by the Baron's bed. The presence of Roxaine and her baby hadn't made it any easier, but the Baron's spirit had joined the rising sun unfettered by any curse or shade. As near as anyone could tell. Loyal gave way to a jaw-cracking yawn, squared his shoulders, and went in.

His father was sitting at the Baron's polished desk. He looked up sharply. "Don't stand there!" he ordered. "Shut the door. And lock it."

Loyal was struck by the fierce expression on his father's face. He looked like one of the strange foreign masks that hung in the glass-fronted case behind him. The Baron's parlor was lined with such cases, filled with carved masks, exotic statues, and the bleached skulls of strange animals. Mounted heads hung above the cabinets. Stuffed birds perched on the mantel. All the blank-eyed faces stared down at the two of them. Loyal frowned in reply. They could all be buried with the Baron, as far as he was concerned.

He locked the door and was turning toward the desk when a harsh voice rang out. "Chain him up! There's a pretty girl!" It was the Baron's parrot, another of his foreign curiosities. He'd loved watching visitors jump when it talked.

"Blast that bird!" his father snapped. "Put the cover on it."

Loyal gladly obeyed. The parrot hissed at him, snapping its beak as he draped the cage. Once covered, it muttered into silence.

Loyal turned back to his father. "What shall I do first?" he asked, eager to show his mettle. There was a funeral to arrange, messages to send to Dunsgow and the other Barons, meetings to reassure vendors and buyers; all that on top of the normal business of managing the Baron's many properties. All complicated by one nettlesome detail: The heir was still an infant.

"Light the fire," his father said.

Loyal's spirits wilted. "Light the fire?"

"You do know how, I assume?"

Loyal quickly reached for tinder and kindling from the scuttle. "I merely wondered what else I could do. To help you, I mean. With the arrangements. The funeral . . . and all." He trailed off under his father's scowl.

"I suppose you can help look for the will," his father said grudgingly.

"You don't have it?" Loyal was amazed. His father was privy to all the Baron's affairs. That should have included the will.

"Would I be looking if I did?" his father snapped. "I signed it as witness, of course, but the Baron kept it among his personal papers. Didn't I tell you to light the fire?"

Loyal hastened to obey. By the time he had it burning, his father had gone through three of the desk drawers. Several small bundles of paper lay on the desk. From the expression on his father's face, none was the will. "Look in those," his father ordered, indicating closed cabinets beneath one of the glass cases. As Loyal was opening them, the door latch rattled. He looked at his father, wondering who else would have a key. His father's scowl deepened.

Roxaine came in. She paused an instant when she saw them, then went straight to the birdcage and took off the cloth. The parrot whistled a greeting.

"Have you found it?" she asked. To Loyal's ears, it sounded like a demand.

"Found what?" his father replied icily.

"The will, of course. Don't play coy with me, Steward."

She opened the cage, and the parrot stepped onto her hand. Since becoming the Baron's consort, she had taken a liking to the blasted thing, and it to her. Now she was the only one who dared handle it. She ran a finger along its beak and around to the red patch behind its green head. It rubbed against her palm and whistled again. Loyal grimaced. Birds of a feather.

"I went over the menu with Liddy Cook," she said, "and sent Hunter out to the park to get a fresh deer. Venison was his favorite."

Jan Steward was livid. "Boar was his favorite," he said through clenched teeth, "and the funeral meal is my concern."

"Your concern should be finding that bloodsucking curse of a so-called mage."

"I have more important things to deal with."

"More important than your Baron's murderer?" She put her hands on her hips. The parrot fled to her shoulder and joined her in glaring at Loyal's father.

Jan Steward stood, looming over the desk. "He did not murder the Baron. He tried to save his life."

"By draining all his blood?"

"Trying to undo the poisons your witch had poured into him."

"My 'witch' has been treating the sick on this estate for thirty years—and healing them! My 'witch' didn't disappear an hour before the Baron died! My 'witch' is still here, in mourning!"

"An easy disguise for the guilty."

"Are you trying to say—?"

"No more than you!" Steward's shout brought her up short. He took a slow breath, then sat back down. "I will send a man to inquire after the healer," he said. "Meanwhile, I have an estate to maintain. Your daughter's estate, I might add; consider that favor the death has done you. She is now master of the River Slow, unless the will says otherwise—"

"It won't."

Steward glared. "Then until she comes of age, I must be her guardian and manage her business. So if you will excuse me, I have a lot to do."

Roxaine raised her eyebrows. "I will manage my daughter's business."

Steward leaned back in the chair, both hands flat on the desk. "As her mother, you can change her diapers, choose her toys, and set her menus all you like. Only a wife can be guardian."

She smiled coldly. "We can take that up with the Council, if you insist. I understand family counts a lot with them. His daughter, my daughter: It should be clear."

She turned to the door but stopped, regarding them both with narrowed eyes. Then she brushed past Loyal, opened one of the cabinets, and took a bundle from the first pigeonhole.

"I think I'll take these for now," she said. "And in case you're wondering, they're my personal papers." She smiled coldly. "Darvin cleared the space for me."

She left then, the parrot glaring back over Roxaine's shoulder. As they went out, it whistled and yelled, "Let her go! Let her go! Pretty girl!"

Jan Steward was pale with rage. "We have to find that will," he snarled.

"Could she really take over the estate?" Loyal's stomach soured at the thought.

"No." His father was emphatic. "She was bluffing. The Council of Barons would never recognize her, mother or not. They'd never let a bondservant sit in Council with them."

"But she's not in bond anymore. Cutter forgave it."

Jan Steward fixed Loyal with a stern look. "He never told me that. Did he ever tell you?"

"No, I—"

"Did you ever hear him tell anyone else?"

"No." Loyal squirmed under his father's gaze. "I . . . we all just assumed."

"Like sheep," his father growled. "He decked her out in expensive clothing. He gave her gifts and liberties. Gave in to her cozening and raised wages. Wasted food on servants. Lightened punishments.

All against my advice! He even took her to bed, so everyone assumed he had forgiven her bond." He turned back to the papers on the desk. "But where is the receipt? Where is the signed receipt, showing he wrote off her bond? I, of all people, should have seen it."

Loyal considered what this could mean. "If there's no receipt . . . ?"

"Receipt, note, title—there should be some document. Cutter signed one to obtain her bond; he had to sign one to release it. He knew it takes more than a promise to forgive a bond."

"Wouldn't she have it?" Loyal asked. "Blazing mages! Her papers! We just let her walk right out wi—"

"Do I look like a fool?" his father snapped. "That was the first place I searched! It wasn't there. And I don't think she has it. She would have produced it by now, to back up her ridiculous statements. *His daughter, my daughter,*" he mocked. "Pah!" He opened another drawer in the desk. "It must be here, among Cutter's papers. Look for it. That and the will. He could've forgiven every bond on the estate through his will, if he'd wanted. Which he didn't. I saw the will. There was no mention of bonds in it."

"But if we don't find one . . . ?"

His father slapped his hand on the desktop, scattering papers. "Then she is still a bondservant! She cannot be guardian."

"That's something, at least. What about the baby girl? She's not in bond. Is she?"

"No. She would still be heir. Despite her breeding." He stared at the fire, lips pressed in an angry line. The silence stretched.

Loyal shifted awkwardly, wondering how he could ease his father's mood. "If only she hadn't been . . ." He trailed off, afraid anything he said would make his father more angry.

"Hadn't been born? Don't think I haven't considered that. The Council of Barons would choose an heir. Not one of themselves; that's forbidden. A Baron can rule no more than one river, to maintain the balance in Council." He stared into the fire a moment, then shook his head abruptly. "The Barons will choose the person most likely to keep affairs running just as they are. A smooth transition, that's what they'll want. I'm sure of it." He paused again, and Loyal wondered how sure he actually felt. "Keep looking! The will and receipt, both of them. We don't run this estate on 'if only's.'"

Loyal turned to the cabinet. It was divided into pigeonholes, each holding a bundle of papers. He started at the upper left, opening each bundle and scanning each sheet. His mind raced with the implications of his father's last words. Had there been no heir, Jan Steward would most likely have been named the next Baron of the River Slow. It had happened once before, many years ago, when the original Miner and his only child had died in a cave-in. The Council of Barons had named his steward the next Miner. It made sense, of course: Who but the steward would know all the details, the transactions and trading alliances? The new Miner's children had followed in the line for over five generations now.

Loyal daydreamed a moment, seeing himself at the Baron's desk. He glanced around the room and couldn't help but frown at the gallery of stuffed heads and carved faces staring back. They would definitely have to go. But Cutter did have an heir. If she lived to maturity . . . He shook his head and reached for the next bundle of papers. His tired mind wandered over inane possibilities as he continued his search. His eyesight blurred with fatigue. He shook it off and slogged to the final bundle in the very last pigeonhole.

It was the will. At first it didn't even register. Loyal scanned the lines mechanically, half asleep. "Now on the third day of the ninth month, by this contract of my own hand and free desire, I, Darvin Cutter, Baron of the River Slow and all its Tributaries . . ." The legalese droned on. Loyal had started to refold it before it finally sank in: "I, Darvin Cutter, Baron . . . do hereby grant and bequeath in this, my last Will and Testament . . ." He snapped alert.

"What is it?" His father was watching him closely.

Loyal held out the papers. "The will," he said proudly.

His father snatched it. His eyes flew over the first page, then jumped to the bottom of the last. His jaw clenched. His face went white, then flushed with anger.

Loyal's mouth went dry. "What is it?" he asked.

"It's a new will. It leaves everything to his daughter. And grants guardianship—complete control—to her!" He stopped, breathing hard.

"Her?" Loyal echoed, aghast. Certainly, he couldn't mean—

"Who do you think?" his father demanded. "His mistress. The blasted servant. He even names her Roxaine *Cutter*. As if they were already married!"

He looked ready to tear it up, but he caught himself. Carefully, he searched both sides of each sheet.

"It hasn't been witnessed," he said quietly. "Or noted."

"What?" Loyal leaned close.

"It hasn't been noted," his father repeated. "There's no seal, no stamp. No witness's signature. No noter's mark of any kind."

"But . . ." Loyal considered the implications. "It's not legal, then. Is it?"

"Even better: No one has seen this but us."

Loyal nodded slowly, unsure he knew his father's mind.

Jan Steward lowered his hand and held the will to the fire. The corner lit. Flame spread along the edges of the sheets, slowly eating inward, turning them red, then black, then ashen. Words flared and disappeared. The last corner flickered. His father finally dropped it, and watched avidly as it disappeared up the chimney. The will was gone.

"No one ever saw it," he repeated. He stared at the tips of his fingers, scorched by the flames. "It never existed."

Loyal regarded his father with amazement. He had been taught all his life to preserve records, so there would be no doubt when reckonings came due. He wondered if he would have had his father's strength of purpose now.

"Don't look so shocked, boy," his father said coldly. "Do you think I'd let that shrew take over the valley and destroy everything I helped Cutter build? Do you think a bondservant could do anything but?"

"Certainly not," Loyal said quickly. "But he did expect to marry her."

"He hardly expected to die so soon." Jan Steward grabbed Loyal's shoulder and shook it. "Think, boy! The woman worked in the laundry, cleaning linens, mopping floors. She's short, coarse, sweaty. Rough hands. A tongue like a fishhook. And a daughter just as nasty. Suddenly, the daughter's fled, a runaway, and this drudge is the Baron's pet, all decked out in velvet and pearls. She's in his bed, whispering in his ear, making changes to the smooth running of our estate. And all at once, the mother of an heir. After fifteen years of marriage to a fine woman produced nothing. Do you think that was natural?"

"Ah." Loyal nodded. "Do you really think . . . ?"

His father shook him again. "Don't be a dolt! Look at the daughter. You saw it yourself: She's a mage, a bird girl. Where do you think she got that talent? From her mother, that's where!"

"But real mages are . . ." Loyal almost said "bedtime stories," but he remembered the raven, the disappearing girl, the stories from Dunsgow. ". . . so rare," he finished lamely. That at least was true.

"No. The woman bewitched Cutter," his father insisted. "Bewitched, bedded, and bore a convenient child." He leaned close, dropped his voice. "Then killed him."

"Killed him?" Loyal's thoughts spun.

"Of course!" his father growled. "How else do you explain it all?"

"But Father, mages can't just bespell someone; all the stories say that. You have to agree to be—"

"She seduced him, fool! Cutter was lonely after his wife died. And he very much wanted an heir. Once he'd agreed in his heart, he was an easy mark for any charm."

Loyal couldn't look away from his father's piercing gaze. "But why would she kill him? He had proposed. Her child was heir."

His father smiled bitterly. "Think of the woman, boy. Think of her temper. Never contented, always demanding, trying to run things, changing this, altering that, the conniving witch!" He shrugged expressively. "Who knows what insult Cutter gave her? Maybe he refused to marry her. But make no mistake about it, Cutter's death was far too convenient to be coincidence."

Loyal nodded. "How can we prove it?"

"We can't," his father said. "And we can't afford to let her appear before the Council. What if she turned her magic on them?" He pointed to the fire. "All we can do is block her."

He went back to the desk and began to tidy the remaining papers. "We have a duty here, boy: a duty to the river, and to ourselves as Stewards. A duty to maintain the values and traditions and business that let all of us prosper. Sometimes that means harsh measures. Sometimes quiet measures." He caught and held Loyal's gaze. "Sometimes both together. The important thing is our duty. Understand?"

"Yes, Father. Absolutely. But what about the bond receipt? If there is one?"

His father glared. "It has to be here. If we didn't find it, it doesn't exist."

"But—"

"It doesn't exist! And without the new will, I will continue as Steward and manage the river as always. Until the Council can meet and make it official. For the child, of course."

"Of course."

"Good. I knew I could count on you. Now, get some sleep."

"Yes, sir."

Loyal fought back a sudden yawn. He was more exhausted than he had ever felt before. He stumbled upstairs, wondering at the sudden turn of fortune. He still worried about the missing receipt and vowed to keep searching. If it existed, he would find it.

And burn it, just like the will. Because his father was right, of course. No one could manage the river properly but them. Certainly not a bondservant. Certainly not one like Roxaine. He, Loyal, would find the receipt. He would block her. And his father would be so proud.

Six

R aven watched the funeral procession from the thick cedars that bordered the cemetery. Roxaine walked behind the bier, carrying tiny Sarita. The baby looked at her with a thoughtful expression, as though the sight of tears were something entirely new. Knowing her mother, Raven thought it probably was. For a moment, she felt some sympathy; then she remembered who had died. She wasn't about to waste any grief on Cutter.

Behind Roxaine came Steward, with his wife and sneering son. The house servants trailed a few steps back. Workers from the farm, meat house, and wharves flanked the lane in untidy groups. Phillipe was there with Hero, Hunter with his surly boy. And she saw Gardener, Cook, Stabler, and a lot of other faces suddenly remembered after the years away. There were a couple of young woman she almost didn't recognize. They'd been girls when she'd left.

The bearers slipped ropes under the coffin and lowered it into the grave. Steward's wife threw in flowers, Cook a sprinkle of grain. Young Steward poured in a cup of river water. His father followed with a handful of earth, then made a little speech that made Raven gag. "Caring and generous" were not words she'd have used about Cutter.

Roxaine made to speak, but Steward elbowed in front of her and launched into a second eulogy. Roxaine stood behind him, waiting with amazing patience. Raven could tell from the look on her face that she'd just as soon push him into the grave.

Steward recited the formal Blessing of the River. People started to turn away, but Roxaine wasn't done yet. Using her own sharp elbows, she sidestepped Steward and began to sing an old grayfolk song. Grayfolk had been living on the middle reach for more generations than anyone could remember. They had fit in, adapted, even intermarried, and few of their old traditions remained: a handful of words, folk tales, lullabies. And the song of final parting. Everyone turned back, surprised. Phillipe joined in quietly, then the other grayfolk. Steward's face went red, his scowl deep as an eagle's.

Roxaine finished her song and closed her eyes, standing for a moment in complete stillness. Finally, she turned and began walking from the grave. Caught off-guard, Steward hurried to catch up, but the other house staff had closed in behind her, blocking him. Raven croaked a bitter laugh. Her mother had just outstewarded Steward.

When everyone had left, Raven flew a roundabout path to the loft of the breeding barn, where she changed form and put on warmer clothes that Phillipe had found for her. Soon Hero came scrambling up the ladder, burdened by a large basket.

"What a feast!" he exclaimed. "There's cakes and creams, a giant roast, must be the biggest cow in the valley, venison, pheasants and hens in walnuts, even the turnips and kale are cooked in butter sauce!" Chattering excitedly, he pulled food from the basket and arranged it around them. Smiling at his easy joy, Raven joined in Cutter's funeral feast, and savored every bite.

She lingered at the estate for almost two weeks. Borly's words had stuck in her mind, and she couldn't stop thinking that her sister was in danger. Keeping watch seemed the best thing to do. She couldn't forget her dream about her mother or the angry words she had thrown out in Sarita's room. She realized she needed to finish the meeting Steward had cut off, to part with her mother on her own terms, without losing her temper. She watched for the moment, but her mother was never alone.

Hero thought it was a great adventure. Many evenings, returning from a late flight, she found him curled up asleep in her makeshift nest among the bales of hay. She didn't sleep well, herself.

There were more visitors than usual, and Raven could only guess what kind of deals Steward was making. He had till midsummer, the next meeting of the full Council of Barons. Meanwhile, her mother and sister seemed to be doing just fine. Roxaine had taken complete charge of the house, firmly shunting Steward's wife aside. She met with Steward every day, forcing him to go over the accounts, wages, work schedules, and all. Watching from the shrubbery, squeezed into the guise of a robin, Raven saw him grit his teeth and part with as little information as he could get away with, clearly stalemated until the Council met. And Raven knew her mother would find a way to attend that session, no matter what Steward might wish. With Sarita in her arms to represent her claim, and a full season's practice running the estate, she'd be impossible to ignore. Whether that would carry any weight with the Council was another question. Raven was no seer, but what she knew of councils made her certain they'd choose whoever they thought would be best for them, not for Cutter's heir or the Slow valley.

The chance to speak with her mother never came. Roxaine was constantly meeting with someone or directing someone else. And when she was alone, she stayed inside. Raven glimpsed her through the windows from time to time, wandering distractedly through the rooms, as though trying to state her claim by sheer presence. Or maybe looking for something: a bit of peace, a moment's rest. Raven didn't envy her. Even when Roxaine was nursing Sarita, old Louella the nursemaid usually stayed near. Only once did Roxaine sit out on the garden bench by herself for a moment. Raven landed, ready to change and confront her, but Roxaine had turned away from the house, hiding her face in her hand. Her shoulders shook. She was crying silently, fighting the tears. Raven flew off, angry for reasons she couldn't explain.

On a sudden sunny day, when a warm breeze blew upriver to clear out a week of drizzle, Raven decided this had all been a fool's errand. Sarita was the heir; she was safe, whichever way the wind blew. It was time to get away from this backbiting business. Her mother could have it. In fact, she seemed made for it. Maybe there really wasn't anything else to say. Raven flew in robin form to the side yard to sneak in a goodbye. Sarita was there, asleep in her basket on the stone bench. Louella sat beside her, knitting. Raven landed in one of the dwarf cedars and looked down at her baby sister.

"Good luck, little Baron," she said. It came out as robin song, but that was all right. "Watch out for Steward and his nasty son. Watch out for our mother, too. Don't believe promises from anyone." Her sister looked up with that serious expression, big eyed and wondering. And so blazingly helpless. "Sorry, little egg, you're on your own in this world. It's best you learn to take care of yourself early."

As Raven spread her wings, her mother came out. Raven settled back onto the branch.

Roxaine came over to the basket. "Hello, little Baron," she said.

Sarita smiled and waved her pudgy arms. Roxaine reached down and held out a finger; Sarita grasped it with both tiny fists and pulled it to her mouth.

Roxaine chuckled. "Hungry, little bird?" She scooped her up and sat on the bench by Louella, opening the flap on her gown so the baby could find her breast. Sarita nuzzled, then fed busily, staring up at her mother's face all the while.

Raven hunkered on her branch, fighting to ignore an unexpected twinge of jealousy.

Suddenly, Steward appeared from the manor, followed by his smirking son and two hulking baronsmen. He strode to the bench, hesitated a moment when he saw what Roxaine was doing, then spoke to the maid.

"Take the child in," he ordered. "I need to speak to her mother."

"Her mother is right here," Roxaine said coldly. "You can speak anytime."

His face reddened. "In private," he growled.

"Then it will have to wait," she said.

Raven enjoyed watching Steward seethe as her mother stroked the baby's hair and let her finish nursing. Young Loyal's face fairly blazed. Finally, Roxaine eased the nipple from her baby's mouth and closed her gown. Standing, she handed little Sarita to Louella. Shrinking under Steward's glare, the poor woman clutched the baby to her chest and hurried into the house.

Roxaine frowned at Steward. "What has you so rushed I can't even feed my baby?"

"Business," he snapped.

"More important than the Baron's dinner?"

"She'll have plenty later."

Roxaine raised a single eyebrow. "Get on with it, then."

Steward smiled stiffly. "You're leaving today," he said. "Now." He held out a document of some kind. A seal flashed in the sunlight. "Baron Stoner now holds your bond."

"What?" Roxaine snatched the document from Steward's hand and scanned it quickly. "This is trash, and you know it." She crumpled it and threw it at him.

He let it bounce and fall. Loyal hurried to pick it up. "It's completely in order," Steward said. "Signed and noted."

"Signed by *you*?" Roxaine said. "You forget, Steward: *I* am the heir's mother. I'm the one who signs the documents."

"You are a bondservant," he said. "The old Cutter's mistress, nothing more."

"My bond was written off. Cutter forgave it." She stood at least a foot shorter than Steward, but she still managed to look down her nose at him.

He glared back. "So you say."

"He signed the receipt," she said.

"Then bring it forth. Show it to me."

She clenched her fists. "Are you calling me a liar, you over-stuffed capon?"

"There is no receipt, signed or otherwise," he barked. He took a breath, calmed himself. "I searched; believe me, I searched very carefully.

Her eyes widened in sudden realization. "I'll bet you did," she growled. "And you found it, didn't you? Here I've been searching all over, while you . . . what? Burned it?"

Steward laughed. "I found nothing. And since you can't produce a copy, you're leaving."

Roxaine turned to the baronsmen. "And you're going to let him get away with this, I suppose?" They shifted uneasily and looked away. She laughed scornfully. "You're going to need support when this gets to the Council, Steward, I can promise you that."

Steward's cold smile returned. "Selling a bond is not a matter for the Council."

"No? You don't think they'll notice you selling the Baron's heir into bondage?"

"The heir is not going," he said. "She's staying here in my care, where she belongs."

For a long moment, Roxaine stood in shocked silence. Then she exploded. "She's my baby!" she cried. She swung a round-house blow that caught Steward completely by surprise. He staggered back, hand to his eye. She pursued him step by step, still swinging. "You thieving, lying crapherd! She's my baby! You will never, ever—" She landed another hard blow before one of the baronsmen grabbed her hand. She turned on him, kicking and hitting. Loyal got behind her and grabbed her other arm.

Raven forgot she was a robin. She launched herself from the cedar, chirping in outrage, and fluttered around the heads of the men. She pecked at them uselessly, completely unnoticed. A flailing arm sent her spinning to the ground. Dazed, she fled under a bush beside the house and watched helplessly as the men subdued her mother. Loyal produced a set of shackles from under his cloak and snapped it onto her wrists.

Roxaine spat at him. *"Zomenswi!"* she hissed. It was from an ancient grayfolk tale: woman stealer. In the story, it could drive a man into exile.

Steward sneered. "Take her to the wharf!" he ordered, rubbing his eye. The baronsmen dragged her away, still kicking and struggling. "Get her things," he snapped at Loyal.

The boy hurried into the house and returned almost immediately, carrying a small bag. He took a look at Steward's purpling eye and pursed his lips. "What if Stoner refuses to take her?"

"Don't worry, you'll be bringing a sweet enough offer," Steward replied. "And more, if he'll send her to his quarries. She'll break soon enough there. Has the wet nurse arrived?"

"Yes, sir."

"Good. Let's hope she can keep the brat quiet."

"You'll tame her, Father, with her mother gone and you guardian."

Steward grunted. "We'll see, boy. A great many things can happen in a childhood. Go on, then, and keep a close watch on her. You have the letter for Stoner?"

"Yes, sir."

"Remember, you represent the River Slow. When you meet him, you are Cutter."

"Yes, sir." Loyal hurried off, smiling.

Raven watched in rage as Steward went back into the house. She knew what the blazing bag of offal meant. It wouldn't happen right away, not so soon after shipping off her mother, but sometime little Sarita would have an accident, leaving that maggoty cow pile free to become Baron. Her mother could take care of herself, but Sarita couldn't. Sarita needed to get out of here. It was time to get out of this useless body and come up with a plan. She took wing, heading for the breeding barn to wait for darkness.

When Hero brought her dinner that evening, she wrapped up

most of it in the napkin and tied it into a bundle she could carry. He watched with sharp eyes.

"You're going after your mam," he said.

"You know about it already?"

"Everybody knows," he said. "Steward is giving her to Stoner."

"That's right." She jerked the knot tight and pulled the cloak over her shoulders, then picked up the bundle.

"You're not flying?" he said.

"I've got to carry my sister," she replied.

Hero blinked. "Your sister? She's all right. Steward kept her."

"Only until he can figure out how to get rid of her. She's the one I've got to rescue."

"But what about your mother?"

"She's going to have to take care of herself."

His eyes went wide. "But she's your mother. You can't let them send her off. Besides, you'll need her help."

"I stopped needing her help years ago," Raven snapped.

"Well, you need her to feed the baby."

Raven stopped with her foot on the top rung of the ladder. The little nuthatch was right. Her mind raced. She could try changing Sarita into a bird, but that could be hard on both of them. If the change went wrong . . . "I'll steal milk," she said finally. "Until I can wean her. Then I'll chew her food for her, like a bird."

"You'll still need help," he said. "Someone to watch her while you find food." He came toward the ladder.

"No," Raven said. "I'm better off alone. It's less risky."

His face fell. "But I want—"

"No! You're too young. It's too dangerous. Your father was right."

Raven hurried down the ladder and out of the barn before he could argue more. She crept across the twilit fields to the back gate of the manor. There was no breeze and no sound from the dogs. She sneaked through the darkness to a spot below her sister's room. All stayed quiet. She set down her bundle and shed her cloak. She was a big raven when she changed, but not that big. Sarita would be more than double her weight then, far too heavy to fly with. Raven would have to risk sneaking out through the house, then reclaim her gear and steal off. After that . . . well, it was one step at a time, and jump when she had to.

She changed to raven. Now she could hear faint noises from within: the kitchen help cleaning up, footsteps in a hallway, but no sound of alarm. She flew to the windowsill and peered inside. The room was dark and still. Remembering her awkward change the first time she went in this way, Raven spread her wings hard against the window frame. She focused on her hands and feet and tried to change faster than she'd ever done before. It still took a few seconds, almost long enough for her to lose her balance and topple outward. But then she had hands and could hold on to the wooden trim while the rest of her changed.

Good trick, she thought: hands and feet first. I'll have to remember it.

She pushed open the window and stepped inside in one quick move. Then stumbled back as her foot landed not on floor but on a soft belly. There was a grunt, a sudden shriek of fear. A body heaved beneath her.

Raven fell backward out the window. She grabbed for the trim and missed. Had a moment's realization that she'd stepped on the wet nurse, took another to realize she was falling. She flapped her arms uselessly, began the spell to change. But never had time to finish. She hit, and the world went black.

Seven

Loyal had traveled on the river before, but not without his father. Now he was on his own, an envoy to Baron Stoner. He had a baronsman along to help guard Roxaine, but he, Loyal, was completely in charge. Here at last was the opportunity to show his father his worth. He thrilled with responsibility, staying up half the night after they left Cutter's Landing and rising before dawn to inspect the boat.

When he stepped out of his cabin, the deck and rail were wet with chill dew. The engine was cold, the paddle wheel still. They were on the *Lady Slow,* Cutter's personal steamboat. Roxaine was locked in the Baron's big cabin up front. Loyal had the larger of the two staff cabins; the baronsman shared the other with the boatman. The others were still asleep. Loyal could hear the soft snores of the fireboy, curled up by the coal bin. He pursed his lips. It was just as his father said: They were all as lazy as you'd let them be. And what would his father do now? Loyal smiled. This decision to wake them was his. Well, he could afford to give them a few minutes' more rest. He savored the moment.

A slight breeze stirred the water along the hull and shivered the dark bulk of the big maple they had tied up to. As Loyal walked forward, he heard a sound from the door to the big cabin: scratching at the lock. He knocked sharply.

"What is it, woman?" he demanded. "What are you doing?"

Roxaine replied without a beat. "Trying to get out, what do you think? I have to pee."

"Use the chamber pot," he ordered.

"It's full. I've been locked in here since yesterday, if you'll recall." Her tone could have sliced iron.

Loyal flushed. Trust her to fill the whole pot in less than a day. "I'll let you out, but you'll empty it yourself," he said. "Then you're going right back in." He waited, but she didn't reply. "Understand?" he demanded.

"Yes, Lord Jailer. Just open the door; I'm about to burst."

Loyal slipped the key ring from his belt and fumbled in the dim light for the lock. He could hear her shoe tapping impatiently just inside. As soon as the lock clicked, she pushed her way out. The pot was indeed full, and it reeked. Loyal curled his lip and stepped back. Roxaine stumbled and the pot almost slipped from her hands, which were still bound in his father's shackles. A gob of stinking liquid slopped over the edge and soaked his knee.

"You clumsy drudge! Be more careful!" He wanted to slap her.

"So sorry," she said. "These irons do make it a bit awkward." She made it the rest of the way to the rail without mishap and dumped the contents over the side. She paused and looked upriver.

"Back inside," he snapped.

She glared at him. "I'm just getting a little air."

"You've gotten enough."

She sighed, then stalked back to the door. Just outside, she made as if to stumble. The pot fell; its fetid dregs spotted Loyal's other knee.

"You stupid—" He cut himself off. He would not get trapped in her games. "Pick it up," he ordered. "If it's broken . . ."

"What?" she drawled. "You'll charge it to my bond?" She scooped up the chamber pot and eyed it. "Lucky me, still in one piece."

"Inside!" He slammed the door behind her.

As he was locking it, his baronsman hurried around the deckhouse, cudgel in hand.

"Everything all right, young sir?" he asked, looking from Loyal to the cabin door.

"It's fine," Loyal snapped. "She just needed to . . . talk." He kept his body turned so the man wouldn't see the wet spots on his breeches.

"If she gives you trouble, call me." The baronsman tapped the cudgel on his palm.

"I doubt we'll need to club her," Loyal said irritably.

The man scowled. "I wouldn't be too sure. She's a fighter. Near took my eyes out yesterday. I wouldn't take those shackles off, if I were you."

"I'll be the judge of that," Loyal replied coldly.

The man stiffened. "Whatever you say, sir."

Loyal gave him a curt nod and hurried aft to his cabin to find a towel and clean off his knees as best he could. The smell lingered, and he realized he'd have to save his other pair of breeches for his meeting with Baron Stoner. Cursing, he scrubbed some more. By the time he reemerged, the fireboy had the boiler heating, and the boatman was throwing together a rough meal of porridge and leftover beef. Loyal watched the baronsman take a bowl to Roxaine. She almost dropped it trying to deal with the shackles and cursed vividly.

"She has a tongue in her," the boatman remarked. "I'm surprised the Baron stood it."

"She charmed him, right enough," Loyal replied, happy to encourage the rumor.

"Well, at least she gave him an heir," the boatman said. "And just in time. Odd how things work out. The Baron's dead, she's off to Stoner, and your father's raising the girl."

"You can't trust a bondservant to raise a Baron."

"Particularly one like her," the boatman agreed. "That temper she has . . ."

"That's not it," Loyal protested. "It's a steward's job. For the good of the river."

"Absolutely."

Loyal flushed. He felt he was being humored. "My father knows what he's doing," he said.

"I've no doubt he does, young sir," the boatman said.

There was no way to argue with someone who kept agreeing with you. "Good," Loyal said lamely. He poked his spoon at the last of his porridge, no longer hungry. "Time we got under way," he snapped. He thrust his bowl at the baronsman, just returning from the bow. "Get hers, too," he ordered.

The man gave him a wooden look, then took the bowl and went forward again to knock at the cabin door. The boatman went aft to check on the fireboy.

Loyal stewed at the rail until the big stern wheel began to churn up the surface of the river. Soon they were surging through the center of the channel. Loyal went to the bow, where the light wind of their passage joined an upriver spring breeze to stroke his face. The Slow was still high, and he could see over the banks into the adjoining fields, where farmers were spreading manure and tilling stubble into the rich soil. They steamed past low, broad fishing rafts and flatboats poling upstream with the aid of small square sails. A flock of ducks paddled out of their way, and the boatman let off his whistle, startling them into loud, splashing flight.

Loyal laughed. He could get used to traveling like this, his father's envoy, on his own special boat. Until his father was old enough to step aside and let Loyal take his place. The Steward of the River Slow. This was perfect training, a chance to see the world. Meet the Barons and do business with them. The *other* Barons. Yes, it was still possible: He might be Baron someday. But first this: envoy. Bearing his father's greetings to Stoner. Delivering his package.

Package. Loyal liked that term. He glanced at the cabin door, where the baronsman stood guard.

"You," he called, feeling magnanimous. "Take a break. I'll keep watch awhile."

"If you say, sir," the man replied. "But you might want to check on her. It's awful quiet in there."

"She lost the fight," Loyal said. "I daresay she's finally realized it."

"Maybe. But I wouldn't put it past her to be slitting the pillows just for spite. You want to keep close watch on her."

Loyal fumed. Did this lout think he was too young and stupid to deal with a lone woman? In shackles? Who was the Steward's son here and who the wagehand? He used one of his father's tactics, a cold smile. "Thank you. You can go now. I know how to handle her."

"Whatever you say, young sir," the man replied. He turned and went aft.

Loyal stared sourly at the riverbanks. They passed another steamboat coming upstream, pushing a long tow loaded high with empty casks on their way to the meat house. The boatmen traded whistles, discordant shrieks. There were more fishing boats and rafts, more fields ripe with manure, more banks lined with trees, the occasional farm landing, a small town. The Slow seemed to be living up to its name.

Finally, it was time for the midday meal, such as it was: bread and cheese and carrots sliced up quickly by the fireboy. Loyal told the baronsman to take a plate up to the boatman, then took a plate to Roxaine himself. When he unlocked and opened the door, he found her sitting dispiritedly in a chair by the front window, staring out at the riverbanks as they constantly disappeared aft. She had wrapped herself in a heavy traveling cloak, as though chilled.

Well and good, he thought. It's about time she learned her place. "Here's your meal," he said. "I've decided you can come out on deck to eat."

She regarded him listlessly, then sighed and took the plate. "Thank you," she said.

He indicated the open door, and she sighed again as she stepped into the sun. She stared a long time upriver, then shuffled toward the bow. Loyal was struck by how small she seemed. Without her fiery temper to sustain her, she had contracted into something shapeless and weak. She stopped at the corner of the railing and tried to balance her wooden plate with her leg so she could bring the food to her mouth. With the shackles on, there was no other way she could eat. She managed two bites before the plate fell into the river. She watched in slumped resignation as it bobbed in their wake.

Loyal muttered a quiet curse. "I'll get you another," he said. "Don't move."

He stalked back to the galley, to find the baronsman watching with an expression of disapproval. Loyal ordered him to slice more food onto another plate. The man complied stiffly. Let him stew, Loyal thought. The woman is my charge, and I will decide her treatment.

Roxaine was exactly where he had left her, staring down at the water with an unfocused gaze. He held out the plate. She took it awkwardly in her shackled hands.

"I'll take those off for the meal," he allowed. "But if you drop this one, you'll eat from the deck."

She smiled wanly and thanked him again. As the shackles came off, she rubbed her wrists, then began to eat slowly and quietly. Loyal glanced at the baronsman, vindicated. He wished his father were here to see.

When she was done, Roxaine handed back the plate and held out her wrists. Her face was resigned, eyes down.

"We'll leave them off for now," he allowed, looping the shackles through his belt. "You can stay out here for a while."

She nodded, smiled slightly, and turned to the river with yet another sigh.

Loyal strolled back to the galley. "Keep an eye on her," he ordered the baronsman.

"And if she jumps in?"

"In that gown? Not likely. But if she does, you'd better go in after her. You wouldn't want to be charged for her bond if she drowned."

Pleased at his quick retort, Loyal went to his cabin. When he glanced out a few minutes later, the baronsman was leaning against the rail, arms crossed, watching Roxaine closely. Loyal decided to leave him there for the rest of the afternoon to teach him a lesson. He got out his quills and ink and began a journal, a record for his father, but his mind kept straying to the leather wallet entrusted to him. Finally, he couldn't resist any longer. He opened it and read the letter to Stoner.

Then he read it again, amazed. His father was offering Stoner half price on all beef for the next five years. In addition, he made an offer to purchase building stone for three new warehouses, at full price. To seal the bargain, he offered one bondservant for Stoner's household or, if he preferred, for his quarries, in which case, and after the Council had confirmed him as guardian to Cutter's heir, Jan Steward would be pleased to reconsider the length of the arrangement, as well as to commission a new wing on the manor and statuary for a garden. The bondservant was never named, though the properly noted receipt for her bond was enclosed.

It was an offer Stoner could hardly refuse, but it would pinch the Cutter purse for many years. Once again, Loyal wondered if he would have had his father's strength of purpose to send off the heir's mother without sounding out Stoner first. He carefully replaced the papers. Feeling very proud to be the chosen courier, he strode to the cabin door to look out on his charge. He had a moment's panic when he didn't see Roxaine, but spotted her sitting in a chair by the cabin door. Just then the baronsman looked up. Loyal stepped quickly to the rail and stretched, as though he had simply come out for some air. In truth, he felt invigorated, with no desire to go back inside. He went to the baronsman.

"I'll watch now," he said. "You take a break."

"Yes, sir," the baronsman replied. He stifled a yawn, and Loyal enjoyed another moment of vindication. The man finally seemed to realize Roxaine was no longer a problem.

Loyal sauntered to the bow, nodding politely to Roxaine as he went by. She nodded back, then pulled the cloak more tightly around her shoulders. Loyal leaned against the rail. The late sun was just above the distant valley wall. Soon they would be in shadow. Already the air felt cooler, and he shivered a little. He almost envied Roxaine her heavy cloak. He glanced at her, so pleasingly small and listless in her chair. As he watched, the shadow line passed over them, and the temperature dropped another several degrees. She seemed completely unaware of it.

He turned back to the river. Another boat was coming toward them. The boatmen traded whistles, and Loyal walked across the bow to watch its churning wake dance on the river. When he strolled back to his spot at the rail, the distant hills were silhouetted by the afterglow of the dipping sun. He gaze traveled aft, into the shadow by the cabin door. He blinked, half blinded by the afterimage of the hills. He blinked again, searching the doorway. The chair was empty, the heavy cloak discarded on the deck.

Roxaine was gone.

Eight

Raven hurt. Her head, her neck, her back; everything right down to her feet hurt. She moaned.

"She's waking up," someone said. The words stabbed the insides of her ears.

"Lie still," another voice said. Raven thought it might be her mother's maid, Louella. "You took quite a fall."

A fall. Raven remembered falling. She couldn't remember landing. She opened her eyes and winced at the blinding lamplight. Wincing made her wince even more. She closed her eyes again and tried to go back to sleep.

The door burst open: more light, more pain. Steward strode into the room. His footsteps drummed in Raven's head. He loomed over the bed, twirling a black feather in his fingers. One of her flight feathers. Anger burned in her throat. She tried to lift her head, but it hurt too much. She sank back.

He chuckled. "Not so quick to flee now, little blackbird?"

Raven tried to ignore him.

"Can she walk?" he asked.

"She shouldn't."

"Move her out to the cell," he ordered. "Let her mend in there, where she can't fly away." He leaned so close that Raven could smell his breath. "You owe us a great deal, little bird: a boat, a fireboy, not to mention your own bond. I promise you, I will collect every bit."

Raven forced out a single word, Roxaine's curse: *"Zomenswi."*

"Just like her mother," he sneered.

Am not, she thought, too weak to say it aloud.

"Get her out of here," he snapped.

"She really shouldn't be moved," the maid said. "She almost died."

"Unfortunate. She would have looked good on the mantel with Cutter's trophies." He strode away, slamming the door hard enough to rattle Raven's teeth.

The maid held a cup of water to Raven's lips. Then four men appeared with a litter. Every joint in her body cried out as they shifted her from the bed. She fainted.

When she woke again, it was completely dark. Her body still ached. Her throat was parched. She reached out, but her hand jolted against a stone wall, sending a hot stab up her neck. She reached out her other hand and bumped a bowl. Gratefully, she rolled over, took it in both hands, and downed a long, healing sip. She fell back, but the movement actually seemed to have helped. Cautiously, she reached out farther. And hit another wall. She ran her hand over the coarse stones. Her heart beat faster. She knew exactly how small this place was. She had been here before, as a girl, locked in more than once by Steward or his wife for talking back, for spoiling laundry, for hiding, for any trifling reason the snake-hearted family could invent.

Raven drew her arms over her chest. She was panting. She closed her staring eyes and tried to slow her pounding heart. Tried to think of somewhere else. But she hurt too much. She lay there, breathing stiffly, all too aware of the walls, until the pounding ache faded into gray and she lapsed back into sleep.

She woke again to more pounding. No, it was tapping. Someone at the door.

Raven sat up too quickly. A sharp pain ran up her spine and kicked the back of her head. She slowed way down, rolling to her knees so she could crawl the two short steps to the door. Silvery light seeped through the cracks. The tapping continued.

"Raven." A high whisper from the gap beneath the door. "Wake up!" It was Hero. The little jackdaw had followed her. She didn't know if that was good or bad.

"Quiet," she whispered, bending close to the gap. "I'm awake."

He spoke even louder. "Are you all right? The maid said you were almost dead."

"Close enough," she said, feeling all the aches anew.

"You were asleep for a whole day!"

"That long?"

"And half tonight! I thought you'd never wake up."

"Hush! You're too loud." Or maybe it was just her headache. She huddled by the gap, breathing in the cool night, trying to ignore the tight stone cage around her.

"Stay awake!" he demanded. "We've got to get you out."

"Whenever you're ready," she said. "What's the plan?"

There was a pause. Then: "Can't you just change and fly out?"

"Change into what? I can't fly through stone."

"Well, if it was me, I'd change into something real small and crawl under the door. Like a mouse or something."

"I'm a bird mage, Calf Wit. I can't change into a mouse."

"Oh." He sounded disappointed. "A . . . a hummingbird?"

Raven thought about it, then felt the gap under the door. It was wide enough to slide a bowl through. It wouldn't fit a raven, but . . .

"I can try," she said. "Here."

She slid off the blanket and fed the corner under the door. Hero pulled it through. Shivering, she closed her eyes and tried to blot out the ache in her head, the lingering pains in her joints. She had never changed herself to anything so small before, never smaller than a robin, and that had felt tight enough. But certainly no worse than the pressure of this tiny stone cell. She just had to concentrate, blank out the walls, forget the pain.

She imagined a hummingbird as clearly as she could. She spoke aloud the words of change, carefully shaping the gestures her mistress had drummed into her head over three years of apprenticeship—a ritual she could almost ignore when she changed to raven. Her bones crackled as she started to shrink. Her brain felt squeezed. The pressure increased and her pain grew worse, as if she were being jammed headfirst into a small jar. She stopped, the spell only half made. Left on its own, her body changed back. She was on her knees, head down, panting.

"Raven?" Hero's voice seemed far away.

You can do this, she told herself. You have to.

Not so small, idiot, she argued back. You'll kill yourself.

She took a deep breath and tried again. She pictured a robin, because she knew she could manage that. She spoke each word carefully. She tried to ignore the popping joints, the growing pain. She had to do this. And somehow, she did.

"Raven? Are you all right?" The question echoed in the dark room, deep and slow.

No, she chirped. She hopped uncertainly to the gap under the door. She ducked her head and sidled under. The rough edges of the planks pressed on her back. Her legs collapsed. She was wedged between the door and the cold stone threshold. She struggled, cheeping feebly.

Huge hands reached under the door and grabbed her, squeezing her wings against her sides. Hero pulled, and she skidded free, leaving at least one feather stuck in a crack in the wood.

"Got you," he crooned, voice booming right beside her.

She chirped angrily.

"Sorry," he boomed.

He set her down on the grass. Raven settled to the ground, closed her eyes. She had to fight to think, to remember words. She forced out the reversing spell. The change back was agony. She was down on her knees again. Tears stung her eyes.

"Blazing mages," Hero whispered.

"Aching mages," she groaned. "Give me the blanket. And food. Do you have food?"

He had brought a sack with bread, cheese, and nuts, along with a flask of water. She gobbled it all in the shadow of the cell. "Now let's get out of here," she said.

"What bird?" Hero asked. "Owls? I was going to say wildcats or maybe foxes, but you only change into birds, so I guess we have to be—"

"Keep your pants on, midge," Raven said. "You're not changing into anything. We're sneaking over this wall and back to your father."

Outraged, he stood straighter, trying to stretch an arm's length into a fathom. "I can take care of myself," he declared loudly. "I got you out of that cell, didn't I? I brought you food and, look, a rope." He held out a coil. "And a knife and—"

A dog began to bark in the kennels. Then another.

"Hush!" she said. "Stop shouting!"

"I am not shouting!"

A light appeared in a window of the house. Raven groaned.

"Hurry!" Hero cried. "Change us!"

A door banged open. A light bobbed into the yard.

"No time," Raven said. "Over the wall."

She shoved him against the stones and pushed him onto the roof of the cell, then dragged herself after. The blanket tangled in her arms and legs and she was forced to abandon it, along with his bag. Hero scrambled to the peak like a cat.

"Keep going!" she snarled, groping for handholds. Hero grabbed her shift, slipped, then sank his fingers into her hair. Raven yelped but managed to snag the edge of the wall and hoist herself up.

"Jump!" she ordered, and he grabbed her hand and did.

The jolt made her cry out again. Hero heaved her up, and together they raced for the windbreak. The bright moonlight lit them plainly as they fled. A voice shouted behind them. Another answered from the gate. Then Raven saw something move at the very edge of the trees ahead of them; a man. She cursed.

"It's my father!" Hero panted.

Raven couldn't see how he knew, but she dragged herself the last few steps into the windbreak. It was indeed Phillipe.

"This way," he said, his low voice amazingly calm. He led them through the trees, then stopped at the other edge and pointed right. "Go that way," he said. "I'll lead them off."

She grasped his arm, shaking her head. "They'll catch you," she panted.

"I can deal with them," he said. "They need me too much in the barns." He glanced toward Hero, then back to Raven, his gentle eyes suddenly fierce. "Him they'd send to the prison farm as soon as blink. Go! Get my Leo away!" Before she could argue, he turned and charged off, making a terrible racket in the branches.

"Wait!" Hero called, and would have raced after his father.

Raven grabbed his arm just in time. "No!" she whispered. "He's right. They've seen you. Steward will have you whipped in an instant, and then locked up. This way. And quietly!"

She pulled him in the other direction. He cast one last look after his father, then turned and followed. His eyes shone brightly in the moonlight.

They hadn't gone more than ten paces before their pursuers crashed into the trees. Raven and Hero flopped to the ground in the shadows and lay still, listening as the men hared off after Phillipe. Raven thanked the mages that they hadn't loosed the dogs yet. She gave them a good head start, then pulled Hero deeper into the shadows.

"Don't say one word," she whispered.

She led him along the windbreak until it ended at the lane to the barns. There was no sign of pursuit.

"Ready?" she whispered. "We're going to make a run for the next line of trees. We have to find a place where we can hide for a while."

"What about your sister?" he demanded.

"I can't try that again. They'll be watching for me."

"What about your mother?"

"I told you—"

"She's your sister's mother, too, you know!" he cried. "And she *can* help you, no matter what you say. Besides, they're watching for you now; you just said so yourself. Maybe by the time we save your mother, they won't be watching anymore."

"Hush!" Raven didn't know what to do. She couldn't leave Hero here; Phillipe was right about that. Even if they hadn't seen Hero clearly, their pursuers would guess as soon as they captured Phillipe. She was pretty sure Steward would send both of them to the prison farm, breedmaster or not. Maybe it did make sense to rescue her mother. Together they could rescue Phillipe, and then the four of them could save Sarita. Assuming Sarita lived that long.

"You ought to at least try," Hero said.

"Kah!" There were too many maybes! No matter which way she went, someone was likely to suffer. Her mother, at least, was on a boat downriver, with that dolt Loyal Steward, who had no idea of what had happened here at the manor. That gave her the element of surprise. So: her mother first, then Phillipe, then her sister. And then to the high reach, no matter what!

"Right. My mother. Take off your tunic and breeches," she ordered.

Hero's smile flashed white. "You're going to change me?"

"We have to move fast if we're going to catch up with her," she said. "Come on, down to your shirt. Let's hope it's light enough."

He began yanking off his tunic. "Owls?" he asked hopefully.

"No," she snapped. She couldn't imagine Hero turned into something as ornery as an owl. "I don't have time to shape the spell. I'm going to let you change into your natural bird form, whatever it is. Something small and quick, I hope. Think about something small and quick."

"I'll try."

"Don't just try, do it. I've never changed anyone else before."

His eyes went huge. "You've never . . ." He grew very serious. "Right, I'm ready."

She looked at his little half-naked body and hoped she could make this work. At least he was willing; that was half the battle.

She raised her hands and began sketching symbols in the air over his head, intoning the first words of the spell. She'd had it done to her often enough by her mistress, and had done it to herself more times than she could remember. But this was different: This was Hero. It was mostly a matter of believing she could do it. And him wanting it.

She could feel it working, magic flowing to the tips of her hands, surrounding Hero in a shimmer like heat above burning coals. She felt herself weakening as the shimmer increased. Slowly, Hero contracted. His face grew smaller, his outlines blurred. There was an odd scrunching sound.

"Ouch!" he squeaked.

Raven's arms fell to her sides. She couldn't have held them up longer if she'd wanted to. Her shift was drenched in sweat. Her head throbbed. But there at her feet, almost invisible in the shadows, was an oversized and very surprised-looking chickadee.

"Dee dee," it said.

Raven squatted wearily for a close look and couldn't help smiling. It had worked! Here, on the middle reach, without her mistress mage to help, she had changed Hero to a bird. And somehow it seemed a perfect fit: small, bold, bright, and full of mischief. She held out her hand, but the chickadee refused the offer. He fluttered clumsily to her shoulder.

"Deedee!" he chirped.

"Hush!" she hissed. "It's too dark for bird song."

"Dee dee?" he asked.

Raven realized this was going to be a problem. It had taken her weeks to learn to speak when she'd first become a raven, and ravens had a natural talent for mimicry. Chickadees didn't. They had a fixed set of sounds. He might never learn to speak human words. And she couldn't command him the way she could a real bird, sensing its thoughts and directing it by will. He was still Hero, even if he was shaped like a chickadee. Odds were he couldn't even understand a real chickadee. Blazing mages! There was so much about this she still didn't know. But as long as he listened and did what she said, they should be all right.

"I've got to change now," she said. "Better get off."

"Dee dee." He took off and careened into the trees.

"Don't go too far!" she hissed. "Stay in sight!"

But he was nowhere to be seen.

"Great mages, what am I doing?" she muttered. She took a deep, weary breath and changed herself.

She didn't feel half so bad as a raven. Her insides had taken on a different shape that somehow relieved the pains a little. But she was very tired.

"Hero?" she croaked, peering up into the trees. There was no answer. "Hero!"

With a whir of wings, he flashed out of the branches and landed beside her.

"CHICKA-DEE-DEE-DEE!" he cried merrily.

She jabbed at him with her beak, but he hopped nimbly aside. "Quiet, chatterbox," she croaked. "I told you, chickadees don't chirp at night."

"Dee-dee," he agreed.

She sighed. "Let's get going before they . . ." She couldn't say *catch your father.* "Before they come looking for us," she finished lamely. As if to help make the point, Cutter's hounds began to bark and bay from the manor. Their charging paws rattled the pebbles on the drive leading out the back gate.

"Go!" Raven croaked. She spread her wings, but Hero was already off in a tiny blur. She hurried after him as quickly as her sore body would allow, across the lane and into the next line of trees. Hero swooped from branch to branch down the windbreak, pausing to rest as she caught up, then darting off again. The belling of the hounds fell behind, fading into a frustrated chorus of yips and whines. Now Raven cawed worriedly at Hero to slow down.

There were any number of reasons chickadees didn't chirp at night—hungry owls, for one. As soon as they could chance it, she was going to stop and change him into something a little easier to protect.

By dawn they were well downriver. Hero was finally slowing down, and she actually managed to catch up and grab his tail feathers in her beak. He settled his wings meekly.

"Time for a break," she mumbled through his feathers. "Understand?"

He nodded, and she let go warily. He stayed there, with what might have been a penitent expression in his little black eyes.

"*Dee-dee dee?*" he asked, cocking his head.

"What?" she groused.

He spread his wings and fluffed his feathers.

"You're cold?"

He shook his head.

"You're hungry?"

He started to shake his head, then stopped and nodded vigorously.

"I am, too. But first I need some sleep. We'll find something at the next cottage."

She led him higher and deeper into the tree, then hunkered down and tucked her head under her wing. He leaned against her and tucked his own head in with her. Raven was too tired to chase him out. Her last thought was how strange they must look. Any other raven would have swallowed him whole.

She awoke with a start a few hours later. The sun was high and the day almost warm. She looked around blearily, wondering what had roused her. Then she realized—Hero was gone!

She croaked his name and heard a faint *chicka-dee-dee-dee* some distance off. Raven flapped hard toward the call and came to a small farmstead with a paddock behind the barn and a whole flock of chickadees darting in and out to snatch grain from a feed trough for an old plow horse. Raven spiraled above them in dismay, trying to figure out which one was Hero. Then she spotted him, a bit bigger and the only one sitting still. He was right on top of the pile of feed, stuffing himself, ignoring the placid horse as it nibbled around him. And totally oblivious of the ragged farm cat creeping along the shadow of the paddock fence.

"Hero!" she croaked.

He chirped a happy *dee-dee* and went on gorging himself.

The cat put its ears forward and kneaded the ground, eyes intent on the tempting fat chickadee waiting in the trough. Its tail twitched. Its hindquarters shimmied.

"Fly, you twitter-brained dolt!" Raven screamed.

She stooped on the trough just as the cat pounced. They reached Hero at the same instant, only he was gone, whirring away in a flash of little wings and a chorus of indignant chirps from all the other chickadees. Raven found herself gripping the cat's tail in her talons. It yowled in outrage. She flapped madly backward, yanking the tail to keep the cat off balance. A paw caught the side of her head. Raven croaked and swooped away before it could get in another swipe. She flew to the ridge of the barn and threw a stream of curses at the cat and Hero both.

"Dee dee?"

A chickadee had landed at the other end of the roof and was eyeing her uncertainly.

"You had better be Hero," she croaked, "or I'm going to have chickadee for breakfast."

The little bird hung its head.

"You'll be sorry, all right, you little stuff-guts. Follow me!"

She led him back into the trees and landed on the ground. As soon as he landed beside her, she changed back to human, then changed him. She was dismayed at how it tired her, but soon enough he stood in the broken light under the trees, boy again.

"Hoi," he said, stretching. "My head hurts! That's too small."

"Serves you right," she told him. "Now, get this straight: If you are going to come with me, you will do what I say and only what I say. You were a pinfeather from being cat food!"

71

"I knew he was there," he said. "The horse told me."

"The horse—?"

"Besides, I could hear him mumbling when he got close."

Raven stared at him. She remembered him with the bull and calf in the breeding barn. Maybe he did have his own talent.

"That doesn't matter," she snapped. "You still waited too long, gorging yourself. Blazing mages, do you know what it would have done to you? Cats like to play with their food before they kill it! And a fox will take you live back to its young. Even a red squirrel will eat a chickadee, if it can catch one sitting still like a fat, lazy, brainless pile of dinner! When I say fly, you fly! Understand?"

He nodded silently, eyes down, the picture of contrition.

"Right," she said. "You have to be something else, something not quite so easy to catch. So I'm going to change you to a raven. Then we can fly together, and you can at least take on a cat with some hope of escaping the menu. Get it?" He nodded. "Good. Now, concentrate. Think about what you want to become."

She began the spell, wearily closing her eyes to picture a raven. The image of a cat mauling a chickadee popped into her head. She shuddered and forced it aside. She felt magic tingling in her hands, and tingling back from Hero, as if reflected. No: even stronger, as if he were making the magic himself. She was sure then that he had mage talent. She almost stopped in amazement, but the spell was going too well. She welcomed his talent and let it mingle with hers, grateful for the help.

Finally, it was done and she opened her eyes, panting from the effort.

There on the ground before her crouched a snarling black cat.

Nine

R aven yelped and jumped back. The cat was twice the size of a barn cat; its paws were huge. Its tail stuck up straight, like a fat black rod. Raven's first impulse was to flee, but the cat just looked at her curiously.

"No," she pleaded, looking around quickly for Hero.

"Rowr," said the cat.

"Hero?" she said weakly.

The cat purred.

"Sweet spirit of the River, how . . . ?"

The cat shrugged.

Raven touched its thick, furry ears, mind spinning. The little jackdaw really was a mage! But how could he use her spell to change into a cat? It wasn't possible.

How do you know? she asked herself. You're no expert.

She stared at Hero. He stared back with a cat's inscrutable smug smile. Obviously, it was possible. Then another worry hit her: What if she couldn't change him back?

She raised her hands and began to reverse the spell. Hero yowled and shook his head. She did it anyway. The cat body shifted and grew. Its tail shrank; its fur began to fuse. She could feel Hero fighting her, but reversing a spell was putting things aright. He made it hard, but he couldn't refuse her. Finally, he was back to Hero, and looking sulky.

"Don't give me that look," she said. "You could have been stuck like that!"

"Then why did you make me a cat in the first place?" he countered.

"I didn't do it, Fur Brain. You did."

"I did? What do you mean?"

"You're the one who made the cat happen," Raven said. "All I did was say the spell."

Hero's mouth fell open. And then curled upward in a huge grin. "I did it? I made myself into a cat? I'm . . . I'm a . . . I'm a mage?" He quivered with excitement.

"Slow down, Cat Boy," Raven said. "You've got talent—I could feel it pouring out of you—but you're a long way from being a mage. I doubt if you can change yourself yet."

Hero frowned. He set his jaw, closed his eyes tight, and clenched his whole body. A minute passed. His face darkened.

"Hoi! Breathe!" Raven cried.

Hero let out his breath in a rush, then gasped in a lungful. He looked down at his little body, crestfallen. "You're right. I couldn't do it."

"Well, don't cry about it," Raven told him. "It takes training."

"Teach me!" he cried, bouncing back at once. "Teach me how!"

Raven groaned. "We don't really have time right now, Hero. My mother. Your father. My sister. Remember?"

"But if I can change myself, I can help even more." His eyes gleamed. "I could be a wildcat, or a wolf or a bear! I could save them and protect you and—"

"First we have to get there," Raven pointed out. "And for that, we need to fly."

"I don't need to fly," he argued. "I can run. I'm a beast mage!"

"You're not a mage yet," she repeated. "You're not even an apprentice. You're a little kid who managed to turn himself into a cat when he was supposed to be a raven."

He glared at her. "You said think about what *you* want to be. Well, I like cats."

She glared back. "It's not a matter of what you do or don't like. It's a matter of getting somewhere fast, without getting eaten."

"Cats are fast, and nobody eats them."

"You think not? A couple of dogs can kill a cat in a trice."

"If they could catch me," he said.

"Cats are sprinters; dogs can run all day. They'd catch you, all right."

"I'd run up a tree."

"And be stuck there," she snapped. "A raven could fly away, at least."

"I don't want to be a raven!" he yelled.

"All right! You don't have to be a raven! Sweet mother of a failed curse . . ." She took a deep breath and tried to reason with him. "Right, not a raven. But we have to be able to move quickly, or we'll never catch up with that steamboat. You can't be a cat. Understand?"

He frowned, but he nodded.

"Good. Right." She took another breath, this time in relief. "Here we go."

She raised her hands, shut her eyes. Said the spell. Again, she felt the tingle of magic streaming from Hero, hastening the change. Not easing it, just speeding it. She opened her eyes.

He was a cat again.

She groaned and changed him back. Her head ached.

"I tried!" he said quickly. "I didn't think about a cat."

Raven rubbed her eyes. "What did you think about?"

"A horse," he said. "A big fast one!"

"Either you didn't think hard enough or you're not meant to be a horse," she said wearily. "Try it again. Or think of something else. Something fast. With stamina. Big enough to take care of itself. I'm only going to do this one more time. Then I'm going to fly downriver, whether you can keep up with me or not. Get it?"

He nodded again, face set. "Got it," he muttered.

She marshaled her strength and went carefully through the spell, eyes wide open.

The change was phenomenal. He started to lengthen. Then fur began to show. A horse tail burst from his backside, tipped with black. But then the change stopped. His face was distorted: a horselike snout, Hero's wide eyes, half a mane, long ears. He grunted. The muscles stood out on his neck. Raven repeated the spell, trying to make the change continue. Instead, he began to shrink. His ears became small and pointed. His snout shortened. Long whiskers appeared. The tail . . .

Raven stopped, but it was too late; Hero was a cat again. He looked down at himself, back up at her, and shrugged.

"That's it," she said, throwing up her hands. "I couldn't go through that again if I wanted to."

She sat on the ground and buried her face in her hands. Her forehead was covered with sweat. She wiped it away disgustedly. Suddenly, she felt fur brushing her knee. Hero was sidling against her, ears back, amber eyes somber. She felt like swatting him.

She stood quickly. "Right," she said. "I hope you're happy. And you'd better hope you can keep up."

She went through her own change and finished it strung out and famished.

"I'm going for some food," she croaked. "Wait here. And I mean it!"

Hero nodded solemnly.

She managed to catch a couple of mice in short order and washed them down with a refreshing drink from a clear brook. She hurried back, half expecting Hero to have wandered off, but he was dutifully waiting where she had left him. She settled on a branch above him. He glanced pointedly between his front feet. A dead mouse lay there.

"That's for me?" she asked.

He snarled—or maybe it was a grin—and said, *"Reour."*

"Kah," she grumbled. "Keep this up and I might have to learn to trust you." Hero's eyes went wide. "Kitty eyes aren't going to help, Furball." She dropped from the branch and ate the mouse. "Well, I was hungrier than I thought, I guess. Thanks. Now, let's get moving."

She jumped into the air and flapped toward the river. Hero darted ahead in a gallop. Raven kept pace with him, but he slowed to a trot in less than a hundred strides. She couldn't fly that slowly, so she landed in the next tree, lifting off again as he reached it. They played leapfrog like that for almost a league. Raven kept to the trees at the edges of the fields, ignoring the rough lanes and narrow canals that connected the widespread farms. When she flew high enough, she could see the river winding in great loops and oxbows off to their right. The bends in the river gave her and Hero a small chance of catching up, but only a small one.

Eventually, Hero lagged to a walk. Raven dropped below the treetops and flared into a stall overhead.

"You're slowing down," she croaked.

He gave her an irritated look and walked faster, panting as the sun peeked above the trees. Then they came to a canal that cut across their route. Hero took one look and plopped down in the shade of a thick bush. Raven landed beside him.

"Don't tell me you're afraid of getting wet?" she said.

Hero glared. He heaved himself to his paws and went to the edge of the water. He lapped up several swallows, then stepped in. And stepped right back out, shaking his paws with disgust.

"I knew it," Raven complained.

Hero gave her another glare and splashed into the canal. In moments it was over his head, but he laid back his ears and paddled furiously. The spring current pulled him downstream at a quick rate. He turned upstream, fighting it.

"Don't worry about where you land!" Raven cried. "Just get across!" She took to the air and flew to a spot farther down on the opposite bank. "Come to me! Here!"

Hero turned toward her and was immediately swept past. The canal wasn't that wide, but he was still barely halfway across, teeth bared, coughing and sneezing as water splashed into his mouth. He began to founder.

"Blazing mages!" Raven muttered. "Keep paddling, Hero!"

Quickly she changed herself back to human, cast off her shift, and dove into the water. She came up gasping; it was icy! Cursing cats and water both, she struck out for Hero's bobbing head. She was no great swimmer—in fact, she hated it—but she managed to catch him. Gasping, eyes wide with panic, he tried to climb onto her back.

"Ouch!" she cried. "Keep those cursed claws in!"

She got an arm around his middle and pulled him against her. He was shaking violently. Rolling onto her side, she pulled toward shore with an awkward one-handed stroke and kick. Finally, they reached the shallows. She tried to stand, but Hero was soggy and dripping and heavy as a tub of laundry. She splashed to her knees. He jumped from her arms, scratching her again.

"Ow!" she yelled. "Sheathe the knives!"

Hero ignored her. He shook himself all over again and again, sputtering and hissing in his own spray. Then he sat down and began to lick himself dry. Raven dragged herself onto the grass and tried to wipe off as much of the water as she could. Despite the bright sunlight, she was shivering.

"I'm going back for my shift," she told him. "Wait here."

As soon as she started to walk off, he staggered after her and kept close the whole way. He went back to licking himself as she pulled on her shift. The brief walk had dried her off, but he was still sopping.

"That's a waste of time," she said. Her arms felt like lead, but she reversed the spell. Hero emerged from his soaked fur and huddled in the small puddle left by the runoff. His shirt was soaked, too.

"Brr," he complained. "I think this is even colder."

"Get used to it," she said. "I'm not turning you into a cat again."

"Why not?" he demanded.

"You're too slow!" she replied. "You're too . . . too . . . stuck on the ground! You can't gallop; you can hardly walk fast for any length of time. You have to go around things, or climb over them. And then there are the canals!"

"I can swim the canals," he muttered.

"Is that what you call it?" she exclaimed. "It sure looked like drowning to me!"

"It was just so cold!" he cried. "And I was tireder than I thought. And I . . . I got scared." He stared at the ground, biting his lip. "Maybe you could change me when we got to a canal and I could swim across that way."

She shook her head. "Too many changes. Magic is work, you know, and there's a canal every couple of leagues from here down to Broadmeet. She shook her head again. "No. You're going to have to fly."

"How about a dog?" he suggested.

"We tried a horse; what makes you think a dog will be any different?"

"I don't know!" he cried. "You're the mage! You tell me!" He was on the verge of tears.

Raven stopped herself from shouting back. He was just a kid. Besides, it wasn't his fault she didn't know everything a mage should. She tried to explain what she did know. "Everyone has a natural form, right? I'm a raven. Your natural bird is a chickadee. You natural beast form must be a cat."

"But you can be other birds," he said.

"That's because I change birds. Dogs aren't birds."

"Right, you're a bird mage," he said, with something close to disgust. Raven almost whapped him. "Maybe if you had a wand," he said. "Don't mages always have wands?"

"My mistress did; so did my friend Carver, but I never needed one. The wand is just there to help you concentrate and . . ." She sighed. "I wouldn't know what to do with a wand anyway."

"How about if you made me a small cat, a kitten? Then you could carry me."

"How about a small bird?" she countered. "Then you could fly." His chin came forward in a stubborn frown. "Blazing mages! What have you got against birds?"

"That's your talent," he said. "Mine is different. I'm an animal mage."

"Birds are animals, too," she snapped.

"You know what I mean. Birds have feathers; animals have fur. Besides, I felt all scrunched up as a bird. My head ached. I didn't feel right."

"That's because you were so small. A kitten would be just as bad!" But Raven could understand what he meant. She couldn't imagine being something other than a bird. Sometimes she even felt strange as a girl. "If you want to be a beast, you'll have to figure out how to do it yourself."

"How did you figure it out?"

Raven shrugged. "I was desperate. When I ran away, I made it all the way to the middle cliff without a sight or sound of Hunter. I thought I'd given him the slip. But there I was at the cliff, trying to find a way up, when his loudmouthed hounds started howling right behind me. It scared the blazing bees out of me. I started scrambling up the cliff face. I hadn't made it more than two fathoms before they came out of the woods and started leaping after me. The cliff was too steep for them, but I was stuck on a tiny ledge, with no place to go." She paused, caught up in the memory.

"What happened?" Hero demanded.

"I changed," she said. "Well, there was more to it than that. I was desperate, like I said, and frightened out of my wits, trying to scramble up higher when I could barely cling to the ledge. I almost fell, and that scared me even more. I saw some birds—ravens, it turned out, but that was just coincidence—and I wished so hard that I could fly away with them that I did." She smiled wryly. "Of course, then I was stuck, because I had no idea how I'd done it or how to change back. A real idiot. Lucky, but still an idiot. If my mistress hadn't found me, I'd probably be living with that gang of ravens now."

"Hoi," Hero breathed. "That's amazing."

"Desperation and sheer luck," Raven repeated. "And maybe I

was still too young. Mage talent shows up at different ages in different people. You can calm animals already, but the rest of it hasn't come yet. My friend Carver is a weather mage, but he didn't have any idea until he was thirteen. His mother didn't find out about her talent till she was over twenty. I had no clue at all until it happened. Maybe I was so desperate, I jumped ahead a few years. I sure couldn't do it again until my mistress found me and showed me how."

"Show me what she showed you. Your spell. How it works."

"It's a bird spell," she said. "Your talent is furry beasts." But why not? she thought. It can't hurt. I hope. "Right. But remember, this is a talent, not a craft that anyone can learn. It's more like art than . . . carpentry or baking cakes. It's not a recipe, it's a feeling."

She taught him her spell, all the words and gestures, and explained how she envisioned each change. He nodded and repeated everything slowly. Then he tried, five times, until he was panting from the effort. Nothing happened.

"That's it, I guess," Raven said. "Sorry. Unless you can get more desperate, or grow up really quickly, you're just going to have to settle for feathers."

Hero sighed. "All right," he said dejectedly. "I'll be a bird. But not a chickadee!"

"It'll be your choice," Raven assured him, but then had to add, "as long as it's not a hawk or an owl or an eagle or a vulture."

"That's all the fun ones!"

"They're too mean and hungry. They . . . how do I explain this? They tend to take over. Did you notice how much you felt like a cat when you were shaped like one?"

Hero nodded slowly. "I guess I did."

"You have to fight that sometimes, and it's worse with a headstrong mind. It can be hard to change back."

"Blazing mages," he said.

"That's right. Now, are you ready to try this?"

"I suppose." He set his jaw. "A stupid bird it is."

Raven bit back a sharp reply, took another long breath. She looked at Hero, with his eyes clenched shut in concentration: clever, well meaning, even likeable, but so blasted worrisome. And then there was her baby sister. And her mother. And Phillipe. How could anyone fly with such burdens?

Ten

roadmeet spread along the riverside in the golden light of the afternoon. The walls of its close-packed buildings shone in a bright palette of color beneath a gray sheen of slate roofs. Boats of every description lined the long wooden landings and stone quays that jutted into the channel, from the first small warehouses to the tall beacon on the point where the River Slow met the Stoney in a swirl of blending water.

Loyal admired the squat tower of the town hall, lifting its elaborate clock and arched belfries above the rooftops. His sister, Berna, had her office there. She was Cutter's clerk in Broadmeet and captain of his squad of baronsmen. She had chosen that path instead of staying at the manor to follow in their father's line. Normally, a functionary's career of that sort would have been Loyal's lot, as second child, but Berna had chafed under their father's guidance. She'd wanted authority of her own long before he'd been ready to grant it. To Loyal's secret delight, she had asked the Baron to let her serve him elsewhere, and he had agreed.

The *Lady Slow* needed to recoal at Broadmeet; as soon as they tied up, Loyal planned to drop in on Berna. And not as her little brother. He was the assistant steward now, the envoy from his father, with duties and responsibilities to match hers. Besides, Roxaine was more trouble in one small body than Berna got from an entire burgh.

He scowled at the memory. By the time he'd noticed her empty cloak lying on the deck, Roxaine had already made some distance from the boat, swimming strongly. Loyal almost jumped in after her, but reason stopped him. She had too much of a head start. Instead, he called to the boatman, pointing at Roxaine. The man swung the wheel hard over. The river was half a league wide there, or more. They had plenty of room to catch her. Loyal's shout also brought out the baronsman. He hurried to the rail and shook his head. Loyal's face burned.

The boat looped around and came back upstream to cut her off. The boatman slowed. She watched, treading water. Even at that distance, Loyal could see the glint in her eyes. As the big stern wheel reversed, she turned and began swimming toward the other shore. Loyal swore. They were much closer to that bank, and now the boat was at a dead stop. He completely forgot the baronsman at his command. He kicked off his boots and dove over the rail.

The water was ice cold. Loyal came up gasping, wondering how the shrew could stand it. He kicked as hard as he could, forcing his long limbs through the freezing water in a rapid crawl. He would not let her slip away! The current pulled him sideways, but it was pulling her, too, and she was flagging. He gained steadily. She glanced back, and again he saw the glint in her eyes. That was how she stood the cold, he thought; she held it off with spite. He fought it with anger. And the thought of his father's scorn if she ever reached the shore.

He came up behind her, grabbed her leg. She kicked madly, splashing great waves into his face. He choked and fell back. She surged ahead, kicking and flailing with feet and fists. Blinded by spray, he lunged forward, swinging hard. He hit flesh and bone.

"Animal!" she cursed, gasping for breath.

She struck out again and again, but he managed to grab one arm, then hooked a leg around her thighs. She went under with him on top, but still she kept fighting, twisting and jerking like an eel on a hook. She grabbed his throat with her free hand, choking him. He hit her again. They bobbed up, both gasping for air. Amazingly, she was still spitting curses.

"Toady! Pig spawn! Sty-born son of a child-thieving—"

She went under again, and this time Loyal held her there. He burned with rage. He twisted her arm back so he could hold both wrists, locked his legs around her, held her down. She bucked and writhed, thrusting her head toward the surface. He pushed her deeper. He clenched her wrists, feeling her strain. Feeling her weaken.

It came to him then—he was drowning her.

As she deserves! he thought.

But another voice said, No, what about Father's plan, his deal with Stoner?

A bad bargain, he argued. But his will weakened. He could never say that to his father, never justify why he had drowned her. And never go through with it anyway, now that his rage had passed.

Loyal pulled Roxaine to the surface. She gasped and coughed, spewing water from her mouth. She clenched her teeth and heaved up more water. A single sob shook her. Then she went limp, shivering violently. He didn't loosen his grip. She had tricked him once; he would not be tricked again. His face still burned. He clenched her wrists and trod water, hardly noticing the cold, till the *Lady Slow* came around and he could hand her up to the baronsman.

In the two days since, he had kept Roxaine shackled in the cabin. He had ordered the boatman to nail shutters over the windows. He'd ordered the baronsman to take in her food and empty the chamber pot. He himself had stayed away from her, so he wouldn't have to hear her insults again. He remembered her striking his father, but Jan Steward had controlled his anger. He had dealt with her coolly, correctly. Loyal swore he would be like that.

Now the boatman blew his whistle as he swung the bow toward the quays of Broadmeet. The *Lady Slow* rocked in the tangled wakes of all the other boats on the river. The fireboy ran to the rail and prepared the mooring lines. The baronsman went to help. Since Roxaine's attempt at escape, a disgusted scowl had never left his face. Loyal hated it.

They docked alongside the three massive warehouses at the Baron's wharf, between two other steamboats, each yoked to a long cargo barge. The engines stopped with a great, steamy wheeze. Loyal went to his cabin to get his bag; it was time to visit Berna. In his mind, he was already going over his greeting, how he would hold himself, what he would say—and not say—about the events of the journey.

When he went back on deck, the baronsman was standing by the gangplank, watching the boatman and fireboy head into town.

"I'll have my sister send back another guard," Loyal allowed. "We've earned a break."

"Thank you, sir," the baronsman replied stiffly.

Loyal frowned; the lout could have shown a little more gratitude. He stalked across the wharf and around the nearest warehouse to the cobbled street. It was like passing into a different world. His mood lifted in the swirl of people bustling along between the bright buildings. Slanting sunlight painted one side of the street in slashes of gold, the other in shadow. People in all manner of dress moved in and out of the light, changing from gray to bright in a single stride. Loyal dodged a goat cart and turned toward the center of town.

As he climbed the street, a dog came over and sniffed his heels, then darted across the street toward the interesting scent from a pushcart filled with meat pies. The smell made Loyal's mouth water, but he was distracted by the sound of a drum. He came out into a small square. In the center, under a broad tree that was just starting to bud, a large spread of a woman was beating a quick rhythm on a hand drum. Beside her, a husky man with a floppy paunch was tootling on a flute. Both wore bright motley waistcoats over tight-fitting breeches that only accentuated their meaty limbs. A small crowd had stopped to watch a lanky boy in similar costume who stood before them juggling.

Loyal stopped, amazed. The lad was flipping several long knives, a hatchet, and a great fat carrot. They spun high into the branches of the outstretched tree, then fell, twirling wickedly, only to be snatched up and flung aloft again. The juggler caught the carrot, took a quick bite, and flipped it high among the twirling blades. The crowd laughed and clapped. Loyal applauded with them, entranced.

Suddenly, a hand fell on his shoulder: his baronsman.

"She's gone!" the man gasped. "The witch is gone!"

Loyal felt as if he'd been slapped. "How?" he demanded. "What happened?"

"I don't know," the man replied. "I went to check, and the cabin was empty."

"Blast you! You searched the boat?" Loyal was already hurrying down the street, the man at his heels.

"Yes, sir. I looked everywhere."

Loyal cursed through clenched teeth. The woman *was* a witch!

In a few minutes, they were back at the boat. Loyal ran into the cabin. He tore open the small cupboard and peered under the bed, but Roxaine was truly gone. There was no sign of his father's shackles, either. She won't get far with those on, he thought grimly. He went back to the door and checked the lock. There were scratch marks all around the keyhole and gouges in the molding around the catch. He cursed again.

"She found something to use as a lock pick," he said accusingly.

"It couldn't have been her spoon, sir," the baronsman said. "I got it back every meal."

"Blazing mages, man, it doesn't matter what she used! You've let her sneak off!"

"I'll run up to the town hall, sir," the baronsman said. "We'll get the squad after her."

"No!" Loyal snapped. That would mean telling Berna. His face burned at the mere thought. "No, they have their own problems to deal with. We'll find her ourselves."

"We can't search the whole city alone," the man protested. "We'll never find her."

"I tell you we will!" Loyal barked. "Come on!" He hurried back onto the wharf, the baronsman trailing reluctantly. "Go that way," he ordered, pointing upstream. "She's wearing that orange cloak. Ask people. Someone is bound to have seen her." He hurried the other way.

He asked every passerby, with no luck. He asked the shopkeepers, but none had seen her. He hurried from person to person, scanning side alleys, peering into storefronts. His anger built, but also a sense of panic. Broadmeet was a warren of streets and buildings, some as tall as four stories. It stretched for at least a league along the banks of two rivers. She had hundreds, thousands of places to hide. But she was wearing shackles; someone was bound to spot her. He held to that one slim hope. Because if he failed, he would have to admit to his sister that he'd lost her. And she would tell his father.

Soon he was back at the square. The big man and woman were performing some clumsy acrobatics while the young juggler played the drum. Their audience had thinned to a few idlers. Loyal hurried over and accosted them, describing Roxaine, demanding to know if they'd seen her.

"She's a runaway," Loyal finished. "A bondservant runaway."

"Is there a reward?" the fat male acrobat asked.

Loyal glared at him. "Runaways are criminals; it's everyone's duty to recapture them. But I suppose there could be a reward. If she's found quickly."

"I haven't seen her," the woman replied.

"I haven't either," the young juggler said. He kept flipping a knife behind his back, a show of unconcern that irritated Loyal as much as the tumbler's greed. He tried to ignore it.

"Well . . . ," the man said, "I might have."

"I don't reward 'might haves,'" Loyal snapped. "Did you see her or not?"

"Well . . ."

Loyal fought the urge to grab the man's fat throat and shake him. "Well what?" he demanded. "Did you see her or not?"

"We—" The man noticed something past Loyal's shoulder and stopped dead.

Loyal spun, begging luck and all the mages it was Roxaine. Instead, it was Berna, striding across the square toward him, flanked by half a dozen of her squad.

"Hello, little brother," she called. "I've been expecting you since I heard you'd arrived on the *Lady Slow*. What's kept you?"

Eleven

R aven studied Broadmeet from high above. The *Lady Slow,* docked between the other boats at Cutter's wharf, appeared to be completely deserted.

"I'm going down for a closer look," she said.

Hero trilled an agreement.

He'd settled on a catbird finally. The name soothed his pride a little. He couldn't fly at a raven's steady pace, but he was still much better at eating up distance than a real cat. It had made the difference; they had caught up with the boat carrying Roxaine.

Raven wheeled slowly toward the wharf, watching the *Lady Slow* intently for any signs of activity. Hero darted ahead.

"Slow down, pip-squeak!" she croaked. "Stay behind me!"

He made a rude noise she didn't know any bird could make.

Two gulls swooped close and eyed Hero hungrily. Raven had dealt with their kind before: all stomach and no brain. It was no hard task to charm them. Now she used her talent to call more, until a thick flock swirled around them. She directed them downward, a gray-and-white screen, till she and Hero landed in the engine well on the *Lady Slow.* Released, the gulls drifted away. There was no sound on the boat.

"I'm going forward," she muttered, but Hero was already hopping along the deck. She hopped after him, snapping at his tail. He dodged nimbly. Cursing, she changed, then reversed the spell on him. The catbird ballooned into an indignant boy.

"Hoi!" he exclaimed. Then he winced and stretched. "Still too small," he muttered.

She shushed him and scurried forward, keeping below the railing. "Someone could come out of one of these cabins at any minute," she whispered. "Stay behind me!"

She checked the two small cabins at the rear, but they were empty. When she came out of the second, she realized Hero was creeping toward the door of the main cabin.

"I said stay—"

"She's in here," he whispered, pointing to the door. It was ajar.

"How do you know?" Raven whispered back, creeping forward to join him.

"Because she smells like you. Only kind of . . . milky, I guess."

"What?"

Hero shrugged. "Ever since I was a cat, I've really noticed how things smell."

Raven didn't know which bothered her more: that she smelled enough to notice, or that she smelled like her mother.

She tiptoed to the doorway and peered in. Hero peered under her arm. She whacked him on the ear.

He dodged into the cabin and glared at her, eyes glistening. "Why are you being so mean to me?" he said. "I'm just trying to help."

"I'm not being mean!" She took a breath and lowered her voice. "I'm just trying to protect you."

"I don't need protecting."

"This isn't an adventure story, Fur Brain. If they catch you, they'll send you away. And they'll whip you first. Blazing mages! I ought to be taking you someplace safe. But I can't, not if I'm going to free my mother—which, I'll remind you, was your idea. There's no place safe to hide you, so I have to bring you with me. And that means you have to let me be the leader. If I say stop, you stop. If I say hide, you hide. Get it?"

He nodded grudgingly.

She felt as if she'd said it all before, with about the same result. "Right," she sighed. "Let's look around."

Roxaine had obviously been there: a few of her clothes spilled out of a bag that had been dumped on the floor; her comb lay on the table by the bed. But the cupboard door hung open, the blankets were pulled all awry, and the chair had been knocked over.

"Looks like a fight," Hero said.

Raven nodded grimly. "She must have tried to escape. They've probably got her locked up in the town jail. Come on."

She started toward the door, then froze. Someone had just come on board. Footsteps meandered toward the stern. Raven was about to sneak out around the front when another set of footsteps rattled over the gangplank and hurried forward toward the cabin. She pulled Hero against the wall beside the door.

"Hoi!" a voice called from the stern. "What's all the rush?"

The footsteps stopped just outside. "The witch is gone!" a man answered. "She picked the lock and snuck into the town!" He went toward the stern. Raven pressed her ear to the crack of the door, heart racing.

"Does young Steward know?" the first voice asked.

"Yes, he's out looking, but it's no use. No one's seen her and night's coming. We'll have to get help."

"He hasn't sent to his sister already?"

The second man snorted scornfully. "The little whelp doesn't want her to know. Too blasted proud to admit he's lost his treasured prisoner."

"Well, that's foolish," the other said. "She could be anywhere. He's going to need more men, and dogs, too, I warrant. I'll go find Boatman and the other crews—they'll help."

"I'm going to the captain," the other replied, "to fetch the squad whether the young fool likes it or not."

They clattered off the boat

Raven turned to Hero with a wild grin. "She's escaped!" she hissed excitedly. "We've just got to find her first!"

She looked out. The sun was settling below the line of hills. Soon it would be too dim to search from the air.

"Clothes," she muttered, turning back to the darkening room. She found the bag on the floor and rummaged out a dress.

It was short at the ankles and full in the chest, but it fit well enough.

"What about me?" Hero said, holding up a skirt with a look of disgust.

"We'll find you a hat," she told him. "You can pretend you're a girl."

She yanked the skirt over his head and covered his short hair with a pillowcase. The result was ridiculous. "Kah! You'll stick out like a wart on a bum."

"You could change me," he said. "I could smell her out. Track her down."

"It's a dog we need, not a cat."

"Cats can smell really good," he protested. "They just don't use it the same way dogs do. They can hear good, too. And they can see better!"

"Right, right," Raven said. "Spare me the lecture." She stared at him appraisingly. "Do you really think . . . ?"

His grin flashed in the darkness. "I know I could smell her out. She smells just like you, remember?"

In a few moments, he was once again the big black cat. He quickly toured the room, touching his nose to the clothes, the bedding, even her comb. He put his ears back and narrowed his eyes, mouth half open, as though tasting the smells. Then he trotted to the door and looked back, tail flicking. His expression clearly said, "Right, I'm ready, hurry up."

"Don't get out of my sight," she ordered, but he was off as soon as she moved.

He padded across the wharf, touched his nose to a stack of barrels, tasted the scent, then sidled along the wall of the warehouse to an alley that led to the street. He looked back once to make sure she was coming, then lifted his nose and slipped into the street. He wove among the feet of the pedestrians like an eel among reeds, forcing her to bump and dodge along behind. People glared. She glared back, feeling overdressed and conspicuous.

Suddenly, Hero made a sharp turn into a shadowed alleyway.

Raven tried to follow but was caught between a fat tradesman and a goat cart filled with a reeking pile of half-tanned hides. When she finally squeezed past, she couldn't see Hero anywhere. As her eyes adjusted to the gloom, she spotted him perched on a door stoop with a rangy ginger tabby. She was struck again by how big he was compared to a normal cat. The two of them were staring eye to eye, but with none of the hissing and fluffing she would have expected. After a moment, they touched noses, and Hero came over.

"What?" she asked, kneeling. "Did he see her?"

Hero nodded and trotted out of the alley. Raven hurried after.

Suddenly, a lean brindled dog leaped out of a doorway, barking and snarling. It was on Hero in an instant. He spun, spitting, swiping at the dog with a big paw. It stopped with a yelp, and he stared it down. Its snarls sank to silence. Its tail gave a tentative wag. Then another dog appeared out of the crowd and attacked Hero from the rear. A third cur followed. Overwhelmed, he turned and ran. The two newcomers hared after him, yipping madly. People yelled and jumped aside, stumbling into each other. The goat cart lurched as Hero ran between the wheels. The dogs upended it, spilling its stinking load onto the cobbles. The bleating goat kicked and bucked in its harness. The tradesman swore.

"Hero!" Raven cried. She tried to push through the milling crowd.

It parted in a rush, and there was Hero, pelting toward her, fur up, tail bushed, ears back. The two dogs raced behind, barking and yipping still. Hero climbed her dress and perched on her shoulders as though she were a tree. His claws dug through the cloth and into her skin. She yelped, then yelped again as the dogs skidded to a snarling, gnashing stop against her legs.

"Get back, you mangy curs!" she yelled. "Pea-brained, tail-sniffing flea bags! Get back!" She kicked out, at the same time trying to pry Hero from her shoulders. Neither move worked. The dogs danced aside, then surged forward again, barking madly. Hero clung tightly to her dress, hissing ferociously.

"Use your talent!" she snapped, kicking again. "Control the idiots!"

He went still, and one dog began to whine. It looked from Hero to its companion, obviously confused, then gave what looked very much like a shrug and slipped away. The other kept up a racket that slowly subsided to muted snarling and finally to anxious muttering. With a look of canine apology, it tucked its tail and slunk off. Hero began smoothing his fur.

"It took you long enough," Raven grumbled. "Some beast mage."

He gave his leg a final lick and started to jump down.

"No, you don't," she said, grabbing his tail. "You stay up there where it's safe."

She started up the street and realized that everyone was staring at them. People moved aside to let her pass. She glimpsed one little girl making a sign against evil.

Wonderful, she thought. We've become a spectacle: the weird girl with the big black cat. Every baronsman in the town will be looking for us.

Hero let himself droop across her shoulders like a furry shawl and began to purr.

The street opened onto a small square ringed by shops and an inn. In its center stood a broad, spreading tree that was just starting to bud. Raven froze, then ducked back into the shadow of the street. The place was crawling with baronsmen! There was a clot of them near the tree, surrounding a trio of street performers dressed in motley. Loyal Steward was with them. And the big blond woman beside him wearing the captain's badge had to be his sister.

"Are you sure this is the way?" Raven whispered. Hero nodded. "Blast!"

There were still enough people out and about in the twilight to provide decent cover. Hugging the buildings, Raven made her way around the next corner to the opposite side of the square. When they reached the far corner unnoticed and turned up the street, she dared to breathe again. But Hero pressed a half-sheathed claw against her cheek. She stopped. He lifted his head, tasting the scents. He swiveled toward the square. Raven turned back with a sinking heart.

A tinker's hand wagon stood this side of the big tree. An awning and brightly painted canvas flaps made the wagon into a low tent. The tree blocked Raven's view of Loyal and his sister, but the baronsmen and tumblers were in plain sight. The paunchy male performer was pulling at his chin in a servile manner, talking furiously. The lanky boy stood to one side, idly flipping a knife from hand to hand.

Raven stooped and shrugged Hero onto the cobbles. "Go ahead," she whispered. "Signal when you find her."

Hero trotted briskly to the makeshift tent and nosed under the skirt. He looked back, nodded. Tail flicking furiously, he disappeared beneath the wagon. With a quick glance at the baronsmen, Raven started across the square. She was halfway there when Loyal's sister said something brusque. Raven's heart froze, but the words weren't aimed at her. She hurried on, until the big tree shielded her from view of the rest of the baronsmen. All she could hear now was a fawning mutter from the tumbler. She reached the wagon and ducked under the canvas.

It was dark. Raven hit her head on the axle and went down on all fours. Her left hand pressed into something soft that jerked aside with a muffled curse. Angry hands grabbed her hair. A foot kicked her thigh.

"Ow!" Raven gasped. "Mam, it's me!"

Her mother went still. "Penelope?" she whispered. "What on the five rivers are you doing here?"

"Saving you," Raven whispered back. "In case you didn't notice, the captain and her whole squad are out looking for you."

"I know they're out there," Roxaine replied. "What I want to know is why . . . Oh, never mind." She sat up, a dim shape in the gloom under the dark floor of the wagon. Something jangled.

Raven peered at her mother's wrists. "You're shackled!"

"That's right, Pigeon. I'd have been long gone otherwise."

"I'm surprised you got this far."

"Well, I did, Miss Know-It-All."

"I didn't mean . . . Right. We've got to get you out of here."

"Just say where." Roxaine jangled the manacles. "But I hope it has a hacksaw. Do you have friends here who can hide us?"

Raven could only stew in frustration.

Roxaine sighed. "No plan?"

"Not as such," Raven replied. "What's *your* plan, lady Baron?"

"I didn't mean—"

An angry voice rose outside. "That's enough, man. Blazing mages, but you've wasted our time, haven't you?" It was Steward's sister.

"Hush!" Roxaine breathed.

They lay still while the captain gave orders to her squad. Lights flickered beyond the skirting as they lit torches.

"I think it's time to leave," Raven muttered.

"Not you, Pigeon," Roxaine replied, and she slapped Raven hard across the face.

Raven recoiled, blinded by tears. In that moment, Roxaine scrambled under the canvas, shackles jangling. There was a shout, then feet pounded past the wagon. Raven started to follow, but Hero grabbed her dress, growling furiously. She rubbed her stinging cheek and smeared the tears from her eyes.

Curse her! she thought. She's not supposed to save me! She shook off Hero and scrambled into the open.

The torches were congregating at the far corner of the square, silhouetting a jumble of figures. She heard an angry shout from her mother and took two steps toward it.

"Hoi! There's another one!" It was the paunchy tumbler. He

was still by the tree, waving a torch and pointing his free hand at her.

Faces turned. Roxaine glared. Loyal Steward stood beside her, his mouth a dark O of surprise. Raven shook both fists at him, then turned and ran.

Twelve

L oyal stared dumbfounded at the grayfolk girl shaking her fists at him. It was Roxaine's runaway daughter, the bird girl. He charged after her. Two baronsmen were already on the chase. Loyal passed the first before they reached the street, and matched the second a few strides later. The girl fled up the cobbles, her skirts flapping heavily. They were gaining.

Suddenly, a big black cat darted between Loyal's legs. He stumbled, sprawling forward. The baronsman lumbered into him, and they went down together in a tangle. Loyal kicked his way clear. He caught a glimpse of skirts disappearing into an alley and rolled to his feet, careening into the rough wall as he turned the corner. He could hear the girl's footsteps slapping down the dark alleyway. There was a crash, and suddenly a pile of empty crates scattered across his path. He leaped the first one, only to smash into the next. As he yanked his foot free of the splintered wood, the big cat reappeared, jumped onto his back, and started shredding his coat. He had to stop and shake it off. Spitting and hissing, it clawed at his hands and legs. Then the baronsmen caught up. One aimed a hard kick at the cat, but it dodged off into the shadows. The boot cracked on Loyal's shin.

"You blundering oaf!" he cried, hopping on the other foot. "I'll have your—"

He was cut off by a harsh croak. Pain forgotten, he dashed to the end of the alley, a blank brick wall. A velvet gown lay piled in a heap in the dirt.

"Blast!" He snatched up the gown in his fist. "Blast the little witch!"

***

Loyal left Broadmeet as early as he could the next morning. He couldn't endure his sister's chiding. She was ten years older, and now she made him feel like a child. He had explained his mission, thinking its importance would impress her. He was wrong.

"This is a risky venture, this playing loose with the heir's mother," she remarked, with a scowl very much like their father's.

"Of course it is," he replied, "but think of what we gain."

"If Stoner agrees. And the Council turns a blind eye. And you even manage to get her that far."

He flushed. "She won't get out of that cabin again. She'll never be alone."

She regarded him closely. "Be careful, little brother," she said finally. "The Council could still decide in her favor. Make sure no harm comes to her. And, by the River, make use of this opportunity. Look around you. Talk to people. There is more to life than Cutter's Landing."

"I'm not a simple bumpkin," he said. "I've been downriver before."

"But you still have a lot to learn. With luck, being out from under Father's thumb will open your eyes, if not your mind."

"Father knows what he's doing!" he snapped. "And if you'll excuse me, I'll be on my way."

He did accept her offer of a baronswoman from her squad, so they could watch Roxaine day and night. He also added ankle irons to the wrist shackles. But Roxaine's story spread. Come daylight, a crowd gathered to watch the infamous mother of the new Baron being led in chains to the wharves. Roxaine marched proudly down the street. Loyal tried to hurry her, furious at the crowd's notice. He could imagine his father's face when he heard.

Finally, they steamed away from the city. Roxaine was secured in her cabin with a newly installed lock and Berna's guard inside with her. Loyal stood at the bow, his back to the lingering crowd. He felt their stares all the way to the point of land where the Slow and the Stoney River met. The boatman swung them through the bend. The *Lady Slow* dipped and bobbed in the swirling currents, the paddle wheel churned, and they were heading upriver into Baron Stoner's valley. Loyal stared ahead, ready for anything that would take his mind off the fiasco in Broadmeet.

The Stoney River quickly narrowed into a gorge flanked by the ridges that separated the river valleys. They passed through the cleft and almost immediately came to a roiling cataract broken by the tall, jagged islands of stone that gave the river its name. A small village stretched the length of the rapids, beside a canal with locks that lifted boats into the next stretch of river. They picked up a river pilot at the top of the canal and steamed on, weaving in tight curves around great rocks and eddies. Small fields and groves perched on narrow terraces that stepped up to the forest capping the ridge line. Rugged quarries scored the hillsides overhanging the narrow river valley. They encountered several boats loaded with stone blocks, surging downstream in the rapid current.

Evenings, they tied up in safe eddies known to the pilot. Loyal and the two baronsmen stood watches through the night. Loyal kept Roxaine locked in and warily studied every raven that soared along the rocky hills above the Stoney. He was sure one of them had to be her daughter. He hated them all.

It took them eight days, two more recoaling stops, and fourteen canals with a total of eighty-three locks to reach Baron Stoner's estate. Loyal kept count. They arrived in late morning in a fine, cold drizzle that made it seem they had moved back a month toward winter. Loyal sent a baronsman ahead to announce his arrival. Then he changed into his best clothes, checked that the receipt and letter were in place, and went to fetch Roxaine. She stood, chains clinking, and began to put on her heavy cloak. Loyal grimaced, remembering how she had huddled so pitifully in that cloak before jumping into the river to escape.

"The Council is bound to ask what happened to me," she said. "I hope you realize, your father is digging his own grave. And yours."

Loyal bristled. "My father knows exactly what he's doing. The Council will favor a guardian who can keep things running smoothly." He quoted his father: "A smooth transition, that's what they'll want."

"It's common knowledge that Darvin forgave my bond and planned to marry me."

"But he didn't marry you," Loyal snapped, "and there is no receipt for your bond. Except this one." He brandished the leather wallet.

"So you say," she replied. "Let me guess: You found it—ever your father's diligent tool—then stood by and watched while he burned it."

Her near hit unnerved him. He remembered how she had bewitched Cutter. "Magecraft won't help you," he snapped.

"I'm no mage and you know it. It's my daughter your father's afraid of."

"My father is not afrai—"

"He can't stand the thought of serving her! Bossed around by the daughter of a bondservant? He quakes at the thought. His fat-faced pride couldn't take it." Roxaine clenched the chain between her shackled wrists. "He thinks with me gone he can rule her, bend her to his leeching will."

"Quiet!" Loyal shouted. "I only hope Baron Stoner sends you to his prison quarry, like the foul-mouthed runaway you are."

"We'll see about that, boy." She pushed past him to the door.

"Yes, we will!" he replied, but he was speaking to her back. Seething, he hurried after.

By the time they had made their way from the wharf to the manor, Loyal felt more in control again. After all, she was the one in chains. He had his father's letter and a new bond receipt in hand. He also knew now exactly what he was going to say to prime the pump. He was so busy rehearsing the speech in his mind that he hardly noticed the graceful stone buildings that made up the estate or the marble statues that flanked the entrance. Inside, the foyer was dominated by a stone fountain on a black-and-white marble floor. Stone vases stood in the corners, and a stone stairway led up to a stone balustrade. Even the chairs along the wall were carved from stone.

A servant led them down a columned hallway to an ornate door. As the woman knocked, Loyal told his baronsmen to keep Roxaine in the hallway. He didn't want her to take over the meeting from the very start. She gave him a condescending look. He smiled back. She'd see where her sharp tongue got her.

The reception room was tiled with stone, chilly and damp despite bright hangings and the coals glowing in a large stone fireplace. Baron Stoner stood by the fire. A woman in a sumptuous blue gown rose from a tall chair beside him as Loyal entered.

"Ah, young Steward," Stoner said affably. "What a pleasant surprise. Do come in."

Loyal strode over and bowed slightly, standing exactly three paces away, as his father had instructed. "Thank you, Baron Stoner," he said. "The Baron and her guardian send their greetings." He held out the leather wallet that contained the letter and receipt. An attendant quickly stepped forward to take it.

Stoner smiled. "First let me present the Lady Stoner: my wife, Clarissa."

She offered Loyal her hand. He took it and bowed, admiring the several large rings that glittered on her fingers. She was a tall woman and quite attractive, with shiny black hair, olive skin, and large eyes. She squeezed his hand firmly, and he blushed.

"Welcome to our river, young man," she said. "Your father never mentioned his son was so handsome."

Loyal bowed again, at a loss for words.

Stoner chuckled. "Don't let it go to your head, young Steward. She says that to all the boys. Now, what have you got for me?"

The attendant presented the wallet. Stoner took out the letter, scanned it quickly, then glanced thoughtfully at the receipt for

Roxaine. He was a match to his wife: dark-haired, large, florid, and quite well turned out. Rings dotted his fingers, too.

"Well, that's a very interesting offer," he remarked, handing the papers back to the attendant. "Where is the famous would-be lady? She didn't drown on the way, I hope."

Loyal stifled a smile. Stoner had provided the perfect opening. "I'm afraid she came very close to it, my lord Baron," he said with a precise edge of regret in his voice.

"What?" Stoner exclaimed.

"She tried to escape, my lord. In fact, she tried to escape twice, and the second time was almost hanged for it in Broadmeet." He shrugged. "Luckily, my sister, Berna, is clerk and captain of the baronsmen there. I was able to convince her otherwise."

"Tried to escape twice?" Lady Stoner remarked. "This is quite a *servant*."

"I most humbly apologize," Loyal said. "We had no idea. Of course, she has always been strong willed. I think her fiery nature is what so attracted the Baron . . ." He paused and swallowed. ". . . our good, late Baron Cutter. Though, I admit, we had a glimpse of her deviousness when she . . . became his consort. Looking back, I realize she took advantage of her standing, lording over all the other house servants, even my mother." He shrugged. "Of course, she has no notion of how to manage people, but she had her wiles and a way to make our Baron happy."

"And to provide an heir," Stoner added dryly. "Well, let's see this pig in a poke."

The baronsmen escorted Roxaine into the room. She went straight to Stoner, ignoring Loyal completely.

"My lord Baron," she said, sketching an awkward curtsey, "I'm sorry I can't offer my hand in a proper greeting. As you can see, I'm a bit inconvenienced." She held up her hands to show the shackles. "My daughter's very own steward had me abducted."

Stoner frowned. "Abducted?"

"Abducted," she repeated. "So he can control the River Slow

by controlling Darvin's heir, my daughter. I am her guardian, by birth and by my husband's wishes."

"Yes, well," Stoner replied. He appeared somewhat taken aback.

Loyal stepped in. "She was never Baron Cutter's wife," he said quickly. "She was merely his consort, his sometime companion. A bondservant, nothing more."

"Darvin forgave my bond!" Roxaine exclaimed.

"Cutter forgive a bond? That seems unlikely," Stoner drawled.

"We were engaged to be married." She was fighting to control herself. Loyal was delighted.

"You and Cutter engaged?" Lady Stoner gave a humorless smile. "How unusual."

"We fell in love," Roxaine said. "Is that so unusual?"

"Not at all," Lady Stoner replied. "But that's not the same, is it?"

"What do you mean?"

"Stoner here falls in love with servants regularly. That doesn't mean they're engaged."

"*We* had a child. My daughter is Cutter's heir."

"But you are still a bondservant."

"I told you, Darvin forgave my bond!" Roxaine caught herself. With a visible effort, she lowered her voice and turned her attention back to the Baron. "I don't know what this boy and his conniving father have done with the original receipt, nor do I know what sort of bargain he has offered you to keep me here, but that's no matter. I can offer a better arrangement, I'm sure."

"Nonsense," Lady Stoner snapped. "What bargain can a bondservant offer, other than what you already gave to Cutter? We've no need of that here. Take her out."

Roxaine finally lost her temper. "You overdressed, jewel-stuffed baggage! You can't keep me from my daughter!"

"Take her out! Now!"

Loyal hid his smile.

The baronsmen grabbed Roxaine's arms and dragged her,

shouting, through the door. They could hear her insults fade down the corridor.

"Well!" Stoner remarked. "What do you think, my dear? Can you tame her?"

"And bear that tongue day after day? Not worth a dozen new servants. Besides"—Lady Stoner gave him an empty smile—"she's far too pretty."

"Hmm. Can't say I noticed," Stoner replied, with a wink at Loyal. "Still, this is a delicate matter, not to be decided merely on looks. Squint!" he called. "What do you see for her?"

A man bustled out of an alcove in a swish of brocade robe, his attempt at drama spoiled by the quivering of pink pudgy cheeks. His eyes peered from folds of flesh. "Yes, my lord," he wheezed. "The woman."

He produced a bulging leather pouch from beneath his sack of a robe and brought it close to his face to undo the knot. He held it out, and Stoner reached in to take something. Squint held the bag out to Lady Stoner. She grimaced and reached in. To Loyal's surprise, the fleshy little man offered him the bag, too. He eyed it suspiciously.

"Go on, lad," Stoner said. "It won't bite you."

Loyal reached in and felt a jumble of slick, cold shapes. He drew one out tentatively. It was a small bone, smooth and yellow with age. He stared at it with mixed distaste and fascination; it looked very much like a finger bone. A strange mark was painted on one side.

Squint took it in a pudgy hand and peered at it. He went to the Baron and to Lady Stoner, studied their bones, then turned to the fireplace and stared at the coals. He mumbled, shaking the three bones in his thick fingers. He dropped them onto the marble tiles, watching as they clicked and skittered into a pattern, which he studied some more. Loyal glanced at Lady Stoner; she was studying the bones as avidly as Squint.

Baron Stoner gave another wink. "Don't worry, lad," he said quietly. "Squint has been right often enough."

Loyal watched with growing apprehension. This Squint reminded him far too much of the supposed healer mage who had overseen Cutter's demise. Could the fate of his father's plan actually rest in the pattern of a few dried bones thrown by this quivering blob?

Finally, with a great wheeze, Squint stooped and collected his bones. "Well," he said, straightening with another wheeze. He glanced quickly at Lady Stoner's frown. "She will be nothing but trouble, my lord."

Baron Stoner looked a little disappointed. Loyal breathed a sigh of relief.

"Not surprising," Lady Stoner said briskly. "Nicco." Yet another attendant appeared. "We've no use for her type here at the manor." She flashed her husband a low-lidded smile. "Don't worry, dear, I'll make it up to you. Nicco, have her taken to the *back* quarry. At once."

"Yes, lady." The man bowed and slipped away.

"There," she said, resuming her seat in the tall chair. "The best solution all around."

Loyal bowed.

Thirteen

aven watched from a tree in Stoner's garden as the two baronsmen dragged her mother, kicking and yelling, from the manor. Then, with an effort, Roxaine calmed herself and stood stiffly between the baronsmen in the shelter of the manor's portico, head raised defiantly. Raven hunched against the drizzle. Hero huddled beside her, shivering. What a cold, ugly tomb of a place! She wished they'd hurry and put her mother somewhere. As long as it had a window, Raven could fly in, change her, and fly out; you couldn't ask for a simpler plan than that.

Finally, one of Stoner's people appeared and spoke to the baronsmen. After more waiting, a horse cart pulled out from the stables, driven by two of Stoner's baronsmen. Raven watched in growing frustration as they loaded Roxaine onto the cart and rattled away. Steward's guard dogs went back inside.

"Great mages, now what?" Raven muttered. Hero cooed miserably. He had asked to be a pigeon at the last changing. He said the catbird was still too small and made his head hurt. That was fine with Raven; pigeons might be stupid and sloppy, but they could fly fast and far without tiring. The change was easier with a bigger bird, too. She shook off the wet and took to the air. Hero cooed dismally and followed.

The cart trundled from terrace to terrace, angling steadily up-river and uphill. People tilling the fields glanced from beneath broad, dripping hats as it passed. Roxaine stood wedged in a corner, staring forward with jaw clenched, the picture of unbending pride. Midday passed with no break in the weather and no meal. They came to a quarry, deep, bare, and glistening. The air rang with the sound of hammers and the grating of stone on stone. The cart passed it by. After several more tiresome leagues, they reached the top of the terraced land. The track skirted the edge of the forest, veering around outcrops and steep ravines. Finally, the cart rounded a sharp bend and passed through a tall palisade onto the floor of another quarry.

Bare walls of streaked marble stretched in a broad, uneven W carved into the hillside. The back face fell in a sheer drop from its treed rim to the rubble-strewn floor. Groups of smooth, nearly round holes pocked the walls here and there. Ragged people toiled on several levels, cutting away massive blocks with heavy hammers and iron drills. Others levered cut stone onto flat wooden skids, or carried log rollers, or labored down sagging ladders with baskets of rubble on their backs, all under the eyes of surly guards in dirty red tunics. A steam engine spewed muddy smoke into the dripping gloom, shrieking metallically when its gears engaged to pull a skid toward the loading ramp. Foremen shouted orders. A whip cracked. Raven flinched as a luckless worker gasped in pain. The guard hit him again.

"Cur!" she muttered. "Filthy, blood-licking cur."

Hero cooed indignantly.

Raven clacked her beak. "Right," she muttered. "A cur is sweet by comparison."

The cart swung toward a cluster of crude stone buildings piled against the quarry wall. Stoner's two baronsmen pulled Roxaine out and dragged her into the longest block. They emerged alone a few minutes later, carrying bread and cheese. They clambered into the cart and set off toward the gate as if they couldn't wait to get out. Raven croaked a curse at their fleeing backs, then settled onto a ledge for another miserable wait.

Before too long, Roxaine was led out by a hefty woman guard. The shackles were finally gone. Roxaine kept pace with the guard, head still high. Raven felt a grudging admiration. The guard marched her to the end of the building and unlocked a small low door. Privy muck spilled out. She pointed her whip at a shovel beside the door. Roxaine turned her back. The guard snapped the whip across her shoulders.

Roxaine yelped. The guard shouted an order and raised the whip menacingly. Roxaine lowered her head and picked up the shovel. Raven growled. She reached out her talent, searching for birds to send against the guard. Before she could sense even one, her mother jabbed the shovel into the guard's gut. The woman bent double. Quick as a striking snake, the shovel came down on her head. She sprawled onto the wet stone below the little door. Muck tumbled onto her head. Roxaine leaned on the shovel with a grim smile. Raven croaked gleefully.

The victory was short-lived. Shaking her head, the guard hauled herself to her feet and backed away, whip ready. Roxaine sneered at her. Instead of attacking, the guard pulled a whistle from her tunic and blew three short blasts. More guards came running, whistling in reply. Roxaine let the shovel fall and waited, arms crossed, wearing a look of contempt. In moments, they had her arms pulled behind her back. The guard she had bested hit her across the face with the butt of her whip; the others chained her to the quarry wall with her wrists so high, she had to stand on tiptoe. The woman guard snarled a long string of threats into her face. Roxaine glared. The guard jerked up her whip handle. Roxaine flinched, and the woman laughed, then spat on Roxaine's bedraggled gown. Still laughing, she and the others returned to their posts.

Raven bit back futile curses. She called a flock of starlings over the quarry to rain droppings on the guards, but sent them off after one pass. It felt weak and silly. She studied the quarry and the palisade, the guard shack and tower. They needed night; then they could fly out. Escape would be the best revenge.

Twilight came early in the damp overcast. The guards shut down the steam engine and herded the prisoners into the buildings. The woman who had hit Roxaine came out with a bowl of food. She stood in front of Roxaine and ate every bite, then belched. With a satisfied smile, she went back inside. Roxaine sagged against the irons.

When it was too dark to see her, Raven nudged Hero and dropped from the ledge. The ground loomed suddenly beneath her, and she braked just in time, croaking a warning to Hero. Her night vision was terrible. She wondered if she dared try to turn her mother into an owl. A whippoorwill would be less ornery. No: Better to let her take her natural form, whatever that might be. Raven changed herself, shivering immediately in the dampness, then took a deep breath and reversed the spell on Hero.

He let out a huge groan. "Hoi, that was too scrunched!"

"Hush!" Raven peered into the darkness.

"I can't see a thing," Hero muttered.

"Me neither," Raven replied. "I think it's time for you to be a cat."

"Finally!" Hero exclaimed, bouncing beside her.

"Settle," she hissed. "We have to do this carefully. Stay right beside me, because I won't be able to see you."

"Right!" he whispered. "I'm ready!" He was almost glowing with excitement.

The change was so easy, Raven wasn't even sure it had happened. "All done?" she whispered.

Hero brushed against her leg. She stroked his smooth back. He was the big cat again. His long tail was a perfect handhold, and he led her across the gritty floor to the wall. Despite his help, she almost ran into her mother.

"What now, warder? Too drunk to find the privy?" Her mother's voice rasped.

"It's me, Mam. Raven."

"Oh, no. Don't tell me they caught you, too?"

"Not me, Mam. I flew in."

"Flew? What do you mean?"

"I'm a mage, Mam. A bird mage."

There was moment of silence. Finally, Roxaine forced a chuckle. "Honestly, Pigeon, this is no time for jokes."

Raven clenched her fists. "How do you think I caught up to you in Broadmeet? By swimming?"

"I guess I didn't really think about it."

"And I don't expect you even care. But I am a mage. I have a real talent. A strong talent. A talent you couldn't even imagine."

"You always had a talent, Pigeon—for making trouble."

"Like your talent for insults?" Raven snapped.

"Which you seem to have inherited," Roxaine rasped. "No, forget that. I'm sorry, Pigeon. I'm not in the best mood for great revelations right now."

Raven gritted her teeth. "I'm sorry, too, Mam. But I really am a mage."

"A mage? That's impos— Well, I'm in no position to argue. You can fly? Really?"

"I can," Raven insisted. "*We* can. As birds. Together. I've come to get you out."

Roxaine gave a sigh that ended in a moan. "What about these chains. Can you make them disappear?"

"No, but I can get you out of them. Are you ready?"

"Ready for what?"

"I'm going to change you."

"Change me? Into a bird? You really can do that?"

"Yes, I can! It's not that hard to understand, Mam. You'll slip right out of those shackles. Trust me for once, right?"

Her mother paused. "Right," she said finally. "Just get me out of here."

Raven braced herself and began the spell. Immediately, she realized how much Hero had been helping with his own transformations. This was like flying through mud. Her arms struggled through the motions. Even her tongue labored over the words. Dimly, she heard her mother gasp, then moan, then let out a pained grunt as she slid to the ground.

"Blazing mages, what are you doing to me?" Her voice was half human, a panicked squawk.

The resistance increased. Raven struggled against it, but it was no use. Her mother refused to change. There was nothing Raven, or any mage, could do against a person's will.

Raven's arms fell to her sides, shaking. She leaned against the wall. Her mother was a dark, groaning lump, huddled on the stone floor. She was free; the change had gone that far, at least.

"Are you all right?" Raven asked. She touched for her mother's shoulder.

Roxaine moaned. "Sweet spirit of the River, it hurts."

"What's the matter?" Raven felt panic in her own voice. Had her spell gone wrong? Had she somehow damaged her mother in the botched change?

"You saw what those filthy curs did to me," Roxaine muttered. "My arms and hands are dead. I can't even hold them up, never mind fly."

Raven cursed. "I'm sorry, Mam. I didn't realize . . ."

"Rowr?" A furry body brushed against Raven's side.

"Hush!" Roxaine whispered. "What's that noise?"

"It's all right, Mam. It's just Hero."

"Hero? A hero cat?"

"I'll explain later. Can you walk at least?"

"In a minute. My legs are fine. I just ache. You started to shrink me."

"I told you: into a bird. If you just let it happen, it doesn't hurt."

"Mrragh," Hero disagreed.

"You be quiet," Raven snapped. "Come on, Mam. If you're sure you're all right."

"Except now I'm freezing, too." Her tone was wretched. "When you shrank me, you didn't shrink my dress, only my shift."

"Well, that's all I can do with clothes," Raven admitted. "Be grateful I didn't shrink the chains, too, or you'd still be in them. Your dress is right here."

"I can't pick it up," Roxaine said. "My arms—"

Her reply was cut off by the bang of a door being thrown open. Light shafted through the gloom. They all froze.

". . . fetch the maggot in. The Baron'll have our teeth if she freezes to death on her first night here." A thick figure emerged, bearing a flickering lantern. It wavered toward them through the gloom. Hero growled deep in his throat.

Raven grabbed the front of Roxaine's shift and pulled her deeper into the shadows. Roxaine stifled a moan.

The approaching guard held up the lantern with a sour laugh. "Not feeling so high and mighty now, eh, m'lady?"

The light fell across the dangling chains. The guard stumbled to a halt, gawping, then swore a filthy stream. She ran back toward the cell block, shattering the silence with a shrill blast from her whistle.

"That's done it!" Raven muttered. She took hold of Hero's tail again. "Work around to the other side, where the palisade meets the stone."

Hero gave a little growl and started off so quickly that Raven almost lost her grip on his tail. Roxaine stumbled after them, pulled by her shift. They hadn't gone five steps before torches and lanterns began to fill the dark behind them. A fire flared up by the gate. Voices called. Torches hurried to the far end of the palisade, cutting off escape. Hero veered toward the back of the quarry. Raven knew there wasn't much there but piles of rubble.

The torches zigzagged toward them, getting closer. Hero veered to the left. His tail writhed in Raven's grasp. The position hurt: half stooped, one arm pulled back straight to clench her mother's shift. Raven stumbled on some sharp rubble and crashed against the back wall of the quarry. They had reached a dead end. Raven moaned. Once again she had failed to save her mother. She could only change, flee, and wait for another chance.

Suddenly, Hero was right beside her face. *"Rowr."* His growl echoed flatly. An earthy breeze washed past her.

She reached out and found a smooth opening in the stone. It was a cave!

"Come on, Mam," she said, turning to pull her to the edge. "Inside."

Roxaine hesitated a moment, then let Raven boost her through. She gave another pained grunt and slipped from Raven's grasp. There was a scratching, sliding sound, a moment of silence, a dull thud, a dull groan. Cursing, Raven hoisted herself into the hole and pitched forward.

She slid down a gritty slope into nothing. Her heart had time for one frantic pulse before she flopped in a heap on top of her mother.

"Nice aim," Roxaine muttered.

"You could have moved."

A hound yelped. Another whistle shrilled.

"Over here!" a hoarse voice cried. "By the caves!"

There was whining and scrabbling outside. Light leaked down the scoured shaft.

"This way!" Roxaine hooked Raven's arm with her elbow and pulled her toward a small dark hole in the wall of the chamber. Hero disappeared into the tiny opening. Roxaine flopped onto her belly, groaned, and dragged herself after him with her elbows. Raven hesitated, heart pounding. Her legs trembled. She sank to her hands and knees. The light in the entrance loomed. The scrabbling became frantic. Raven cursed miserably, swallowed her fear, and crawled into the narrow dark.

Fourteen

Loyal was eating the midday meal with Baron and Lady Stoner when Nicco hurried in. Loyal wondered what could be so important as to interrupt the Baron at a meal. Even the morning's breakfast had taken an hour to eat. He marveled that the Baron and his lady weren't as fat as their seer, Squint. It was a waste of time and food, he thought, but a part of him also enjoyed being singled out as their guest. Nicco, their own steward, did not eat with the Baron and lady.

As Nicco whispered into Stoner's ear, the Baron almost inhaled his food. He grabbed his goblet and downed a great swallow of wine, then bellowed, "Bring in this Warder woman! I want details! And find Seeker! Now!" Nicco hurried out.

"What is it, my dear?" Lady Stoner asked. "Surely it can't be worth choking over."

"She's gone!" he exclaimed. "Cutter's little fire sprite. She's escaped the quarry."

Loyal swallowed hard.

Lady Stoner gasped. "However could she? No one has ever escaped!"

"No one indeed!" Stoner frowned, and Loyal was suddenly reminded of his father.

He flushed. "I'm as amazed as you, my lord. I had thought that, after two failed attempts . . ."

"Pah! One expects a prisoner to try. The question is, how did she manage it?"

Loyal thought he knew, but he was saved the embarrassment of admitting it by the return of Nicco, followed by a woman dressed in a mud-spattered tunic the color of dried blood. She doffed her hat and made an ungainly bow. Under Stoner's growled interrogation, she described the events of the night before.

"Into a cave?" Stoner demanded. "In my prison quarry? What sort of a failed curse let that happen, Warder?"

"A-a-all the quarries have c-c-caves in them, sir," the woman stammered. "The marble is like that."

"I know that!" he growled. "It should have been blocked! Did anyone go in after her?"

"Of course, lord Baron, sir," Warder said. "They searched half the night and more, came back out just before I left. They were down to their last candle stubs."

"Was she alone?" Loyal interrupted. They all turned to look at him. "Well, uh, are all the other prisoners accounted for?"

"Yes, young sir, they are," the woman assured him.

"Did she have a light?" Loyal persisted. "A lantern, a torch?"

Warder hesitated. "Well, no, I don't think so, now you mention it. There was no sign of light when I heard her down the hole."

"What did you hear?" Loyal asked.

She glanced at Lady Stoner. "Well, to be honest, young sir, it was something I wouldn't want to repeat right here."

"That sounds like her, all right," Lady Stoner remarked.

"You're sure it sounded like her voice?" Loyal pressed.

"That's hard to say," Warder admitted, "what with the echoes and the dogs barking and the . . ." She trailed off.

"Yes? There was something more?" Loyal frowned at her reticence.

"Well, there was this hiss. Almost like a cat or something. Only bigger."

Loyal blanched. He could only guess what it meant, and none of the guesses were pleasant. "I suppose it could have been the sound of her crawling away?" he asked.

"Whatever the blasted noise was, she's gone," Stoner growled. "Where does the cave come out? Does anyone know that, at least?"

"Oh, nowhere, sir," Warder said quickly. "We've been all over the ground around the quarry. There's no hole big enough to let a person through, even a stringy wench like her."

"Good," Stoner said. "Then we have only to wait for her to come back out, begging for food and light."

"Unless she gets lost inside and starves to death," Lady Stoner remarked dryly.

Stoner frowned at the thought. "Well, Seeker will find her. She's as good as caught, in that trap." He stabbed another bite and shoved it angrily into his mouth, then threw down his fork in disgust and swallowed without even chewing. He followed it with another gulp of wine. "Don't you worry, lad," he said to Loyal. "My seeker is the best huntsman on the five rivers. He'll sniff her out."

"I'm sure, my lord," Loyal said, trying to sound enthusiastic. He remembered his futile search for her daughter. If Roxaine shared that talent . . . No, she would have flown away by now. But how did she escape? Did she have some other magecraft at her call? He could well imagine her changing to a giant snake and slithering away through the depths of the earth, only to pop back out in the courtyard of Cutter's manor. Loyal shuddered. A bondservant *and* a mage: It would be a disaster. His father would blame him, of course.

Nicco returned, this time with a weathered man in mottled leather.

"M'lord, lady." The man gave Stoner and his wife each a quick bob of the head.

"We have a runaway, Seeker," Stoner growled. "From the prison quarry."

The seeker listened to the tale with his head thrust out and shaggy brows raised. He had a long, pointed nose and an overbite so pronounced, it seemed he had no chin at all. To Loyal, he looked like a tanned spaniel on point. In fact, the man looked stupid; certainly, no match for Roxaine if it came to a game of wits.

Halfway through the telling, Nicco returned yet again, trailed by a red-faced, wheezing Squint.

"Squint!" Stoner barked. "The woman's escaped. Escaped, do you hear! What kind of sight is that, eh? Well? What do you have to say for yourself?"

Squint glanced at Lady Stoner, but she gave him only a cold frown. "My lord," he said smoothly, squinting even more than usual, "I never advised sending her away. I said she would be nothing but trouble. I definitely saw trouble. You see? It is as I said. And saw."

"Said, saw: You knew what I meant!" Stoner slapped the table.

Squint's eyes almost closed. His fingers twitched as though he were casting bones. "I certainly thought I did, my lord. I asked of my sight the question: 'Should she be sent to the quarry?' Perhaps you were thinking more on the lines of 'What if I keep her here?' Assuming I was answering *that* question, you also assumed she should go to the quarry, whereas I—"

"Fah!" Stoner threw up his hands. "You and your blasted questions! All I wanted was a straight answer!" He grabbed his goblet and downed the remaining wine.

"My lord," Squint protested, "there can't be an answer without a question."

"Then answer this question, bone man: Where is the woman? Eh? Where is she?"

Squint fumbled under his robe for his leather pouch. "Certainly, my lord, though—"

Seeker snorted. "Old bones aren't going to help," he said. "It's tracking you need. Honest skill."

Squint fixed him with a piggish glare. "Just because your dim mind can't understand the subtleties of my talent—"

"Mumbles and riddles, you mean. 'Tisn't talent, that's for sure. Magecraft!" He snorted again.

Squint drew himself to his full, round height. One narrow eye twitched. "You are an insult," he wheezed. "A living, breathing insult to the intelligence. Go, then; go find her. Sniff at her tracks on your hands and knees. You'll get no help from me." Clutching his bag, he huffed toward the door.

"Squint!" Stoner bellowed. The seer stopped in his tracks. "Get back here."

"Let him go," Seeker grumbled. "Don't need his old bones."

"Be quiet, both of you!" Stoner growled. "No one escapes our punishment! Seeker, you will indeed sniff the ground, if that's what it takes. And Squint, you will use whatever talent your fat head holds to help him. Where is she? That is your only question from now until you have her back in chains. Do you understand?"

Seeker's face drooped like a whipped dog's. Squint's had gone from pink to white. His jowls quivered. Neither dared meet Stoner's glare.

"Yes, m'lord," Seeker muttered. "I'll find her for you."

Squint's fingers worked on the pouch. "I will make sure he does," he wheezed.

"You'd better, both of you," Stoner warned. "Go! And you, Warder!" The woman had retreated to a corner by the door. Now she jerked to attention. "Go with them. You let her get loose; you can very well help get her caught."

"Yes, my lord." She stared at the floor in resignation.

Stoner waved them all out in disgust and reattacked his cold meal.

"Well, young Steward," Lady Stoner said, "you've handed us quite a piece of work." She regarded him as if he were an odd lump floating in her meat sauce. "No wonder you were so quick to part with her bond."

Loyal flushed again. "My father made everything clear in his letter."

"Everything except the nature of the beast."

Baron Stoner waved a hand. "Fah! Jan Steward proposed a bargain. If I didn't demand a look in the horse's mouth, well, there were reasons for haste, eh, lad? If he slipped me a nag in a pure-bred's blanket . . ."

"The woman is young, healthy," Loyal protested. "A hard worker."

"Is she?" Lady Stoner drawled. "How will we ever know, my young Steward?"

Loyal was sick and tired of being referred to as "young." And "lad." And even "boy" on one occasion. Now they were as good as calling him a young thief!

He gave them a smile as empty as the lady's. "I'm sorry if you think you've been cheated. I will make sure you receive the full value of the bargain."

"Blast it, I want the woman back!" Stoner growled. "I won't have people thinking they can escape from my prison quarry."

Loyal stood and threw down his napkin. "Then I will go help find her."

"Oh, don't be ridiculous," Lady Stoner said.

"I will go," he repeated. He drew himself up, trying to look and sound older. Affronted. As correct and commanding as his father. "I insist on it. As you have pointed out, I knew the woman was troublesome before I delivered her. Therefore, it is my duty, to my father and my river, to make good on a fair bargain and bring her back."

Baron Stoner regarded him with amusement. "A pretty speech. Very well, go catch her."

"I will make an example of her, you can be su—"

"It wouldn't do to have her missing," Stoner went on, stabbing another forkful. "Selling her bond is one thing; losing her in a quarry is quite another. Looks too convenient. Miner, Miller—they'd be quick to question this bargain of yours then, eh? No, we need her. We may have to produce her when the Council meets."

Loyal blanched. Produce her at the Council? They couldn't let her speak to the Council. What if she charmed them, as she had

Cutter, and they made her guardian? Or even Baron? A bondservant Baron? It was against nature!

Loyal eyed Stoner in a new light. Had Roxaine already charmed him somehow? Obviously, the man couldn't be trusted. "Yes, of course. My lord," he finally managed.

"Well, don't just stand there dithering, boy. Get on with it."

Fifteen

R aven and her mother huddled against the wall of the cave. Hero lay across their laps, the only spot of warmth in the damp darkness. Their thin clothes were soaked, their bodies slick with mud. Roxaine shivered violently; then Raven started. It took a long time to stop. Hero made a worried sound, half growl, half mew.

"We'll be all right," Raven told him, trying hard not to chatter.

"That's not a real cat, is it," Roxaine said.

"No," Raven replied. "That's Hero . . . Leo. His father is Phillipe, the breedmaster."

"Sweet mages," Roxaine breathed. "What have you done to him?"

Raven gave a wry laugh. "Nothing he didn't want." She started to explain about his talent but was interrupted by another harsh bout of the shivers.

"We'd better move around," her mother said.

Raven could hear pain in her voice. The last stretch had been a long, tight crack with two right-angle bends. Roxaine had barely been able to haul herself through on her bad wrists. It had been almost impossible for Raven, squeezed by the rock, forcing herself forward with fingers and toes as the crack narrowed and pressed all the air from her lungs. Fleeing from unseen scrabbling and swearing behind: two or three guards in pursuit. It was their faint light from behind that had let Hero find any path at all. Raven gave thanks for the eyes of a cat.

The guards had missed the low slit Hero had spotted. They went the more obvious way, taking the light with them. That had been a long time ago, while Raven, Roxaine, and Hero lay silently in the tight crack in the rock. For Raven, it had been a constant battle against a panic that squeezed her more tightly than the stone. Finally, Hero led them a few more lengths, and the narrow passage widened into a chamber of sorts. Nothing they could see—there was no light at all now, only a vague mirage at the back of the eyes—but tall enough to stand in. The floor was a slab of slimy rock that sloped uncomfortably into the darkness. Somewhere nearby, water dripped slowly, one drop every hundred heartbeats. Raven realized how thirsty she was. And hungry. And sore. And how very cold. She shivered again.

"Come on," Roxaine ordered. "Move. Help me stand."

Muttering a curse, Raven eased Hero off her legs and forced herself up. She turned, found her mother's arm in the darkness, and tried not to pull too hard.

Roxaine groaned, but once on her feet, she shook off Raven's hand. "Stretch," she said. "Shake your arms. Swing around. We've got to stay warm."

Irked at being bossed about, Raven swung her arms hard and whacked the wall. "Blast! I hate this!"

"I don't like it any more than you do," Roxaine replied. "Ow!"

Raven grinned in the darkness, then felt guilty. Her mother hadn't been so stupid as to hit the wall; she simply couldn't move her arms without pain. Raven inched carefully down the sloped floor, hands held out in front of her. The chamber seemed to be larger than she'd thought. That made her feel a little better. Not being able to see helped, actually. She could pretend it was a big space. Lots of room. Not a tight hole, like a cell, with no windows and hardly a door—

She stopped the thought with an effort of will. Her heart was racing. She swung her arms again and bent to right and left, concentrating on the movement. Suddenly, her feet slipped on the slimy rock. She yelped and flailed the air, sliding flat-footed down the slope, expecting to smash into the opposite wall at any instant.

Instead, she splashed into a pool of cold water. She came to rest ankle deep, her toes buried in soft silt.

"Are you all right, Pigeon?"

Raven gritted her teeth. "I'm fine, Mam!" she snapped. "I just slipped a little. Not our biggest worry right now."

"Now, there's an understatement," Roxaine said. "Did I hear a splash?"

"Yes, I splashed! There happens to be a pool of water in this mucky, dripping snake hole, imagine that!"

"Well, that's good, isn't it? I'm thirsty. Watch out, I'm coming down."

"Oh. Right." Raven felt stupid, and even more irritated. "Just be careful; that floor is like a sheet of ice. We don't need you any more hurt than you are."

"Your splash was a warning. I'll be carefu—"

Roxaine gave a little cry. There was a slurping sound, then a splash, then a curse in the darkness.

Raven grinned. "I see you found the pool."

Roxaine didn't even try to reply. Raven heard her gulping water, and bent to drink. It was silty but wonderful. She marveled that she could be so wet and still so thirsty.

"Well, that's surely better," Roxaine remarked. "Now, if we could just stumble into a pool of warm soup."

"I'd settle for a few bites of cold meat," Raven said.

"Might as well wish for the best."

"If wishes were fishes . . ." Raven began.

". . . we'd be up to our necks in trout." Roxaine splashed over and took Raven's arm. "No sense standing in the drinking bowl. Help me out of here."

Together they slid their way up and over till they found a relatively level patch of rock just above the edge of the pool. They sagged against each other in the dark. Hero found them and rubbed against their legs, meowing.

"How about it, Cat Boy?" Roxaine asked. "Think you can find a way out?"

He gave an agitated *yeow*.

"Sounds like he's willing to try," she said.

"They'll just be waiting for us at the cave mouth," Raven said.

"Have you got a better plan?"

"There has to be another way out of this hole. Ouch! Sheath those claws, Fur Brain!"

"We aren't going to find it in the dark, Pigeon. We'll be lucky even to follow our own tracks back. Little Hero here is the only hope we've got."

"I'm not going to just walk into their arms."

"They don't know about you. I'll go out first and give myself up, then—"

"Hush!" Raven clenched her mother's arm, startled by an odd noise nearby.

"What?" Roxaine whispered. "Is it them?"

"No," Raven whispered back. "Something else. Overhead." She strained her ears. She could hear better than most, but not as well as a raven. Water dripped. In between, the silence was as deep as the darkness.

"I don't hear anything," Roxaine said. "Maybe it was an echo."

Hero growled.

"You heard it, too, didn't you," Raven said.

Then she heard it again: an odd fluttering sound. Faint, shrill chirps almost beyond the edge of her hearing. "Just bats, Mam."

Hero meowed.

"Forget it," she said. "You'll never catch them in this dark."

He yowled, pawing at her leg.

"Ow! Keep those fishhooks in! And, no, you can't go hunting bats." Then it sank in. "Bats . . . that means there's another way out!"

Hero yowled so loudly, the bats began to chitter and flutter around the top of the cave.

"I think he's trying to tell you something," Roxaine said.

"Well, he can blasted well tell me in words!" Raven began to unspell him.

"What are you doing? You're not going to bemagic him, are you?"

"He already is bemagicked," Raven replied wearily. "I told you: He's a boy in cat form. A mage, like me, only a different kind. I'm a bird mage, but he's an animal mage."

"Birds are animals too."

"I know that! He's a *furry* animal mage, all right? A beast mage."

"A beast ma— You mean he can be a bat?"

Hero yowled in agreement.

"Keep wishing," Raven muttered. "He can only be a cat, and only if I change him."

Hero growled and took a swipe at her leg.

"Ow!" Raven yelp. "That does it, you mangy tail licker. I'm changing you now!"

Hero was talking even before she'd finished. "I kept trying to tell you: There are bats here; there's another way out. But you wouldn't listen. Blazing mages! Argue, argue, argue!"

"We were not arguing," Raven said. "We were . . . discussing. And it's a bit hard to listen to you when you can't even talk."

"I talked," he retorted. "You just didn't understand me."

"We can understand you now, Hero," Roxaine said. "Can you be a bat?"

"Of course I can. I'm a beast mage. I think. I might be just a cat mage."

"He's tried being a horse and a dog," Raven put in, "but it didn't work."

"That was then," he countered. "I wasn't desperate enough."

"What's that got to do with it?" Roxaine asked.

"It's a long story," Raven said. "And right now, *I'm* feeling a little too desperate to go through it again, right?"

"If you say so," Roxaine replied. "Hero, if you were a bat, how would we follow you? We can't fly. We can't even see."

"I'll lead you where you can walk," he said. "Or crawl at least."

"Are you sure we'll fit?"

"Well . . . I think so. The bats don't have any trouble."

"Bats are a lot smaller than we are," Raven pointed out.

"They need enough room to fly," he replied.

"I wasn't worried about that," she said. "What about the headache? Are you desperate enough for that?"

"I don't know!" he cried. "Just let me try!"

"Yes," Roxaine agreed. "Unless you've got another idea."

"Of course I don't!" Raven snapped. "I only . . . Blast it, I hate this place as much as you do. Even more! But I don't . . . He . . ." She trailed off. Maybe they were both desperate enough.

"Can we just stop talking and try?" Hero begged. "Mages, it's cold in here!"

"You're the one getting the fur," she grumbled, raising her hands to begin.

This change was the hardest ever. Raven didn't know much about bats; she had to rely completely on Hero's talent to guide the spell. She couldn't even watch to see if it was going right. But it sounded awful, as if all his bones were breaking. He said ouch, and then ouch again, and again, and then constantly, his voice rising to a squeak and a peep and a chirp, until she could hardly hear it at all through the pounding pulse in her ears. But he never gave up, never resisted enough to stop the spell. She dug her way through it, as if she were squeezing through the tightest part of the cave. Sweat ran down her already-soaked face. When it was done, she sank to the floor, weak and clammy.

"What's happened?" Roxaine demanded. "Is he all right?"

"I don't know," Raven admitted.

Something very light landed on her head. She was too tired to be startled.

"Is that you?" she asked. He chirped in reply. "He's all right," she said.

Roxaine sighed with relief. "You really are a hero."

Raven hauled herself up. "Isn't he, now. Well, let's see if this works."

It was a long, hard scramble. Hero clung to Raven most of the time, flying off only briefly to explore the passage. He steered by pulling her hair. They went up and sideways and even down in a steep pitch that dipped them through a pool under a spine of rock. They disturbed other bats, who chirped and brushed them with their wings, sending chills down Raven's spine. They stumbled through a stinking bed of guano that squirmed with some kind of bug. The hours stretched as tight and thin as the cracks they forced themselves through. They had to stop several times to rest. Raven fought back her panic, not once, but again and again.

Finally, when she thought they must be going in circles, Raven realized she could see. She stared at the rock a hand span from her nose: white, grainy marble, streaked with black and smeared with gray mud.

"Light," she whispered. "Mam, there's light coming in. I can see the rock!"

"Bless the River, you're right," Roxaine replied. "I can, too."

"Come on!" Raven cried. "Hurry!"

Now that she could see, the walls closed in. She peered ahead, trying to spot the opening, but the passageway twisted and turned, a rippled, oval tube barely the thickness of her body. She began to scramble forward as fast as she could. Hero flew ahead and disappeared around the bend. Raven slithered after him, but there was only more rock, more passageway. She stifled a curse that was half a sob and kept crawling. The passage twisted again. The light grew. She scurried faster.

And then she made a final turn and was almost blinded. Suddenly, it was roots and mud and she was squeezing through an arm's length of dirt. She grabbed and pulled and kicked, and then she was rolling onto her back on dried leaves. She drew in a sobbing breath and stared up, wincing. Light filtered through overhanging trees. The sky above them was blue. And she could smell the scent of plants and drying rain and the tang of open air. She had never smelled anything so wonderful before.

Hero fluttered down to land on her chest. He was chirping frantically, brushing her cheeks with his wings. She started to hug him but realized she could crush him with the slightest squeeze. She cupped his little body in her hands and sat up. His tiny ugly face twisted in agony.

"Is it the light?" She was still half blinded herself. "I'll change you. Just a minute."

Roxaine was calling from the cave opening, and Raven put Hero down to help her squeeze out. Roxaine flopped onto her back, gasping, staring at the sky as Raven had.

"Beautiful sunshine," she breathed. "And sweet, sweet air. You smell that?"

But Hero was chirping and fluttering around Raven's face again.

"Right," she said. "I haven't forgotten you. Settle down."

Hero fluttered to the ground like a wounded bird. Raven took a breath and steadied herself. Then she reversed the spell.

Hero almost burst out of the bat shape to boy. He cried out, his tiny chirp swelling quickly to a wail. "Ow!" he cried. "Ow, ow, ow." And it didn't stop, even when all his joints had stopped cracking.

Raven realized he was crying. He huddled on the ground, sobbing.

"Are you all right?" she asked.

"It hurt," he sobbed. "Too small. Too, too small."

"It'll get better," she said. "Come on, get up. Move around. Stretch."

He only sobbed harder.

"Give him some time," Roxaine said. She sat by him and took him in her arms. "Come here, little Hero," she whispered. "Brave

Hero. You led us out. You did good." He curled against her chest and cried into her ruined shift. She stroked his hair, crooning a simple melody.

Raven stood stiffly, watching her mother rock Hero against her breast. She felt stupid. And useless. And she hated it. She looked around. The edge of the trees was just behind them. "We're not all that far from the quarry," she said. "We need to get away from here."

"I know, I know." Roxaine sighed. "He just needs a moment. I do, too. Mages save us, dear, we don't all have your thick skin, you know."

Raven bit back an angry retort. "Right," she said. "We're all pretty bruised after that. I'll go get some food. That's half the problem, right? We're hungry." Roxaine nodded. "Don't let him go anywhere. He . . ." She trailed off. Hero had stopped sobbing. In fact, he seemed to have fallen asleep. Her mother waved her away. Feeling dismissed, Raven turned and plodded deeper into the woods to change in private.

Sixteen

I t was twilight by the time Loyal arrived at the quarry, riding in company with Seeker, Squint, and Warder, the guard. He had sent his own people back to Cutter's Landing on the *Lady Slow* with a letter explaining the situation. He hoped to follow soon after, and impress his father with a speedy capture. By the time his party straggled through the quarry gate, hope had succumbed to saddle sores. He slid from the pony gratefully, only to gasp at the pain in his legs. He hobbled after Warder and Seeker, leaving Squint to wheeze along in his wake.

A miserable mass of prisoners was shuffling toward the cell blocks, herded by guards. Loyal's lip curled at the smell.

"Look at them!" Squint exclaimed. "Their clothes are rags. They're filthy. This is a terrible way to treat people!"

The seeker gave him a blank stare. "Just runaways," he muttered.

"And I suppose you put half of them here," Squint said acidly.

Warder ignored them, pushing her way through the throng with a few sharp whacks from a long cudgel. Loyal followed, brandishing a slender cane baton he had picked up from one of Stoner's baronsmen. He was not only sore, he was ravenous; Stoner's big meals had worn off during the long ride.

But Seeker made Warder take them right to the cave. He knelt and studied the ground leading up to the entrance, growling his displeasure when he saw the jumble of tracks in the sparse rock dust. Holding a lantern low, he worked his way back toward the cell block in a zigzagging path that ended at a set of manacles hanging from the wall of the quarry. He carefully studied the dirt gathered at the base of the wall. To Loyal's disgust, he even knelt and sniffed it.

"Cat," he said. He glanced up at Warder. "You keep cats here?"

"Cook's got a cat," she replied. "Why?"

He didn't answer. He worked his way back to the cave, this time more directly.

"Right," Seeker said after one final look at the lip of the entrance. "Get some food first. Then we go inside."

Loyal looked at the small oval opening set shoulder high in the marble wall of the quarry. Cold air breathed slowly from the darkness inside. "Yes," he said, hiding his reluctance. "Food first. Then we catch her."

The seeker was an annoyingly quick eater. Surprisingly, Squint hardly touched his portion. He followed them stoically back to the cave mouth, frowning and muttering. He had brought an ornate staff along, topped with a rough, milky crystal. It tapped loudly at every heavy step. When they reached the cave, he held a lantern behind the crystal and peered into the stone, muttering even more. His little eyes flickered in the odd light cast through the crystal. His pudgy cheeks shook. He finished his incantation with something like a cough, blinking as though newly awake.

"It will do you no good to go into this cave," he intoned.

"Pah!" Seeker huffed. "They went in, didn't come out."

Squint brushed him off. "You can sniff tracks all you want, huntsman. I'm telling you what I saw—to wit: It will do you no good to go into that cave."

"What exactly did you see?" Loyal asked. "Enlighten us."

"I saw an empty hole," Squint said, repeating with great emphasis: "Empty."

Seeker snorted. "Are you coming, lad?"

"The name is Steward," Loyal insisted. They seemed to take turns irritating him.

"Right, then, young Steward, are you coming or not?"

"One question more. Squint, did you 'see' where to find the woman?"

Squint rubbed a florid cheek. "Well, no, I can't say that I did, young sir."

"That would be a far more useful sight, don't you think? Why don't you work on it while we're inside." Loyal flashed him a cold smile. "Just in case, eh?"

Loyal and the seeker each took a lantern and a handful of candles. Loyal carried a leather shoulder bag as well, with two sparkers and a flask of water, along with his baton. Seeker had a coil of rope and a pair of manacles. He also carried a cudgel and his long hunting knife. Reluctantly, he entrusted his firearm to the guard.

"There will be no shooting in any case," Loyal stated. "Baron Stoner wants her alive."

Seeker shrugged, then levered himself nimbly into the hole and slid feetfirst into the darkness. Loyal looked at the narrow shaft and silently cursed Roxaine. She would work in this quarry forever if he had anything to say about it. Setting his jaw, he scrambled awkwardly into the hole and slid after Seeker.

Seeker followed the trail deeper and deeper into the cave. It was slimy going. They crawled through low tunnels as round as smokestacks and walked through angled slots between huge slabs of stone that had cracked and shifted somehow in the deep grasp of the earth. They splashed through puddles of remarkably clear water. They got wet and filthy and cold.

The seeker kept his eyes on the path the whole time, sometimes bending low to check a side passage but never looking up from the tracks and smears that led them on. He spoke only once, to complain about Squint.

"Useless, that man. Wands and runes and bones and whatnot: useless. No skill in it, no honest craft. Pig's wash."

Loyal was almost inclined to agree but for Roxaine's daughter, the raven girl. She was no load of pig's wash. A blasted curse, more like it. Shape changing—could Roxaine do it, too? Was she lurking down here in some awful form, just waiting for them? He shivered, suddenly aware of the darkness beyond the feeble glow cast by their flickering lamps.

As if he'd heard Loyal's thought, the seeker stopped and studied a patch of mud to one side of the tunnel. "Cat again," he said. "Big one." He looked down the tunnel, then back the way they'd come. "Strange, that. It's traveling with the woman."

"With the woman?" Loyal echoed. "Are you sure?"

Seeker frowned at him. "I know my craft." He pointed to a smear in the mud. "The woman's print first, the cat's on top, then stomped on by half-blind guards coming behind." He snorted. "Dolts."

He continued down the tunnel. Loyal followed, wondering now which was the cat: Roxaine or her becursed daughter?

They went on in silence until they came to a high, narrow chamber. Loyal straightened his stooped back gratefully. The seeker padded along with his head held low, lantern out, scanning the muddy floor of the cave. Suddenly, he stopped dead. Still bent low, he turned and almost swung his lantern into Loyal's stomach. The candle went out.

"Blazing mages!" Loyal snarled. "Watch what you're doing!"

"I am," Seeker muttered. He grabbed Loyal's lantern and pushed past to creep slowly back up the cave, studying the floor intently.

Loyal picked up Seeker's lantern and fumbled a sparker out of his bag. "What is it?" he demanded. Seeker only grunted. His head swept from side to side, long nose pointing at the trail.

Loyal slapped the sparker against his thigh. It glimmered and died. He struck it again, and again. Finally, he coaxed a meager flame from the little wick, then almost doused it in his hurry to relight the lantern. Finally, he had his own pool of light. He breathed a sigh of relief and hurried after Seeker.

The huntsman was down on his knees by a narrow crack right

at the base of the chamber wall. Even Loyal could see the smears leading beneath the lip of stone.

"In there?" he asked, appalled.

"'S right," Seeker replied. "Slippery one, that cat."

"The cat?"

"Cat's in the lead." He lay on his belly and peered into the slot. "Never did like cats."

He slithered into the crack. Loyal cursed and followed.

It was the worst part of the cave: tight, twisting, unbearably slow. Loyal, face pressed sideways into the mud, could hardly breathe. He had to push his lantern ahead of him, inch by painful inch. All he could see in its shifting glow was muddy rock and the soles of Seeker's boots. The boots stopped at one point. Seeker said something unintelligible, the sound blocked by his own body. The boots moved on. Loyal tried to follow. The rock pinched his shoulders, chest, hips. And held him. He couldn't move. He thrashed in place, unable to go forward or back. His hand hit his lantern, knocking it over. The candle guttered madly.

"Seeker!" Loyal cried. "Wait! I'm stuck!"

"Relax." Seeker's voice sounded flat and distant. "Tighten up and you just get bigger. Breathe."

"How?" Loyal snapped. "It's too small!"

"They made it through," Seeker called. "We can, too."

"I can't! We have to go back, find another way!"

"There is no other way."

"Back!" Loyal yelled. "Push me back!"

"Can't," Seeker replied. "Forward's the only way." His boots slid out of sight.

"Wait!" Loyal cried, but the sound of Seeker's scraping passage faded away.

Cursing, Loyal struggled against the unyielding stone. He managed to shift back the tiniest bit. His groping hand found the fallen lantern and righted it. The light stopped its mad dance. He shifted back another inch.

Blast that Seeker! he thought. Blast them all! Useless, self-serving lackeys! They would never have treated his father like this, deserted him fathoms deep in solid rock and darkness.

But Jan Steward would never have been here in the first place. Loyal could imagine his father's face, glaring in disbelief at the ruin of his plan. Sneering as his own son crawled backward like a worm from the cave, empty-handed. He cursed Seeker again, and Squint and Warder and Stoner, for letting Roxaine escape. For bringing down his father's contempt. He would not take the blame for them. He would make it right. He would show them, his father most of all.

Loyal slowed his breath. He forced himself to calm down and go limp. Then he pushed all the air out of his lungs and wriggled. His chest came free. He slid loose and inched his way forward again.

Finally, he came out in an open room a few strides wide, with a floor that sloped steeply. The ceiling was a blessed two fathoms high. He stood, shaking with rage and relief. Seeker was crouched by a pool at the bottom of the room.

"Two of 'em," he said, as Loyal skated awkwardly down the slope.

"Two of what?" Loyal snapped. The fool was as maddening as the cave.

"Women," Seeker replied. "Two of 'em."

"So. No more cat?"

"Oh, no. Cat's still with 'em."

Loyal swore. "Are you sure?"

"I know my craft," Seeker muttered, "Not like—"

"Leave it!" Loyal scraped drying mud from his face. "Who on the five rivers is the blazing cat?"

Seeker eyed him suspiciously. "'Who?' What are you not telling me?"

"The woman has a daughter," Loyal said. "A runaway, just as bad as her mother. She's a mage."

Seeker's stare deepened into a frown. "A mage?" His lip curled.

"She can turn herself into a raven."

Seeker pondered this. "Haven't seen raven tracks, only cat." He rubbed his narrow chin. "That'd explain how the woman slipped her fetters. Cat's small enough, slide right out. Explains the gown, too."

"The gown?"

Seeker nodded. "Found her gown balled up against the wall where they had her chained. Cat doesn't need a gown. But who's the third?"

"No idea," Loyal said. He sat by the pool, trembling with fatigue and flagging anger.

Seeker looked around the room. He held his lantern high and studied the ceiling. He grunted.

"What?" Loyal asked, looking up.

"Bats," Seeker replied.

He splashed across the shallow pool and studied the wall, clambering up to shine his light into a crack near the ceiling. Loyal could clearly see a pair of tiny brown bodies clinging to the rock nearby. Seeker came back down.

"No cat now," he said. "The women went out that way, but the cat's disappeared. No prints anywhere this side."

"That's impossible," Loyal said.

"Maybe didn't go out a cat," Seeker replied. "Maybe flew." He glanced at the sleeping bats.

"A bat?" Loyal breathed. He cursed and hit the wall.

Seeker studied the high-up crack a moment. "Pah! Mages!" With that, he splashed back across the pool and scrambled up the slope to the entry slit. He got down on his belly, then glanced back at Loyal.

"Hurry up," he growled. "They'll move quick with a guide. Best bet's outside."

"You think you can still find their trail?"

Seeker snorted: half laugh, half disgust—Loyal couldn't tell, but he sensed it was aimed as much at him as at their quarry. "Unless you've decided to let her go."

Loyal's anger rekindled. "Never!"

Seventeen

Nearby an olive thrush called. Another answered from a distance. Raven stirred. It was the brink of dawn; the time just before your eyes realize there's enough light to see by. She shivered, remembering the total darkness in the cave. What a difference, knowing this darkness was temporary. She could already make out the spaces between the branches around her, the pattern of dark and not-so-dark. The thrush called; the answer came again. Then a vireo sang, then a white throat. Suddenly, the air was noticeably gray. A full chorus of birds joined the brave first voices of morning.

Raven stretched her wings and dropped from the branch to land lightly beside Roxaine and Hero, curled together at the base of the tree. Hero . . . She clacked her beak in frustration. When she'd returned the day before, accompanied by a cohort of crows hauling bread and cheese stolen from a farm down on the terraces, Hero was still sound asleep in her mother's lap. Raven dismissed the crows, then changed back to girl.

"Well, that is surely amazing," Roxaine said. "And a bit easier to watch than . . ." Roxaine glanced at Hero. "He had a rough time of it."

"A bat would be hard," Raven said. "It's not his natural form."

"I would think this is his 'natural' form," Roxaine remarked, nodding at Hero.

"I meant his bemagicked form. The cat."

"And you're a raven?"

"Yes."

"It doesn't hurt you to change like that?"

"No," Raven said. She stood straight. "It's my talent. And I'm good at it."

Roxaine shook her head. "Whoever would have guessed? You, changing people to birds and animals."

"Just birds," Raven corrected. "Hero is the beast mage. He can't change himself, but his talent is strong enough to take over when I try to change him. It was all I could do to convince him to be a bird so we could catch up to you. He's a stubborn little rodent."

"Maybe that's the cat in him. What did you try to change me to in the quarry?"

"I don't know," Raven admitted. "I was just letting you go to your natural form."

"Whatever it was, it hurt," Roxaine said.

"That's because you stopped partway," Raven said. "You shouldn't have fought it."

"Well, I didn't know that," Roxaine said dryly. "I'm not the mage."

"That's right, you aren't," Raven said. She was trying to make a point, but somehow it didn't come out right. What was the use? Her mother wouldn't understand anyway. "Do you want some food or not?"

"I certainly do, thank you. Did you eat already?"

"A little." She hadn't been able to resist nibbling on the cheese.

"Well, let's get some into Hero here. He probably needs it the most."

Now Raven felt guilty. She squelched her appetite while Roxaine woke Hero and the two of them ate up everything the crows had brought.

"Come on, have some," Roxaine insisted, but Raven refused.

"I'll hunt later. You can, too, Greedy Guts," she added to Hero.

And that's when the trouble came up.

"I guess," he replied, squirming a little.

"You guess? It's another excuse to be a cat again," she said.

"Right. In a minute." He hunched, shivering.

"Come on, let's get some fur on you," she said. "It'll warm you up."

She started the spell, but it was like pushing on a stone wall. Nothing happened.

"You're not even trying," she said. "What's the matter?"

His shoulders twitched in a shrug, but it changed to a shake, and suddenly he was sobbing again.

Raven stared at him, aghast. "What is it? Are you still sore? It'll go away. Changing is the best thing for it, believe me."

He shook his head harder. "It doesn't hurt," he said. "It . . . it wasn't that. It was just so small. I couldn't . . . I couldn't think. I couldn't remember. I almost forgot I was me!" He sobbed violently.

Raven lifted her arms, then let them drop. "That happens," she said. "My mistress changed me to a swallow once. I almost forgot to come back, it felt so fun to fly like that."

"It wasn't fun!" Hero cried.

"Well, I mean, right, it's not always fun, but . . ." She trailed off helplessly.

Roxaine gave her a look, then went to Hero and put her arms around him.

"A cat is a lot bigger than a little old bat," she said. "You like being a cat, don't you?" Hero shrugged and sketched a nod. "There. You just need to be something bigger."

"Not just bigger," Raven put in. "You have to have enough room inside to be yourself. You were fine as a pigeon, right?"

"No," Hero sniffed. "It felt awful."

"Well, why didn't you say something?"

"I did," he muttered.

Raven clenched her teeth. "You said the catbird was too small, not the pigeon."

"What was I supposed to say? You told me—"

"That's enough," Roxaine said. "What wouldn't be too small,

Hero? Or would you rather not change at all? You could just stay a person, like me."

Raven groaned. What was she planning, to walk all the way back to Cutter's Landing? Sooner or later they were both going to have to be birds.

"Listen, Hero," Raven said, "you can't walk barefoot all the way home. You're going to freeze in just that shirt. You need to hunt. So you have to change; that's all there is to it."

Hero set his jaw and didn't answer. Raven thought he was trying not to cry again. Roxaine knelt and faced him eye to eye.

"Think of it this way, Hero," she said. "We're right in the middle of a big escape. You've had to be braver than you ever imagined, so brave it hurt. The adventure has turned into hard work. What's worse, it's not over yet. It's like being in bond: Every day you have to get up and go to work, even though you know that Steward is pinching your wage so hard, you can barely hope to pay off. But you do keep working, because all you *can* do is hope things will get better. You have to believe they can. You have to do everything you can to make it get better, even if it's only by being kind to another worker, or telling a joke when everyone's sad, or lending a hand when someone else is overwhelmed. That's one reason why I fell in love with Baron Cutter: He was willing to make things better. And that's one reason why I'm determined to get back to Cutter's Landing. My daughter is there, yes, but I am determined to drive out Jan Steward and finish the changes I started with Darvin. Will you help me?"

Hero was watching Roxaine with wide eyes. When she posed the question, he glanced away. Then back. "I guess I have to," he said quietly.

"Thank you," she said. "Remember, you can be as big as that brave heart of yours."

"Blazes!" Raven groused. "What a—"

It wasn't her mother's look that stopped her, it was Hero's. The little furhead had swallowed the speech, worm, hook, and all.

"Right, right," she said, holding up her hands. "Whatever gets you to change. But it's not just a matter of being big. A stork is big, but he's dumb as a post. You need to pick something that fits your mind."

Hero nodded briskly. "Right."

Now, as bird song rang through the trees and the light went from gray to pearl, his paws twitched in his sleep. Roxaine shifted, snuggling against his curved back. He rolled over, pressing his broad paws into her belly, and began to purr. Every bird in the area immediately went silent.

Roxaine's eyes popped open. "Ouch!" she exclaimed, rolling away from Hero's kneading paws.

Raven clacked her beak. "Keep it down, cat man!" she croaked. "You'll wake up the whole valley."

Hero rumbled to a stop, blinked, then opened huge amber eyes. He had chosen to be a wildcat, but he was the biggest wildcat Raven had ever seen, easily as big as some of Hunter's hounds. As big as his purr.

Roxaine felt his broad forehead as if he were a child with a fever. "How are you feeling?" she asked. "Do you need to change back?"

He rumbled and shook his head.

"Well, let us know the moment you feel even a little bit uncomfortable." She stood and looked around at the brightening forest. "Time to move on," she said.

Hero rolled to his feet and stretched backward and forward, just like a house cat. His yawn was framed by fangs as long as a man's thumb. He gave one paw a quick lick and looked at them expectantly, ready to go.

Finally! Raven thought. They had covered less than a league the evening before. Raven had needed a long rest after changing Hero, and Roxaine had insisted on walking. She said her wrists hurt too much to fly. Raven wondered if she was actually afraid of

143

changing after her first, failed attempt and then seeing what had happened to Hero. But Raven had also been too tired to argue. If her mother didn't want to change, she wouldn't, and that was that.

"How are your wrists?" Raven asked.

Roxaine made fists and rolled them around. She gave a sigh. "They're better," she admitted. "I suppose we should try changing me." She glanced at Hero. "You're feeling all right?"

He nodded, flashing a grin full of vicious-looking teeth.

"Right." Roxaine forced a smile. "What do I do?"

"Nothing," Raven said. "It's something I have to do. You just have to relax and let me." If that's at all possible, she added silently. She closed her eyes and changed herself back to a girl. She wished she could stay a raven, but she needed hands to make all the right gestures.

Roxaine's smile faded as she watched Raven emerge from the raven form. "I don't know if I'll ever get used to watching that," she remarked. "It is . . . Am I going to look like . . . ? Never mind. Give me a minute." She rolled her head around, shook her arms, and shrugged her shoulders right up to her ears, finally letting them drop with a great breath.

Hero rolled his eyes.

Raven couldn't share his amusement. She had never felt so nervous before a change. Her stomach crawled.

"I'm ready as I'll ever be," Roxaine said finally. "Do what you have to, Daughter."

Raven took a deep breath and closed her eyes. Slowly, carefully, she began the spell. She didn't try to force her mother into a particular bird; her natural form would be best. Raven was determined to make this as easy for her mother as possible.

It was less effort than she'd expected, maybe because she was so intent. She heard a sudden squawk from her mother and knew it was done. Smiling, she opened her eyes.

A bright-green parrot with red-rimmed eyes glared at her from the forest floor.

Raven stared back in dismay. "You're not a raven," she moaned. For some reason, she'd been sure that her mother would naturally be one.

The parrot bent her head, inspecting herself. A red patch flashed on the back of her neck.

Just my luck, Raven thought. A loud, squawking, headstrong, beady-eyed parrot!

The parrot—her mother, Raven reminded herself—gave a tentative flap of her wings and squawked at Raven. Raven moaned again. She knew parrots could talk, but she had no idea how long it took them to learn. Roxaine squawked again, then whistled in frustration.

"That's right, Mam," Raven said. "You can't talk. I hope you can stand it."

Roxaine raised both wings, fluffed to twice her size, and chattered something that sounded annoyed. Then she gave an obvious shrug and settled her feathers. She stared at Raven, waiting. Raven wondered if she had the energy to force her mother into a different form, then decided it wasn't worth it. Stifling her frustration, she changed herself and flapped up to a low branch.

"Give it a try, Mam," she croaked. Roxaine made a few weak flaps. "Harder!" Raven snapped. "You're not swatting flies, you know."

Roxaine muttered something that sounded rude. She flapped harder and lifted off the ground. She gave a squawk of surprise, and suddenly she was swooping between the trees, a flash of green and red. She whistled exultantly. Hero yowled approval. Raven's relief was soured by irritation; if only her mother had become a raven.

Roxaine flew around a few more trees, then swooped back and landed on a branch. She almost toppled forward but caught herself with a quick flap. She gave a pained *squork* and shook her wings gently.

"Are you sure you can keep this up?" Raven asked worriedly.

Roxaine's red-rimmed eyes looked offended. She threw herself into the air and flapped away. Hero bounded after her.

Raven watched them race through the trees and could only shake her head. A parrot. A parrot and a little kid in a wildcat suit. Somehow, she had to lead them safely back to Cutter's Landing.

Eighteen

Throughout that day and well into the next, they climbed higher into the hills that divided the Stoney River from the Slow. Roxaine's arms tired frequently, and she rested by riding on Hero's back. The two of them made a strange sight: a parrot bobbing along on the back of a huge trotting wildcat. Raven was miffed to see him travel so briskly for her mother after arguing so much with her.

What slowed them now was the land. The trip to the quarry had taken them well into the hills that framed the steep-sided Stoney valley. Those hills had grown into a series of long, broken ridge lines, each one higher and steeper than the one before. The forest was old, the trees widely spaced with little undergrowth beneath. Occasionally, the way was blocked by a brambled clearing or tangled blow-down or highland bog. Raven scouted ahead, trying to find the best path for Hero and reading the surrounding birds for signs of danger. Not that she thought anything in these woods would bother a wildcat as large as Hero, but it wouldn't pay to be surprised by a pack of wolves. Or a hawk with a taste for parrot. Besides, it gave her a brief chance to be on her own. She settled on a branch high in a huge oak tree, shook out her feathers, and preened a little. A gentle breeze made the branch sway. She could almost watch the new leaves breaking from their swelling, red buds. She took a deep breath and closed her eyes, savoring the lull.

"Squawk!"

Raven lurched alert, heart leaping. Her mother peered at her from the next branch.

"Mages, don't sneak up on me like that!" Raven croaked.

Roxaine squawked again, blinking her red-rimmed eyes.

Raven found her mother's constant glare empty and irritating. She always looked angry, and that made Raven feel angry. "Right," she muttered. "Just soften that squawk. You're as loud as a tickled chicken."

Roxaine whistled indignantly.

"Please try to be more quiet," Raven said. "Don't let the parrot take over."

Roxaine shrugged expressively, head cocked.

"I may have changed you," Raven muttered, "but you chose that noisy shape." Then, before her mother could do anything more irritating, she asked, "Where's your little cat pony?"

Roxaine pointed a wing.

Raven clacked her beak. "We'd better get back before he wanders into trouble."

Roxaine made a dismissive razzing sound.

You didn't have to herd him all the way from Cutter's Landing, Raven thought.

She dropped from the branch and swooped downhill. Roxaine whistled and darted past. Raven croaked irritably and sped up, but Roxaine stayed ahead. Mages, she's fast! Raven thought. And getting stronger. If only we could get Hero to fly, we could be there so quickly. But she knew it was a vain hope. She slowed, letting her mother hurry on ahead.

When she reached them, Hero was pulling apart something that looked as if it might have been a squirrel. Roxaine was tearing at a clump of fiddleheads. She bit into a tightly curled morsel with her wickedly hooked beak, then made a disgusted sound and spat out brown shreds. Hero pushed his small carcass toward her, but she shook her head and forced down the remains of the fiddlehead. Hero shrugged and gnawed off another limb.

Later that afternoon, Hero suddenly stopped and began licking his left front paw. When he tried walking again, he flinched at each step. He limped along for several strides before Roxaine flew down and landed beside him. Raven stopped in a tree overhead.

Roxaine made a series of soft, questioning *chirrup*s and *chark*s.

"Neow." Hero gave his paw another couple of licks and set off again. He tried to walk normally, but it was obvious he was hurting.

Roxaine hopped in front of him and whistled sharply.

"Softer, Mam," Raven reminded.

She snapped a curt squawk and turned back to Hero, head cocked.

He lifted his paw. She turned her head this way and that, peering at the pads.

Raven looked too, but couldn't see anything out of place. She reached in with her beak, trying to separate Hero's toes more widely. He growled and snatched back his paw.

"Don't be so touchy, Cat Boy. I can't see a thing, Mam. We need a furless look."

Hero growled a protest, but Roxaine nodded. Raven changed them all.

With human eyes to study a bare-skinned hand, they spotted the problem quickly: a long thorn thrust deeply into the tender flesh between Hero's first and second fingers.

Raven winced. "Ouch."

"Hold still," Roxaine said, reaching for the tip of the thorn. Hero yelped and jerked his hand away. "Sorry," she said. "There's hardly anything to grab on to. Let's try it again."

Reluctantly, Hero offered back his hand. Very gently, Roxaine spread his fingers and pinched the end of the thorn with her nails.

"That beak would be a help here," she remarked. Hero flinched. She gripped his wrist. "Right. I'm going to count to three. Ready?" Hero nodded, eyes clenched. "One, two—"

She jerked the thorn out.

"Ow!" Hero shook his hand wildly, then tried to suck at the

webbing between his fingers. He shot Roxaine an accusing glare. "What happened to three?" he muttered.

"She used to do that to me, too," Raven said.

"And she was just as big a crybaby as you are," Roxaine countered. "Now we need a mullein leaf, or comfrey. It's a bit early for either, I guess, but it won't hurt to look around. Pigeon, see if you can find some food. There's not much for a parrot to eat in these woods. Now that I'm me again, I'm starved."

Raven bit back a reply and set off through the woods. If her mother wanted to play herb witch, that was fine, but Raven was not going to act the part of her servant. She would look for food because she was hungry. And her mother would blazing well eat what she found, or she could just try being a raven, the bossy old jay.

Raven changed herself and flew above the canopy into the fresh air. The sun was already behind the ridge in front of her, but the sky above was still a deep blue. It felt good to be out from under the trees, flying higher and higher into the cooling air. She topped the ridge and saw one more beyond. Long and steep walled, capped with giant trees, it was like an ancient garden thrusting up from a younger land. She knew at once it was the final wall between the river valleys, a piece of the high reach itself. She stared at it, wishing she could fly right there and rest, far above the schemes and plots of barons and stewards. But she couldn't, not till her sister was safe.

She soared higher still, until she flew into the rays of the westering sun. Squinting into the glare, she saw the purpled hills of the Slow valley, hidden in shadow. Two days' flying would take them to the river; no more than that. If only Hero would agree to be a bird. She called out hoarsely, venting her frustration in the echoes.

By the time Raven soared back beneath the trees, Roxaine had made up a poultice of some kind for Hero's hand and, from the look on his face, was making him chew something vile.

"You can spit out the bits when you're done," Roxaine said.

Hero started spitting.

"I said when you're done," she chided. "It's for your own good, you know. For the pain," she explained to Raven. "Willow bark."

"Looks delicious. Meanwhile, I found some actual food: a deer carcass. Still pretty fresh, too; at least, it tasted fine to me."

"You're going to eat carrion?" Roxaine exclaimed.

"It'll taste better than your willow bark," Raven replied. "And if you can't stomach it the way you are, I'll change you."

"A parrot can't eat rotted meat. I need fruit, seeds—"

"You don't have to be a picky parrot! I'll make you a raven, and then we'll all have enough to eat! Right?"

"The parrot is fine, dear," Roxaine replied. "I'll just find some more fiddleheads. And there are lots of other shoots up here."

"Suit yourself," Raven said. "How about you, Hero?"

Hero looked from Raven to Roxaine, then shrugged. "As long as it's fresh," he said.

"You do whatever you need to, to eat," Roxaine said. "I'll be fine."

By the next morning, she wasn't so fine. She had found a few shoots and buds that didn't make her gag outright, but no more fiddleheads. Then it got cold. She huddled against Hero and shivered most of the night. Raven knew because she didn't sleep well either. She was too mad at her mother's pigheadedness. And at the way she fussed over Hero. The little fur face soaked it up, as if she were his own mother. He was welcome to her, Raven thought. But it still made her angry. Not jealous, she told herself. No. Just . . . irritated.

They were all up as soon as the faintest light appeared. Up and edgy. Roxaine grumbled about the cold, the hard ground, Raven's snoring.

"I do not snore!" Raven snapped. "That was your sweet little kitty!"

Hero growled indignantly, stretched, and strolled over to the carcass for breakfast.

"Save some for me, Greedy Guts." Raven dropped from her limb.

Roxaine watched, lips pursed. "Well, leave some for me, too," she said suddenly.

"Are you sure?" Raven asked. "It's a whole night older."

"Yes, I'm sure," Roxaine said. "I've got to eat. Make me something that can. I'll admit I'm nervous about it. You say the parrot is my natural form, and it has seemed a bit easier than the first time. A different bird is going be, well, different. In many ways. Maybe harder."

"What about a raven? It'll be bigger. And warmer."

"You're the mage; whatever you think is best."

Raven felt an unexpected thrill of pride at her mother's compliment and the trust it offered, however grudging. It would be nice to have a raven companion, too. Her mother might even be able to learn some speech. Raven started the change in a much better mood than when she'd woken up.

She didn't get to celebrate long. After many hard minutes she saw her mother began to take on black feathers. Raven redoubled her efforts, but the end result was a crow. Cursing in frustration, Raven changed her mother back to human.

"What was wrong with that, Daughter?" Roxaine demanded. "The deer was looking very tasty."

"You were a crow!" Raven cried.

"Well, so what?"

"You were supposed to be a raven!"

Roxaine studied her appraisingly. "You're really disappointed, aren't you? I'm sorry, Pigeon. I let you down again."

"It wasn't you," Raven growled. "It was me! I wanted you to . . . Oh, never mind."

"Give it another try," Roxaine said. "I'm game. I'll think harder about ravens."

Whether that did the trick Raven couldn't say, but this time her mother did become a raven. With a bright cackle, she spread her wings and hopped to the carcass. Hero moved over so she could get at the thickest remains, and she dug right in. Raven sighed, feeling drained. Even her own change seemed hard.

They all ate their fill and set off, somewhat heartened at first, but Hero's limp returned. Roxaine flapped from tree to tree above him, *kakk*ing encouragement. Raven scouted ahead, looking for the easiest path. When they reached the top of the near ridge, she flew high again, to take another look into the Slow valley. As she circled upward, she was surprised by a croak just below her. It was Roxaine, laboring aloft. She came abreast of Raven and stared across the ridges. Her raven eyes were easy for Raven to read: disappointment, frustration, longing.

"It's not that far, Mam," Raven said. "Two days' flight at most."

Roxaine shook her head and looked down pointedly. Raven could see Hero resting on a rocky outcrop far below.

"Right," Raven admitted. "We're not flying. We're limping."

Roxaine gave a sudden caw that echoed between the ridges, a cry and a curse in one harsh call.

"We'll get there, Mam," Raven said. "And Sarita will be just fine. You'll see."

"*Kah!*" Roxaine dove straight down, disappearing into the trees. Raven almost yelled at her to be careful but stopped herself. She wasn't going to start mothering her own mother.

It was late afternoon by the time they reached the base of the final ridge. Its steep ledges went up in high, broken steps carpeted with ferns and stunted shrubs. Raven and Roxaine each tried to find the easiest path for Hero, but he zigged and zagged his own way from ledge to ledge, moving as much distance sideways as he did upward. Finally, he reached the top and sank gratefully into a thick green bed of moss. Raven and Roxaine landed beside him.

"Good work," Raven said, and Roxaine croaked appreciatively. Hero just grunted.

Roxaine turned to Raven and held out her wings, *kakk*ing insistently.

"You're saying you want to be changed, right?" Raven asked. When Roxaine nodded, she sighed. "This means I have to change, too, you know." But she did, and soon they were both stretched out on the soft moss.

"Thank you," her mother said. "I needed to be myself."

I already was, Raven thought. She peered into the old forest that capped the ridge. The bed of moss extended into the shadows, broken only by an occasional outthrust knob of gray stone furred with lichen: the bones of the land. The boles of the trees were several spans around, the first branches as thick as small trees themselves, arching ten and twelve fathoms overhead. Oak, ash, beech, hornbeam, hickory: These ancient trees were thickly leafed already. Smaller, slender shadbush and rowans guarded the gaps at the edge. The space within seemed veiled, mysterious. Magical. Raven could feel it on her skin, a faint tingling, like a soft breeze. The leaves stirred. She rolled over and closed her eyes. The breeze came again, and she heard something odd. She peered along the ridge toward the sound.

"What is it, Pigeon?" Roxaine asked.

"You don't hear it?" Raven asked. Roxaine and Hero both cocked their heads.

"It sounds like singing," Roxaine said at last.

Raven rose quickly and changed herself. "Stay here," she said, lifting from the moss, but Hero uncoiled and followed, with Roxaine at his heels.

They came to a small stony brooklet that whispered and churled sweetly as it swirled along its rocky bed and tumbled down the ledges.

"It's beautiful," Roxaine murmured hoarsely. She dropped to her knees and dipped her hands into the clear, singing water, scooping up a mouthful. "Delicious, too."

The breeze blew down the brooklet, bringing with it a sound even more like music. Raven found it fascinating, though it had an odd edge to it: high tones that soured the melody. She wondered if her mother could hear them, or if they sounded only in her raven ears. Roxaine led them quickly alongside the brooklet as it meandered amid the massive trees, till they came to a broad clearing, almost perfectly round. In its center lay the source of the brook: a pale-blue circular pond, rimmed with patches of greening reeds. The breeze blew again, and pond and brooklet both seemed to sing for them. Raven tingled. Hero's fur shivered, as if he felt it, too. Roxaine hurried to the edge of the pond, and Raven dropped to the grass beside her. Hero limped up on her other side. All three leaned forward to peer into the singing water.

Nineteen

Singing filled Raven's ears. The surface of the pond pulsed gently in the breeze. Light scattered along the ripples, silver and blue and even gold, swirling in time to the singing. It was too bright, almost sharp. Raven blinked fiercely. Something glinted farther down, among the pebbles on the bottom. She squinted through the glare. The water stilled.

Her own face peered back, reflected in a golden halo. Her own face: girl, not bird. She gasped and leaned back, staring down at her black, feathered breast. Hurriedly, she reversed her spell. Almost instantly, she was human, and the song seemed to swell, all the sour notes and sharp tones gone. She turned back to the water, anxious to see more of what she could only glimpse before. The glare had disappeared; the light was pearly and warm. It danced to the music of the brook. The pond hummed a deep harmony. She saw her face again, smiling back. Blue sky and clouds showed beyond, as if she were floating in a second world beneath the water. Something else was there, something moving just at the edge of the scene. She leaned farther, trying to bring it into view. She glimpsed it, and her heart soared. She leaned even farther.

Pain tore at her shoulder. She was wrenched back from the water. Her eyes blurred with tears. She gave a cry and stared about. Hero was crouched beside her, one broad paw raised, claws spread.

"What—?" she gasped.

He gave an anguished yowl and gestured toward the pond. Raven stared stupidly. Now there was something floating in the water. She wiped away tears. Another light breeze rippled the surface. The singing started again. The thing drifted away from the shore. Raven leaned forward.

Hero slapped her again. She reeled. All at once she knew: The floating thing was her mother! And rising from the water at the far side of the pond was a long, snakelike head. It sought back and forth, then spied her mother. It lifted on the end of an arching neck. And kept rising, to reveal a sleek hull. It moved toward her across the pond, a lean, sharp-prowed boat decorated with a serpent's head. And in the bow stood Loyal Steward.

"Mam!" Raven cried.

Steward leered. He hefted a long gaff and stretched the wicked hook toward her mother. Raven howled a curse and ran into the water. Steward laughed, a rippling sound that echoed in and through the singing of the pond. And there, behind him at the tiller, was his fat red-faced father. Raven reached for her mother but stumbled in the loose gravel under the water and went down to her knees. Her mother drifted away.

The singing surged. Raven lunged to her feet and struggled forward. The water was up to her chest, and still her mother drifted just out of reach. The Stewards laughed. Jan Steward strode to the bow, holding high two massive pairs of manacles.

"For you!" he bellowed. The words rang in Raven's ears.

Loyal stretched out his gaff and hooked her mother's clothing. Dragged her from the water. Raven glimpsed her face, slack, draining water from nose and mouth. She felt dizzy. Weak. Terrified.

Laughing, Jan Steward clasped an iron ring around her mother's neck and pulled her over the rail. He snapped the manacles onto her wrists. She hung over the water, drained, lifeless. Raven's guts twisted. She wanted to turn and run.

"Flee!" the song agreed. "Flee, before it's too late."

What cursed magic is this? Raven thought. Panting in fear, she stared at the oncoming boat. Young Steward threatened her with his gaff. Jan Steward shook the manacles. Raven heard Hero yowl-ing behind her, a dim, horrid, mournful sound. Her mother's lolling head turned. Her sightless eyes stared.

"Flee," she rasped. "Fleeeee. . . ."

And the singing water echoed, "Flee."

Raven turned and splashed toward the shore. The water dragged at her ankles. The water held her like chains. Without thinking, she screamed her spell.

Immediately, she turned into a raven. Immediately, she began to sink. But the song had gone sour again. The glare on the water half blinded her. The Stewards' laughter was a hollow echo.

A raven? she cried. In water? You brainless dolt!

Desperate with fear, she did something she had never tried before: She changed from bird to bird.

She knew it could be done; she'd seen her mistress do it. But only once, fully rested and prepared. Raven took a deep breath and closed her eyes, blocking out the image of the boat. She pictured the bird she wanted to be and let the spell bubble from her. She felt her skin tingle, felt strength flow from the bottom of the pond, from the soil and stone of the high reach. The change was odd; things inside moved in unfamiliar ways. Her neck stretched. Her bill bulged and sharpened. Her wings and legs lengthened. She slipped beneath the water. The song dimmed; the terror lessened. But the air in her lungs was too little. She fought the urge to inhale, ignoring everything but the change. Her body swelled. She bobbed to the surface. She gasped in a lungful of air and surged afloat, a great swan. Trumpeting, she glared about, searching for her enemies.

There, wavering in the glare! She could just make out the dark hull, the two leering faces. She charged across the water, wings flapping mightily, head thrusting. She lifted into the air and surged toward Jan Steward's face.

And flew right through. Bewildered, she banked in a tight turn. All she could see were a few faint shadows, fading to nothing as she watched. The song was tinny. The breeze died and the pond stilled, empty. She looped around, confused. Hero yowled from the bank. Her mother was hunched beside him, weeping. Roxaine's arms were crooked in her lap, as if they held something. Every few seconds, she stroked the empty air beneath her face. Hero yowled again and rubbed his big body against her side, but she ignored him.

Raven circled again. A fit of breezes drifted along the surface of the water. A vague shape seemed to drift with it, but it held no terror now. Illusion, she realized. It had all been an illusion. Her swan self could only glimpse it. To her human eyes, it had seemed real and terrible. And her mother was still in its grip.

She swooped to the shore. Hero growled at her, his own fear and anger plain. She couldn't blame him. Her mother remained oblivious, sobbing as though she had lost every hope in the world.

Raven started to change. Fatigue and worry made it difficult to think, but she hardly had to, the magic here was so strong. She was human in an instant. And with the change, the singing reached for her thoughts again. Bits of image flashed at the edge of her sight. The spell was powerful, insistent, but Raven was armed against it now. She ignored the melody and kept her gaze away from the water.

"Mam!" she cried. "Mam, resist it! It's not real, whatever awful thing you're seeing."

It was as though she didn't exist. Her mother rocked back and forth over the invisible thing in her arms, keening. In the mournful flow of tears and moans, Raven picked out one word: Sarita.

"She's all right, Mam," Raven said. She knelt directly in front of her mother and took her chin, forcing her to look up into her face. Her mother's eyes were blank, wild, wept dry. She tried to pull free, to look back down at the illusion in her lap. Raven wouldn't let her.

Her mother's eyes went wide. She stared at Raven in growing terror. She began to gibber nonsense. She shrieked and pulled away. She struck wildly. Raven dodged, but not quickly enough. The blow shook her head.

"Mam!" she yelled. "It's me!" She was almost crying herself.

Her mother struck again, but Raven blocked the blow. And struck back, a hard slap across her mother's face.

It didn't work. Her mother shrieked again and tried to scramble backward on her knees. She flailed the air, blocking illusionary blows.

"Great mages," Raven moaned. "Hero, I need your help." Quickly, she changed him to a boy. "Grab an arm," she said. "We've got to get her away from here."

Just then, the breeze blew again. Hero turned toward the pond, eyes wide.

"No!" Raven yelled, punching his arm hard. "Don't listen to it. You saw what happened to us." He nodded, rubbing his arm. "Refuse it. Pretend it's me trying to turn you into a sparrow." He set his jaw and turned away from the sound.

Her mother had risen to a crouch. She stared at unseen horrors on the water and backed toward the woods.

"Not that way," Raven said. "We've got to get to the other side of the ridge."

She and Hero each took an arm and pulled her mother toward the far side of the clearing. She fought them weakly, exhausted. They passed into the great woods, where a path led in the right direction. Hardly a dozen paces farther, they came to the remains of a small cottage. Its moss-covered roof was half caved in. Its windows gaped. But Raven could feel the faint aura of leftover magic seeping from the ruin.

"Keep moving," she said. "I think that was home to whoever the pond was protecting."

Hero shuddered like a cat ridding water from its fur.

Suddenly, Roxaine sagged against Raven's chest. They were out of earshot of the pond. The illusions seemed to have left her.

"Mam?" Raven asked quietly. "Are you all right?"

She shook her head. Her shoulders kept heaving in time to her dry sobs. Raven and Hero took on most of her weight and pulled her past the cottage and through the darkening woods. It was near twilight by the time they stumbled to the far edge of the ridge. Raven looked down the steep ledges and knew they'd never make it in this drained state.

"We'll have to sleep here tonight," she said, though the thought of staying anywhere near the bemagicked pool made her skin crawl. Hero nodded regretfully. Her mother made no answer; she didn't even open her eyes when they laid her gently on the moss. Raven regarded her with growing dismay. She remembered the floating body, the chains, the certainty her mother was dead. Knowing it had been illusion didn't help; the sense of loss was terrible. She sank to the ground and took one of her mother's hands.

Hero leaned against Raven. "What happened?" he asked. "You kept staring and staring into the pond, and when I tried to get you to stop, you suddenly went wild and ran into the water and you were shouting and crying, and all the time your mother was wailing and—"

"Slow down," Raven moaned.

"But what happened?" He stared at her almost angrily, shocked and confused.

"Illusions. The miserable pool had a spell on it." She shivered violently.

"I thought you couldn't be spelled if you didn't want to be."

"That's why the music was there. It lured us in. When we looked into the water, it showed us scenes that were so beautiful, we kept looking. We never had the chance to decide we didn't want to be spelled."

He cocked his head, puzzled. "Nothing's that beautiful, is it? What did you see?"

"I saw . . ." Raven trailed off. What had she seen? It had been so lovely, so . . . desirable. Something to do with her mother? "I can't remember. Not that part. It was just the lure. What came next was awful: terrible illusions. Steward, both of them. My mother . . . Kah! It was nothing but illusion, ugly, twice-cursed, mind-stealing illusion!"

"But why?" he cried.

"To scare us off," she said. "That cottage—whoever lived there didn't want anyone else to come near the place."

"Who would cast a . . . a mean spell like that?"

"I don't know," Raven said.

"It was evil!"

"There's no magic rule that says mages can't be evil."

"But . . . I just thought . . ." He dug at the moss between his knees. "I don't know what I thought. I can't understand how any-one . . . She was so sad." He softly touched Roxaine's hair.

His concern almost embarrassed Raven; Roxaine wasn't even his mother. He hadn't seen her drowned. She shivered violently.

"How long will that spell last?" he asked.

Raven shrugged. "I don't know," she said again. "Until the mage comes back and removes it, I imagine. Or some other spell cancels it."

"We have to do that," he said. "We have to cancel it. Before it catches someone else."

"How?" she asked wearily.

"Don't you know?" he asked back. "You're a mage."

"I don't know a thing about illusions."

"But—"

"How many times do I have to tell you? I know only my own magic!"

"But—"

"Leave it! There's nothing you can do. You cannot save every-one in the world, Hero. Life isn't like that."

Hero stared at her, aghast. "Shouldn't we even try?" he asked. She glared back. "I'm sorry," he said, dropping his gaze.

"Kah! I'm the sorry one," Raven said. "I should have realized:

the singing, the perfect pool. Blazing mages, I even felt the magic! I should have known."

"I felt it, too," Hero said. "It tingled."

"It's the high reach. Magic is alive here." Raven gave a wry laugh. "I've been thinking all along I should come here, and look what happens the minute I do: tricked by an enchanted puddle."

Roxaine suddenly clenched Raven's hand. Her eyes flickered open. She peered up at them, confused, then seemed to actually see them. Her face fell into a grimace of regret. Tears welled in her eyes. She pulled Raven's hand to her cheek and wept bitterly. "I left her," she sobbed.

"It was a spell, Mam. An illusion. You couldn't help it."

"No. I should have. I should . . . But it was so wonderful. And then so terrible. I . . . I left her. I ran away and left Sarita, I deserted my baby, my own baby." She leaned her head into Raven's hand, soaking it with tears.

Raven wondered about the night she and her mother had been set to run off together. Had it been fear that had made Mam desert her then? And how much of a part had fear played in Raven's anger, in her own decision to leave alone rather than stay to learn the truth? It didn't seem to matter so much now. The spell on the pool had made her relive losing her mother, and it had been much more horrible, the illusionary loss much more real. Raven realized how grateful she was to have her back.

"You didn't really leave her, Mam," she said. "It was just an illusion, a spell, meant to chase you away. And it will never be able to charm you again now that you know. You're safe now."

"Raven's right," Hero told her. "We're safe now." He looked at Raven. "Right?"

"Absolutely," Raven said, trying to sound confident. "We're safe now. Everything is all right."

Roxaine only sobbed harder. "My baby," she whispered. "I can't—"

"You'll have her back soon," Raven said. "You'll have her back before you know it."

Still Roxaine sobbed. "My milk's dried up. It stopped down in the cave. It stopped for good." She took a deep, shuddering breath. "I can't ever nurse my baby again."

"That's all right, Mam. She's got a nursemaid."

"I don't want another woman to feed her!" Roxaine sobbed. "I want to."

Raven stroked her mother's hair, wishing she could somehow ease her sorrow, but she had no idea what to say.

Twenty

S quint drew his pony up on Loyal's right. "We're lost, I imagine," he whispered loudly.

They had come to the base of yet another ridge, only this one rose in sheer ledges, each a dozen fathoms high. The seeker was peering at the forest floor where it met the rock. His nose twitched at Squint's remark, but he said nothing.

"Why don't you cast a few bones, then, or shake that be-jeweled crutch of yours and be of some use?" Loyal snapped.

"There is a great difference between a crutch and a staff," Squint huffed. "One is a mere prop, the other an artist's tool."

The seeker snorted.

Squint waved a hand as if to brush him away. "Go ahead, scoff. Jeer like a kennel hand. A true mage stands above such ignorant insults. And a seer stands above all, peering past the veils of here and now to scry the distant peaks of future and possibility."

Squint wheezed in a breath to feed another onslaught, but Seeker had already remounted and was riding away.

"That's right!" Squint cried. "Flee from what you cannot grasp! Run from—"

Loyal snapped his baton at Squint's pony, making it shy. Squint cut off with a yawp.

"Put a bung in it!" Loyal ordered. "Every beast in the forest will know where we are!"

He turned his pony to follow Seeker. Squint fell in behind with the surly Warder, muttering. Loyal pushed aside an overhanging branch and let it snap back at them. You had to show these people their place.

He caught up with Seeker just as the man dismounted again.

"Went up here," Seeker said, indicating some invisible sign on the rock face. "Leave the ponies; take what you can carry on a shoulder." He pulled off his saddlebags and began sorting his gear.

"What's going on now?" Squint demanded as he rode up. He looked from the seeker to the steep ledge. "He can't be meaning to climb that?"

Loyal, who had been about to make the same protest, slid from his pony. "We're all climbing it," he said. "Take only what you can carry on your shoulders. Now!" he snapped, cutting off a new protest from Squint. "Or I'll be telling your Baron how little you've done to scry out our quarry!"

Blowing in outrage, Squint heaved himself out of the saddle. Warder followed with a resigned sigh. After half an hour of arguing and complaining, they had the gear sorted. By then, it was near twilight, but Seeker scurried up the first pitch without the slightest hesitation.

Loyal followed more slowly, leaving Squint to labor along with Warder. They were all the same: self-serving louts. Seeker deserved a good thrashing himself for leading them on so late. These sheer ledges were dangerous in the dim light. And what would they do in the morning without the ponies? Walk all the way to the River Slow? Cursing the three of them, Loyal scrambled from ledge to ledge. He could just make out Seeker's silhouette above him. Finally, it slid over the top. Seeker reached down, pulling Loyal up and to the side with an amazingly strong grip.

"Don't want you treading where they might have," Seeker grumbled. "Too dark now. Keep clear till dawn."

"I am not sleeping this close to a cliff," Loyal snapped.

"Plenty of space that way," Seeker replied, gesturing. He peered over the edge, waiting for the others.

Loyal resettled the heavy saddlebag on his shoulder and made his way into the trees. It was gloomy under the high branches, but he found a comfortable spot carpeted with thick moss a dozen paces in and threw down his burden. With a huge sigh of relief, he sat and leaned against a hoary trunk.

"Over here!" he called.

"Shh!" Seeker replied, appearing from behind a tree like a night spirit.

"Blazes, man! Don't sneak up on me like that!"

"Shh!" Seeker repeated. "Night sound carries."

"Tell that to Squint when he starts snoring."

"What's that about me?" Squint asked, looming out of the darkness, with the blocky Warder on his heels.

"Keep quiet," Loyal ordered. "Night sound carries. They could be close."

"Not likely," Squint huffed. "I'm sure I would feel it if they were." He squinted between the broad trunks and shivered. "I feel something, but not them."

Seeker snorted and set about clearing a circle in the moss.

"You're not lighting a fire, are you?" Squint demanded. "What if they see it?"

"The trees will shield the light," Loyal said. "And I'm not about to eat a cold supper."

He waited impatiently while Seeker made a small fire and roasted a grouse he had shot earlier in the day. The man was a fine sniper, but Loyal was beginning to doubt his tracking skills. For all he could tell, they were wandering aimlessly up and down the hills. It seemed mad that anyone would choose to flee up this last set of ledges.

As if he were reading Loyal's mind, Squint placed a hand reverently on one of the gray trunks. "O ancient trees," he intoned quietly. "I sense that we are the first people to see this grove in countless generations. We're on the high reach. My very flesh tingles."

"It can't be the high reach," Warder said. "We'd have to cross the upper reach first."

"The high reach stretches down between the valleys like fingers on a great hand," Squint said. "It is the backbone of our land; the rivers, our veins."

"Seeker?" Warder asked.

"'Tis the high reach," Seeker replied gruffly. "Don't know about no fingers."

Warder looked around nervously. "They say magic is strongest on the high reach."

"Oh, it is indeed," Squint said. "The most powerful mages live here, thriving in the constant ebb and flow of magic."

Loyal gave a laugh. "They also say the high reach is filled with magic spirits, ancient hags, talking trees, living stones, and a whole host of evil creatures that lie in wait for the unwary. Are you frightened, Warder?"

The woman glowered. "I wouldn't say frightened. It's just . . . well, we've all heard the tales. They make you think."

"Fables, more like it," Loyal said. "To frighten misbehaving children."

"Not all are fables," Squint warned. "There is more to the high reach than any of us can imagine. That was no mere flock of birds whose tracks we saw outside the cave. And no mere cat that accompanies them. You are witnessing mage talent at first hand. A far greater talent than mine," he added softly, with a surprising look of sadness. "But who knows what greater power bides here on the high reach? Or how a lesser power might grow when given the chance to feed on the very source of magic?" He peered longingly into the dark forest.

"Rather feed on this," Seeker remarked, pulling the spit from the fire.

He cut the bird into quarters. Loyal took his share first, as leader. It seemed hardly more than a mouthful, and he found himself longing for one of Stoner's rich banquets.

"Very tasty," Squint remarked. Food had revived his bluster. He had reduced his portion to a small pile of bones and was reworking them for every last morsel.

"We're hunting bird folk," Seeker said. "Might be we've just eaten one." He held up a wing tip. "What d'you think, seer? Mother or daughter?"

Squint smiled thinly. "Neither. I would have known." He tossed his bones into the fire. "What's the matter, Warder? You've left half of that thigh."

She shrugged. "I'm not all that hungry, I guess."

"Well, if you don't want it . . ."

They bedded down on the moss. Loyal slept fitfully, coming half awake several times to what sounded almost like distant voices. He shrugged it off as the wind soughing in the leaves. He woke for good at the first sign of dawn. He could hear frogs peeping somewhere nearby, but no wind and no voices. Warder was keeping watch by the remains of the fire. She greeted him softly; he grunted a reply. It was too early for speech, particularly after such thin sleep.

As he stumped behind a tree to relieve himself, a light breeze pressed his cheek. Once again, he thought he heard voices, this time mingled with music. He peered toward the sound and was surprised to see the bulbous silhouette of Squint, standing in the gloaming under an arch of branches, staring toward the sound. The breeze rustled again. The singing came more clearly.

"What is it?" Loyal asked.

Squint shook his head. "Something beautiful," he whispered. He took a step toward it. "I think we should go see."

"Better fetch the others first."

Squint turned from the sound reluctantly.

Warder looked surprised when Loyal ordered them up. "You think it's them?"

"Would they be singing?"

"Well, if it ain't them . . ." She glanced nervously in the direction of the music.

Squint was already walking away. Seeker hurried after him. "Watch where you step," he grumbled. He strode ahead, scanning the ground.

The breeze picked up as they went. The music swelled and waned with the movement of the air. They came to a brook where water tumbled and played, making music in its rocky bed.

"Stop!" Seeker barked. He dropped to his knees, searching the bank with his usual disregard for all but the pursuit.

Loyal grabbed Squint's arm, though he found it hard to hold back himself. The seer trembled with impatience. Warder stood a few paces, gripping her cudgel.

"They were here," Seeker said. "Cat, woman, and bird. Went that way." He gestured upstream, toward the singing.

"Could that music be them?" Loyal whispered.

"It's not them," Squint said. "It's . . ." He shook his head. "It's very different." He led them straight toward the sound, leaving Seeker to follow the tracks by the brook. They came out of the trees into a beautiful clearing, glowing in the slanting dawn light. A perfectly round pond sat in the center of the space. Light danced on its silvered surface as the breeze ruffled the water. The singing seemed to come from there. Squint hurried forward and lowered himself to his knees at the edge of the water. Loyal went more slowly, scanning the area for birds or beasts of any shape, still hoping to find their quarry here.

Warder refused to leave the shelter of the forest. "Have a care, young sir," she called. "This can't be natural."

"Don't be ridiculous," he said. "It's just music."

She shook her head. "This place is empty. If we're hearing music, something magic is making it. I don't trust it." She gripped the trunk beside her, as if fighting some pull that threatened to drag her into the clearing.

"Don't be such a biddy," Loyal scoffed, turning to the pool. The music called sweetly. He heard his name: "Loyal. Come, Loyal. Come, Loyal son. Come, Loyal heir. Come, Loyal Steward and Baron-to-be." He hurried to the edge of the water.

Squint was peering into the pool, clutching his staff, muttering hoarsely.

"Quiet!" Loyal growled, trying to hear the singing more clearly. He leaned close. A face appeared in the water. His own face, rippling with the breeze. Then another face, upside down. He gasped and looked up. His father was striding toward him, hand out.

"Loyal!" he called. "Come, my son. My good boy!"

Loyal's heart surged. His father was smiling. His lips moved, but Squint was babbling, almost squealing in Loyal's ear. Words tumbled out, confusing the sweet music, drowning his father's speech.

"Be silent!" Loyal cried. He gave Squint a slap on the shoulder. The seer tumbled into the pool. The music soared in the fresh silence. His father beamed. Loyal stepped forward to meet him, oblivious of the cold water seeping into his boots.

His father kept beaming, but his face was changing. Hardening. His eyes grew cold. His smile became a sneer, then a snarl. He lifted his other hand, and Loyal saw it held a switch tipped with thorns. His father beckoned, face still caught in the rictus of rage and joyful hate. He flicked the switch at Loyal. The thorns snapped inches from his face, each a sharp-tipped flame, hot enough to feel. His father laughed, more growl than human sound. He raised the switch to strike again. The song surged. "Lout, dolt, sniveling, useless, failure. Flee. Flee. Flee!"

Loyal turned and fled.

Twenty-one

R aven jerked awake. Heart beating, she glanced around. Shreds of dream dissolved into early dawn. An image lingered: Steward, chains, a hook. Mam. She rubbed her eyes hard. They were huddled together, all three, beneath a mound of pine browse Hero had gathered in the last moments of twilight. He and Mam were sound asleep, and she herself still felt drained. She wondered what had woken her. Something other than the dream, she was sure.

It came again: a cry from the center of the ridge. From the pool. She jumped up.

"What is it?" Roxaine looked around blearily. Hero groaned and tried to bury his head in the bed of needles.

"Shh. Someone yelled," Raven whispered.

Hero looked out. "Do you think it's the mage of the pool?"

"No idea."

"Change me," he said, scrambling to his feet. "I'll go look."

"No, you won't," Roxaine said, grabbing his arm.

"I'll go," Raven said.

"Change us first, just in case. And be careful. If it's someone from the quarry, they'll be armed."

"From the quarry? Not likely."

"Wildcats leave tracks, and we haven't always been birds. Please, stay out of sight. You got away from me once, child. I'm not going to lose you again."

Or I you, Raven thought. She coughed, her throat suddenly tight with an unexpected happiness. "I'll stay hidden, Mam," she said. She rubbed her face again, trying to scrub away some of the weariness. "Hurry. They're close."

Hero's change was fast and smooth. Even her mother's change seemed easy, in part because Raven let her take her natural form of a parrot. Still, she could feel the power of the high reach strengthening her spells.

"You two head down the ledges," she said. "I'll meet you at the bottom."

"Now wait just a minute—" her mother began, but Raven was already changing, not to a raven, but to a thrush: small, easy to hide, and perfectly normal in woods like these. With a quick trill, she flew into the dark grove.

She went straight to the clearing, only to find her mother was right. There was that loutish guard from the quarry, and Loyal Steward himself. But what a scene: The two were wrestling at the edge of the trees. Steward was yelling, thrashing wildly, trying to pull free. The woman was grunting hoarsely, taking his blows like a stolid ox.

"There's nothing there," she gasped. "It's nothing, young sir. Visions, mage stuff."

Steward ignored her, eyes blank with terror. Raven knew what he was feeling and couldn't help but trill a short laugh.

A dog-faced man dressed in hunter's leathers broke from the trees by the brook. He stared at the struggling bodies, then at the pool. The breeze chose that moment to strengthen. The song rose. The man started toward the water.

"Seeker, no!" the woman shrieked. "Don't listen to it! It's cursed!"

He stopped and half turned toward her, but the pull of the song was too great. He shuffled sideways toward the calling water.

"No!" she cried again. "Fight it, man! Before it drives you mad."

Steward used her distraction to wrench an arm free. She had him by one wrist only, and that was slipping.

"Sorry, lad," she grunted. Then she gave him a roundhouse blow that sent him stumbling against a tree. Raven cheered. Before Steward could recover, the guard grabbed him by belt and collar and marched him over to the still-shuffling huntsman. The man opened his mouth to speak, but she slapped him hard.

"Sorry," she said, then slapped him again. And gave another good wallop to Steward as well. "The blasted pool's cursed. If you listen, you'll go mad. Do you understand? Or do I have to hit you again?"

The huntsman rubbed his cheek. "Two's enough," he muttered.

"Good. Take this one." She thrust Steward into his arms and charged to the side of the pool. Only then did Raven notice the third man, floating face-up in the water. The woman hesitated, obviously terrified. With a curse, she splashed in. She kept her eyes aimed up, groping with her hands to find the fat body. All the time, she chanted a wordless melody, as if to overpower the water's song: "La la la-la-la la laaa la la-la." It sounded horrible, but it seemed to help; Steward sagged against the huntsman, his terror gone.

The woman towed the fat man to the bank and rolled him out and over away from the pool. His face was blue, his narrow eyes blank. She felt for a pulse.

"Blazes, his heart's failed!" she cried.

The huntsman rushed over and pounded on the fat man's chest. On the third try, the fat man gave a great gasp. His eyes went wide. He coughed and gurgled and retched. Steward looked up, lips pursed in a grimace of disgust. His own face was almost as pale as the fat man's, but his eyes were dark with malice.

The huntsman helped the woman hold the fat man on his side till he stopped retching. They sat him up. With a shake that rattled his jowls, he coughed up a last mouthful of watery phlegm. His piggy eyes cleared.

"I . . . I . . ." He wheezed after each word.

The woman squeezed his shoulder. "Go easy, Squint. You almost drowned there."

"What the blazes did you think you were doing, man?" Steward demanded shrilly. "You should have warned us! That thing could have killed us all!"

The man called Squint said something too low for Raven to catch. She flew around the edge of the clearing to a closer branch. The huntsman's head snapped up; his eye followed her. She hopped into the shadows, then crept back along another branch.

". . . beautiful," Squint was saying. "A more mellifluous sound I have never heard. It spoke to me."

"What did it say?" the woman asked. Her voice was edged with fear.

"I can't remember," Squint said. "All I know is that I entered a trance, the deepest, most luminous trance I have ever experienced." His voice thickened. His eyes gleamed. "And I saw," he said.

"Saw what?" the woman whispered.

"It was the sharpest sight I have ever achieved," Squint said, shivering. "A vision of pure clarity, pure truth." He turned his piggish eyes on Steward. "You were there, young sir." His eyes narrowed to slits. He peered inward.

Steward swallowed. "Where was I?" he demanded.

"A room of faces," Squint intoned. "Strange and arcane faces, their eyes peering from the very walls. And beasts, of the woods and sky and places I have no knowing of. A bird with a hooked beak and bright feathers, green and red. They hovered over a fire. You were there, in the light of lamps and fire. You and a tall, pale man. An angry man, red-faced but cold, even in his anger. He spoke to you, you replied."

"What did we say?" Steward asked, but he looked ready to run away again.

"I can't tell you," Squint replied.

"What?" Steward exclaimed. "Tell me. I order you, Squint, te—"

Squint lifted a pudgy hand. "I didn't hear; I only saw. The angry man spoke, you answered. He demanded, you gave. You lit the fire, I remember that now. You lit the fire, and he put something in it. You were looking for something, the two of you. You found it. You gave it to him. He put it in the fire. He burned it. While you watched. Bespelled, you were. In his thrall. In his . . ."

A faint breeze ruffled the surface of the pool. Squint's mouth moved silently. His eyes went wide, focused on the water. Loyal jerked around, as if something had moved there. He swallowed and forced his gaze away.

"It was not enough," Squint said. His voice was flat, completely without emotion. Raven shivered at the sound. "It was not the piece you needed, the payment, the sealed bargain that ends all question, ever sought by you and the angry man. It lurks outside your notice, hidden from sight. Within reach for anyone willing to seek beside the spread of dark reckonings." His voice deepened. "I see you hunting. Too aloof. I see you running. Too slow. I see you shooting. Too . . . too . . ."

Squint fell silent. Raven crept forward, as transfixed as the others.

"Squint?" the woman whispered. He didn't answer. She gave his arm a fearful shake. "Squint?"

He blinked. "Yes? What?"

"What happens next?" the woman asked.

"I beg your pardon?" Squint said.

"The shooting? Who was he shooting at?"

"Shooting?" Squint echoed. "Did I say something about shooting?"

They stared at him. He peered back blearily. They all sighed, disappointed. Except Steward: He stood stiff as a post, watching Squint as if the fat man had changed to a snake.

"When will this happen?" the woman asked, glancing at Steward.

"I don't know," Squint replied slowly. "Alas, the time of my seeing is never clear, even here, in this most magic of places." He regarded Steward with a frown of concern. "Be wary, young sir. Beware that room of faces. Beware the spell of the tall, pale man. He means no good. His cold anger will burn you."

Steward stared back, horrified. He tore away with an abrupt wave of his arm. "Ridiculous!" he snapped.

"You don't know that place?" Squint asked. "That man?"

"Of course not! Sheer invention!" Steward stalked away, gesturing toward the pool. "You were the one bespelled. A weak mind, that's what you have. A weak mind, filled with nonsense by nothing more than a . . . an evil tune! A pool of illusions!"

The others watched his ranting, amazed. But Raven knew that room. Thoughts churning, she flew off.

Raven reached the spot where she'd left her mother and Hero and swooped down the ledges. They weren't at the bottom. She flew a way into the wood, but there was no sign of them. She called, but a thrush's sweet voice was useless. She settled to the ground and tried to change directly to a raven, but she couldn't do it. She wondered briefly if it was because she was now on a lower reach or because she wasn't desperate enough. She changed to a girl and called again, sure they'd hear her human voice.

There was no reply.

She's deserted me again! Raven thought, heart sinking. No, she told herself. Not now. Not after yesterday. I've just missed them. They came down at a different place. They got lost. That's all.

She changed to a raven and soared back up the ledges, searching the stones frantically for some sign of their passage. She called again but still heard no reply. It occurred to her then that they must have followed her, toward the sounds. Right toward Steward and his band.

"Mam!" she groaned. "Can't you follow the plan just once?"

She soared over the high reach, scanning the treetops for a bright flash that might be her mother.

Without warning, a brown blur stooped on her. Raven dodged at the last minute. The blur flashed past, taking a tail feather with it. Raven croaked in pain and cursed whatever it was. She rolled sharply and spotted it swooping back for another strike. A bearded falcon. A mother. And she was mad.

Raven dodged again and sent a volley of curses. *Idiot!* she railed. *Pea-brained, pigeon-eating bully! I don't have time for this!* She croaked a command, but the falcon was deaf to everything but the threat to her chicks. She hissed viciously and grabbed at Raven's face with her talons. Raven dove, leveling out just above the greening leaves. The falcon dove in pursuit, and she was a lot faster. Raven looped, rolled, and came down right on the falcon's back. Grabbing hold, Raven matched her wingbeat for wingbeat, turn for turn, all the while chanting the spell that would calm her. The falcon slowed. Raven could sense her anger turning to confusion. Raven let go, and the falcon flapped toward her nest. Sighing in weariness, Raven settled onto a branch.

A movement came at the corner of her eye. She turned and saw she was right above the deserted cottage. She had just enough time to register people below: Steward, Squint, the guard. The huntsman, with his firearm raised.

She heard the shot.

Twenty-Two

Loyal's heart jumped in his throat as Seeker fired. The raven jerked, then crumpled and fell. Its body twirled like a falling leaf, one wing half open. It caught in the branches, held a moment, fell farther, caught again, then slipped free and tumbled to the ground.

"There's one of them," Seeker growled. He started reloading.

"Blast you, man!" Loyal yelled. "I said I wanted her alive!" Do you? a quiet voice asked. Loyal stopped in midshout, remembering Squint's awful vision. And the illusion of his father. Did he really want her alive? And which one of the cursed women was this?

As if on request, a parrot burst from the trees. Shrieking like a steam engine, it dove at the seeker. He snapped the breech shut and fired. It dodged and dove at his face. Dropping the firearm, he drew his dagger and swung wildly. And missed again. The parrot grazed his right eye with its talons. Yelping, the seeker twirled, fending it off with his blade, the other hand pressed to his bleeding eye.

"Get it!" Loyal yelled. He lunged toward the parrot. It spun and dove at him. He threw himself flat, covering his face with both arms. Talons scoured his head. He rolled away, struggling to his knees, waving his arms madly around his head. He collided with Warder, who was swinging her cudgel at the parrot. It struck his arm with a painful crack. Cursing, he crawled frantically out of range. She followed, trying to help him up, but he shoved her away. Then a huge bobtailed cat bounded from the shadows. It sprang right over Loyal and climbed the seeker's body as though he were a sapling. The seeker howled and fell on his back. The wildcat mauled his arms, tearing slits in his leather sleeves. Warder stumbled toward them.

The parrot squawked. The cat yowled, a cry so shrill and fierce that Warder stopped dead. The parrot swooped past, swiping Loyal's cheek with its sharp bill. He ducked, protecting his head with both arms. When he looked again, the cat had lifted the raven across its back and was loping into the woods. The parrot perched on its shoulder, supporting the bouncing raven with one foot. They disappeared into the dark grove.

Seeker scrambled to his knees, groping on the ground for his firearm. Blood ran from his face. "Where are they?" he snarled. "Which way?"

"Did you see that?" Warder exclaimed. "That wildcat was as big as a hound!"

"Wasn't no wildcat," Seeker growled, staggering to his feet. "'Twas a mage thing, a man cat. Tried to kill me!" He began fumbling at his pouch.

"You killed its companion," Squint pointed out. "What do you expect?"

"Thirty mages blast you, Squint!" Loyal exploded. "Why didn't you foresee *this?* That would have helped us a lot more than that . . . that . . . nonsense you coughed up from the pool! And you, Seeker! Blasting away at everything in feathers! I told you . . . Blast!" Loyal knew which bird was which; the look in the parrot's eyes had been pure Roxaine. Why couldn't Seeker have shot *her?*

"'Twas only birdshot," Seeker muttered. "So high up. Only meant to stun it." He stumbled along the path, searching for the wildcat's tracks.

"Sit down," Warder told him. "We've got to stop that bleeding."

"'S nothing," Seeker mumbled.

"Shut up and let her do it!" Loyal snapped. "We've got to get after them!"

Seeker's leather sleeves had taken the worst of the damage. His arms were hardly scratched. His eye was swollen and ugly, but still whole. Warder took her own sweet time dressing the cuts around it, and Loyal fretted over every wasted second. Then a sudden realization made him smile.

"Squint, if the daughter is dead, what will happen to the parrot mother? Will she be able to change herself back to a person?"

"What a horrible thought," Squint wheezed. "She'd be trapped. A parrot forever."

"Yes, horrible," Loyal agreed dryly. They could keep her in the cage with Cutter's parrot. After cutting her tongue out, of course. Parrots lived a long time; a long time in a cage would do the woman good.

"That's enough, Warder. Move on!"

Seeker surged like a hound on a leash. Muttering, he followed the cat's tracks under the trees. Soon they came to the drop on the other side of the ridge. Seeker sniffed along the ledges, bent almost double, searching with his good eye for the trail down.

Squint stared at the forest beyond the ledges. "That's the Slow valley," he said.

Warder followed his gaze, surprised. "It is?"

He nodded.

Loyal stared across the treetops below. The middle reach of the River Slow. The cat and the parrot were heading right toward Cutter's Landing. They were trying to kidnap the Baron's heir. And his father had no idea.

"Hurry!" he snapped.

"Found it!" Seeker replied. He pointed to some sign Loyal couldn't see and knelt to lower himself down the first sheer step.

"Wait," Squint said. "I'm not going."

"What!" Loyal glared at the fat seer. "What do you mean, you're not going?"

"I'm not going any farther," Squint replied. "The room I saw, the angry man, they're down there somewhere. Waiting for you, young Steward." He shook his head. "I don't want to be there when you meet."

"Your master ordered you to help me," Loyal snarled.

"If I told Stoner what I've seen, he'd order me not to," Squint replied evenly. "I saw evil, young Steward. I saw a danger greater than any escaped servant."

"And I say you saw nonsense!"

"What did *you* see, then? Anything better?"

Loyal's mouth worked, but he couldn't say a word.

Squint regarded him with a knowing look. "I'm not going," he repeated. "And you shouldn't either. What I saw—"

"You have no idea what you saw!" Loyal yelled. He grabbed the front of Squint's cloak. "If you tell Stoner one word of that vision, I swear I will . . ." He trailed off, realizing how frantic he sounded.

"You do know," Squint said. "You know that man."

"Hah!" Loyal turned away. "I know you're a coward, that's what. You let a vision frighten you, like a child in the night." He stalked to the edge of the drop, sneering over his shoulder at Squint. "Go, then. You go on back. Tell your master you deserted us here on the brink of capture."

Warder stepped to Squint's side. "I'm going with him," she said.

"You're—?" Loyal could only stare.

"That's not our valley," she said. "We've got no authority there."

"My father is steward there!" Loyal raged. "What more authority do you need?"

Warder looked away, but she shook her head stubbornly. "Baron Stoner's my master," she said, "not your father. I'm not going any farther."

"When Stoner hears about this . . ."

She shrugged. "I'll tell him myself, lad."

Loyal spun on Seeker. "What about you, eh? Are you frightened of strange places and mad dreams, too?"

Seeker pointed down the ledges. "They went that way," he growled.

"Then what are you waiting for, oaf? After them!"

Twenty-three

Raven was falling. In the dark. She couldn't see anything. She whirled dizzily. Falling. Terrified, she flapped her wings.

Pain stabbed her arm! Her wing. Her head spun faster. She felt sick. Her body bounced and bounced. She had fallen. And bounced. She tried to lift her head.

Pain clubbed her temple. She lifted her hand toward her head. Pain stabbed her arm . . . wing.

What was she? Where was she? In Sarita's room? She had been trying to rescue her sister. She had fallen out the window. Tried to change. Hit. Bounced.

She was still bouncing. In the dark. No, her eyes were closed.

Open them, she thought. Thinking was hard. Go on, thick-wit, open them!

She opened her eyes. The light hurt. Trees blurred, flashing by. Ground, bouncing. Blurred. She couldn't focus. Everything was doubled. She lifted her hand to rub her eyes. Pain stabbed again.

I've broken my wing! she thought.

Terror returned, and with it strange, scattered memories. In no order. No sense. Her head whirled. Her stomach heaved.

A harsh squawk rang beside her ear. She retched harder. The bouncing stopped. Raven rolled sideways and fell. Not far. Landed on something soft. She squinched her eyes open and saw blurred pine needles by her cheek. Strange faces on the other side.

A wildcat! Raven croaked and slashed her beak. Beat her wings. Pain crumpled her. She croaked in agony and tried to drag herself away. Every motion hurt. Her vision swam. A parrot wrapped its wings around her, crooning.

Parrots don't croon, Raven thought. Cutter's parrot would never croon.

Some of the memories rearranged themselves.

"Mam?" she croaked.

The parrot murmured hoarsely. More memories returned: the pool, the terror, her mother's anguish. Then the pool again, young Steward. With a huntsman.

She'd been shot. And some of the pellets were still buried in her wing and scalp. She could feel them. Her head throbbed. Every time she moved her wing, pain blazed all the way up to her neck. She was seeing double. Moving made her stomach heave. And she couldn't fly. Panicked, she tried changing herself to human. She was able to do it, but now she was cold. She lay on her side, panting, afraid to move.

Hero licked her hair, cleaning off dried blood. His big tongue was so rough, it almost tickled, but the gentle touch seemed to ease the pain a little. Roxaine studied the wounds, head cocked. Raven let her eyes close. Her mother's wingtips brushed her hair; it seemed to ease the pain. She started to drift off.

Her mother squawked again. Raven gasped.

"Let me alone," she mumbled, pushing feebly with her good hand.

Roxaine wouldn't. She nipped Raven's wrist and spread her wings, chittering insistently.

"You want to be changed?" Raven moaned. "Now?"

Roxaine whistled and nodded.

"I don't know if I can, Mam."

Roxaine whistled louder. She gestured firmly at Raven's scalp and arm.

"Right, right. I'll try."

She rolled onto her back, moaning again as something grated in her shoulder. She couldn't get up, but she could use one hand at least. She sketched the spell in the air, muttering the words. It wasn't working.

"Hero. Help me."

He laid a paw gently on her forehead. Immediately, she felt stronger. She repeated the gestures and words, grateful that she was reversing the spell, not casting it.

Roxaine emerged slowly from the parrot. She shook herself once, then bent over to study Raven's wounds again. She stroked Raven's hair.

"Lie still, Pigeon. You're hurt."

"Blast it, Mam; don't call me Pigeon."

Her mother pressed her cheek to Raven's. It was wet with tears. "I'm sorry. I just can't forget you're my little girl."

Something—the words or the tears—eased Raven's pain a little. She patted her mother's back awkwardly with her good hand. "I'm your big girl now, Mam," she mumbled. "Sarita's the little one; you can spoil her. But don't you ever call her Pigeon, you hear me? Pigeons! Kah!"

"Well, Hero, I guess she's going to live."

Raven wondered how that could be true.

"Nothing really deep, thank the River," Roxaine continued, carefully parting Raven's thick hair to study her scalp. "Two pellets oozed out when you changed. But that shoulder—it's dislocated. We can't leave it like that." She placed one hand lightly on Raven's shoulder blade, took Raven's elbow in the other.

"What—"

Her mother jerked, shoved, twisted. The shoulder snapped into place. Raven howled as every muscle clenched. She fought down bile. But when her stomach settled, she realized the pain was less.

"Blazing mages," she gasped, "you could have warned me."

"You would have tensed up," Roxaine said. "This was better."

"That's easy for you to say."

"Well, it worked, didn't it?"

Raven tried to sit up, but every movement still pained her arm.

"I can't fly." The thought hurt more than her wounds. She fought against a new surge of panic.

"It'll heal," Roxaine assured her. "It's just going to take time."

"We don't have time, do we? Where are we? Where's Steward?"

"We slowed him down a bit, but I doubt we stopped them."

"Then we'd better keep moving," Raven said, but she couldn't even begin to get up.

Roxaine rubbed her palm along Raven's cheek. "You can take a moment longer, Daughter, but I'm afraid you're going to have to change again. Hero can't carry you like that."

Raven contemplated being a raven. And balked. She couldn't fly. As a human, she could walk at least. If only she could get up.

"I don't know," she mumbled.

"I know you. I've seen what you can do, Daughter. And Hero will help you, right?"

He growled a yes.

"If only he could change to a horse or something," Raven groaned.

"But he can't now. When you're better, you can teach him," Roxaine said.

"Teach him? How? I'm no mistress mage."

"I'm sorry, P— Daughter," Roxaine said. "We can talk about it later."

Hero *yow*ed anxiously.

"Right," Raven muttered. "They're catching up. You first."

"Are you sure? I can walk."

"Not fast enough," Raven moaned. "Come on, Hero. Touch me again."

She just managed the change, and sank back. Her mother brushed her forehead with a wingtip while Raven's breathing steadied. Drawing on her last strength, and whatever she could borrow from Hero, Raven changed herself. With her mother's help, she hauled herself onto Hero's back. Roxaine settled behind her, providing support.

"Go, Hero," Raven muttered. "Show the muck heads your tail."

He growled and set off at a lope.

Hero's wildcat was light-footed, but he still bounced. Raven's head and back ached. Her bad wing sent jolts of pain into her gut. She felt cold to the bone. Then it began to rain. Raven leaned against her mother and clung stubbornly to Hero's back, shivering. Her vision narrowed to a spot of fur. Hero kept moving, all through the day and long into the night, pausing only to drink. Raven blacked out more than once, only to jerk awake in pain at a bad jolt. She started to slip off and was too dulled to try to save herself. Roxaine wrapped her wings around her and held her in place.

"Thanks, Mam," Raven muttered.

"*Shush,*" Roxaine replied.

Everything slowly went dark.

Raven came to in thin daylight. Her mother was holding her. They were perched on the back of a sleeping wildcat. Hero. She tried to wake up her memory. A few more details arose. Steward had that guard woman with him. She'd hit him—Raven almost smiled. And the fat man. Floating in the pool. He was a mage, had a vision of some kind. About Steward, and young Steward. And her mother? Raven wracked her memory but the details wouldn't come. She knew it was something important, but it just wouldn't come. Frustrated, Raven shook her head.

Her mother woke instantly. She cooed softly, brushing Raven with her wings. Hero stirred, yawned, and stretched, almost tumbling them off.

"Where are we?" Raven mumbled. She looked around at rough walls of bark. "A deer blind?" Roxaine nodded, and Raven managed a chuckle. "One hunter chases, the other hides." The joke fell flat, even for herself. Her pain was less, but her wing was still useless.

"I'm going to have to keep riding you, Hero," she said bitterly.

He nodded, regarding her with wide, predatory eyes.

"Kah! Don't give me that look!" she snapped.

Roxaine made a chiding sound.

"Right, right," Raven grouched. "He's a cat. How else can he look? Sorry, Hero."

Roxaine peered closely at Raven's head. Suddenly, she nipped at something.

"Ow!" Raven croaked, pulling away. Roxaine spat out a bit of birdshot. "No more of that, please," Raven begged.

Roxaine shrugged.

"It's my head! Ask first." She was trapped on the ground with an insolent cat, and now her mother was biting her. But they were all still alive, and still ahead of Steward. "We'd better get moving," she said. "Hero, did you try to cover your tracks at all yesterday?"

He bared his fangs.

"Right, you did. Don't strain your face over it," she croaked. "Let's just hope it slows them down." But as Hero padded into the open, she looked around in dismay; the rain had turned to light snow. "Wonderful. Your tracks are clear as paint."

Hero made a rude noise and began trotting downhill. Raven stared glumly at the line of paw prints following them. Not too long after, another wildcat stepped into their path. Raven tensed, all too aware of her useless wing. But the wildcat didn't even seem to notice her and Roxaine. It approached Hero hesitantly. They touched noses, then began to trot together.

Hero ran with the other cat for a long way, crisscrossing its tracks. When they came at last to a good-sized brook, he led the cat into the water and downstream for a hundred paces before sending it off on the other side. He kept to the stream for another hundred paces before climbing out on a fallen trunk. Not too long after that, they came upon a small herd of deer. Hero patiently sat until he had calmed them enough to approach. They traveled in company for several leagues, an unlikely procession. When they came to another stream, Hero took to the water again, then let the herd wander off. All the while, the land dropped steadily and gentled. Suddenly, they came out of the woods into high pasture. Hero loped across the rolling meadow to the next line of trees.

"Wait," Raven said. She was feeling stronger now, though her wing still pained her terribly. "I want to check on the pursuit."

Her mother squawked a query.

"With someone else's wings," Raven replied. She reached out, found a keening dove nearby, and sent it flying back the way they had come, watching as best she could through its eyes. The trees sped by beneath as it climbed farther and farther toward the ridge line. Raven's control grew more and more tenuous. The dove began to wander. Raven gripped Hero's back, drawing on his strength, and bent all her talent on command, on seeing what the dove saw.

Suddenly, she glimpsed movement below. The dove balked, startled by the presence of men. Raven made it dip beneath the branches; she had to be sure. Yes, it was them. The huntsman was already raising his firearm.

Flee! Raven shouted the command. The scene whirled. Raven's eyes flew open. She was panting, heart pounding. She had no idea if the dove had escaped.

"They're coming," she croaked. "That dog-brained huntsman, shooting at everything! And that flat-faced shrike of a steward. If only I could fly . . ."

But she couldn't. She calmed herself. "I don't know how far back they are," she said. "Doves are fast, so I guess as much as a day."

Roxaine whistled in concern.

"I know: Not much time to free Phillipe and steal back Sarita. If we can keep up this pace, we should reach the estate in three or four more days. We should have a plan by then. We'll have to, so we will."

Roxaine whistled agreement. Hero growled.

"At least we've learned some things *not* to do," Raven added.

Twenty-four

L oyal stumbled across the field at a half run. Seeker had already reached the trees at the far side. He was hunched over like an old woman, casting right and left for the tracks of their quarry. He straightened, glanced back at Loyal, and disappeared into the windbreak.

"Blazes, man, wait!" Loyal yelled. It came out a breathless plea.

He slowed to a walk, gulping air. They had been running for most of the past four days. Jogging, trotting, at times sprinting; through rain, sleet, and that miserable snow. They ran from the first glint of dawn till it was too dark to avoid crashing into a tree. The only times Seeker had slowed was when he'd lost the trail. Then Loyal had stewed with ill-suppressed anxiety, even as he blessed the chance to stand still for a while. Seeker had always found the trail, and off he had gone, full tilt.

Since their second day off the high reach, they hadn't seen a single bird, deer, rabbit, or any other animal to shoot and eat. They hadn't even heard a crow or a blue jay. It was that thrice-cursed cat mage, he was sure of it. Somehow, it was warning the game away. Trying to weaken them. Well, it wasn't going to work; they'd come to a farmstead soon enough. If not, he'd take what they needed from the next shepherd he saw. Kill a lamb. Roast it. His mouth began to water. His stomach growled. He reached the trees and was just opening his mouth to yell when Seeker reappeared.

"Can't slow now," the Seeker grumbled. "They're moving faster."

"How far ahead are they?" Loyal asked. He gulped a swig from his water bottle.

Seeker shifted from foot to foot. "Day, day and a half."

Loyal looked back at the hills. "We're four days at least from the manor. Can we catch them in time?"

"Not if we stop here."

"Then what are you waiting for?" Loyal slapped the cork back into his bottle and pushed into the trees.

"Over this way," Seeker growled, trotting past him.

Loyal stifled a groan and forced his aching legs to move faster. In fifty paces they came out on the grassy bank of a stream.

"'Tain't deep," Seeker said, plunging in.

"Wait," Loyal ordered. He had glimpsed a building downstream, half hidden in the trees. "There's a house. We can get some food." He began to hurry along the bank.

Seeker splashed the rest of the way across and caught up on the other side. "We'll lose time," he argued. "We've food enough." He flapped the near empty bag draped over his shoulder.

"For you, maybe," Loyal snapped. "I, for one, do not intend to arrive at the manor a scarecrow." And I'm not going to run any farther if I can help it, he thought.

As they neared the house, Loyal spotted a narrow hull turned upside down on the bank. His spirits soared: Water was the fastest road in the Slow valley. He could beat Roxaine to the estate, trap her, show his father once and for all what he was worth.

He was speeding downstream in hardly more than an hour, seated in the middle of the narrow skiff, eating cold lamb and spring greens. The farmer and his oldest daughter paddled rapidly at bow and stern. Loyal's pouch was lighter by a handful of silver, backed by a promise of gold if he reached the manor in three days.

The seeker was still on the trail. "Press them," Loyal had ordered. "Keep them on the run."

The seeker had replied with no more than a scornful glance at the boat before haring off.

Loyal finished his meal and settled more comfortably on his seat of folded blankets. The farmer and daughter paddled tirelessly. This was the proper way to chase runaways.

They reached a canal at dusk, and the daughter hung a lantern from a pole in the bow. She and her father took turns napping while the other kept them moving. Loyal was pleased to see the effort a few coins could inspire. Of course, they should have been honored to do it for nothing; he was, after all, their assistant steward, on his father's business, acting with the full authority of the infant Baron. If they lost this race, he'd see they got no gold. And repaid the better part of the silver.

He shivered. If they lost the race . . . The image of his father's face loomed in his mind, raging, sneering, raising a fire-tipped switch. Loyal stared at the glowing lantern, the dark riverbank. The face flickered at the corner of his vision, mocking him. As it had every night since he'd first heard the cursed song. He squeezed his eyes shut, till he could see his own pulse in the darkness. Only then did his vision clear. He dozed fitfully.

When dawn came, they paused just long enough for everyone to visit the privacy of the trees. They hurried through a tiny village. They dodged around long, blunt canal boats pulled by stout ponies. They came to a major town, at a junction with a wider canal, where three boats could pass abreast. Loyal sat upright and set their boat lurching.

"Watch yourself, young sir," the farmer said. "A capsize'll slow us down for sure."

Loyal hardly noticed. He was staring at a plume of smoke lifting skyward above the roofs of the town. It could be only one thing.

"Faster!" he cried. "Catch that steamboat!"

Luckily, the steamboat was still tied to the town wharf. Luckier still, the boatman was a bondservant of the manor, a beery lout named Bozer who was only too happy to give Loyal a ride in exchange for the promise of a hefty payment on his bond.

"We don't stop till we reach the manor," Loyal ordered. "Not even at night. Understood?"

The boatman spat over the side. "Clear as a window," he grunted.

"You have enough coal?" Loyal demanded. "You know the river well enough?"

"Yes and yes," the boatman replied. He ran a hairy forearm across his brow. "Don't you worry, young Steward."

"Then what are you waiting for?" Loyal snapped. "Get under way!"

"Just as soon as we got steam up, young sir." The boatman stumped back to the engine well and gave his ancient fireboy a cuff. "You heard him, you lazy git," he bellowed. "Lay on more coal!"

The fireboy hunched his shoulders and mumbled something about smothering the fire, but he clanged open the firebox door and sprinkled a scoop of coal on the glowing heap inside.

"No more'n a minute," the boatman boomed, stumping back to Loyal. "I'll just dodge ashore and let the canalmen know we're leaving."

"And sneak into the nearest alehouse?" Loyal asked. "You'll do nothing of the sort, Bozer. I know your type. Get up to the wheel. I'll clear the lines myself."

The boatman glowered. Loyal glared back till the hairy lout looked aside and climbed to the cabin top, grumbling the whole way.

Loyal went to the stern and loosened the lines. The farmer and daughter were still waiting in their little skiff. He could see the line of canal boats on Bozer's tow beyond them. The boatmen were watching him curiously. He waved.

"Steam's up!" the fireboy yelled.

"About blasted time!" the boatman bellowed back. He let off a shrill blast from the boat's whistle.

Loyal slipped the stern line, untied the towline, and hurried to loose the bow, ignoring the shouts from the farmer and canalmen.

Bozer's canal steamer was smaller than the river craft, but it had a good turn of speed when there was nothing dragging behind. They reached the Slow by evening. Bozer sounded the whistle and turned the prow upstream, hugging the shore to avoid the main current. Loyal went aft to make sure the gray-haired fireboy didn't slack off, and stayed up the night to keep them moving. The lazy louts couldn't be trusted. And he wanted no more dreams.

Midmorning the next day, the carrion reek of Cutter's meat house blew down on the breeze. Loyal inhaled as if it were the sweetest perfume. When they finally reached the wharves of Cutter's Landing that afternoon, he leaped ashore before the boat had even stopped. He ran past the startled wharfhands, clambered onto the seat of an empty wagon, and drove at a gallop toward the manor house, leaving the driver yelling in the lane. The wagon careened through the front gates in a great clatter that set the hounds to howling. Hauling on the reins, Loyal managed to stop the horses just shy of the back wall of the stable. Ostler charged out of a stall, red-faced and cursing, only to stop cold when he saw who it was.

"Watch your tongue!" Loyal snapped, tossing him the reins. He sprinted to the house and burst through the main door.

"Father!" he called. "Father!"

Jan Steward loomed in the doorway to Cutter's parlor. At the sight of his reddening glower, Loyal jerked up short. His heart pounded. For an instant, he'd thought he glimpsed a switch in his father's hand.

"Good day, Father," he said, trying to sound calm and composed.

His father's frown deepened. "This mad entrance had better mean she's back in the quarry. If you have any different news, I'll need a very good reason. Well?"

Loyal swallowed. "She's as good as captured, sir. I—"

"What do you mean 'as good as'? Did you catch her or not?"

Loyal couldn't meet his father's glare. "I've chased her over the high reach and all the way across the Slow valley. She's—"

"You haven't caught her?" Jan Steward stepped closer, and Loyal couldn't help but cringe. "You capering idiot! I sent you off on a simple delivery. One small woman. In shackles. And what did you do? You let her escape! Not once but three times! And now you rush in here all a-thunder to tell me she's still free? Blazing mages, a child could have done it!"

"Father," Loyal pleaded, "listen to me. She's headed here, no more than a day away, probably by toni—"

"Here?" his father bellowed. "You let her get all the way back here? You simpleton! Don't you realize—?"

"Into a trap!" Loyal screamed.

His father pulled back, face flaming with rage.

Loyal dropped his voice, averted his eyes, hurried on. "We know she's coming and we know why: to claim her daughter. That's our bait. She'll risk anything to get her precious, puling little baby back. Don't you see? She's as good as caught."

He stopped, shaking, watching his father's face from the corners of his eyes.

Jan Steward settled back on his heels. "Tonight, you think?" he demanded.

Loyal nodded quickly. "Yes, sir. Tomorrow night at the latest."

His father considered. "Does anyone else know about this?"

"Only the seeker, sir."

"Who in the five rivers is the seeker?" his father snapped.

"Stoner's huntsman. I told him to stay close on her trail, to push her right here."

His father snorted. "Why didn't you just have him catch her? No, spare me your sorry excuses. Come in here." He stalked back into the parlor.

Loyal stopped dead in the doorway and stared at the walls. The mounted heads were gone. The stuffed birds, the skulls, the carved statues—all were gone. In their place hung lists and charts from the steward's office, and one large painting of the manor house, opposite the desk where his father now sat. The changed scene reminded Loyal of Squint's vision. Roxaine's bond receipt was still hidden somewhere here. But where, if not this room? Maybe—

"Don't stand there gawping like a farmhand," his father snapped. "Get in!"

Loyal hurried in. There was one other chair, narrow and hard and straight backed. He perched on the sharp edge of the seat. He realized suddenly that the parrot cage was gone as well. He stifled a thin laugh. He'd find it, to cage Roxaine. And one for her daughter. And then the receipt could stay hidden forever.

"You think we can trap her?" his father demanded.

Loyal jerked himself back to the present. "Yes, sir," he replied, trying to sound assured. "All we have to do is give them the chance to get in."

"Them?" His father eyed him suspiciously. "What do you mean, 'them'?"

"The other daughter's with her—the raven girl—and someone else, a mage of some kind. He changes himself into animals: a wildcat at least, maybe a deer, a snake."

"A beast mage? You've stirred up a rat's nest of trouble, haven't you? And I don't imagine you have the first idea how this trap of yours is going to work."

"I—"

"Quiet! You've done enough damage." His father leaned forward, glaring. "You're not to say a word about this, not to anyone. Understand?"

"Yes, sir, I—"

"I said be quiet! No one else must know she's coming."

"But we need to prepare right away. I should—"

"You'll do nothing!" His father eyed him as if he were bad meat. "No, there is something you can do. How did you come here? By steamboat?"

Loyal began to describe his race down the canals and up the river.

His father cut him off, a grim smile quirking his lips. "You can take the child away. If you think you're up to it. I'd have tiny shackles made, but in your case I doubt it would help."

Loyal flushed with shame. "I can't take the child. I need to be here, to help—"

"To help the witch get away? Not blazing likely. I won't risk you losing her again. Or the child. What if they sneaked in here as mice, eh? They change the daughter, carry her out, change again, fly away, all right under your nose. That idea never occurred to you, did it?"

Loyal looked away, because it hadn't.

"I thought as much," his father growled. "I should adopt the witch's baby. Maybe I'd get a child who could think."

Twenty-five

They crept within view of the manor wall in the early evening. Raven, still forced to ride on Hero's back, peered from the shadows of the same windbreak they had fled through less than a month before. She flexed her shoulder and wished she'd had longer to heal. The one other time she'd dared charm a bird and send it back to spy, the shoot-happy huntsman was still there, barely a day behind. She'd sent the bird fleeing at the first glimpse, and warned Hero they had no time to waste. He had kept on relentlessly.

Now her mother settled quietly into the shrub overhead.

"See anything?" Raven whispered.

Roxaine made a sad noise that could have been yes or no. She sighed, and Raven knew she'd be crying if she had human eyes.

"You'll have her back soon, Mam. Don't worry."

Roxaine dropped to the ground and spread her wings, pointing at her chest. Hero slipped deeper into the shadow. Raven hopped off, changed herself, and then her mother.

"Louella had her out on the bench. With a wet nurse." Roxaine's tone was brittle. "They took her back to the same room. I saw the lamp come on and made sure."

Raven flexed her injured arm. "We'll have to sneak up the stairs."

"I'll have to carry her downstairs anyway," her mother pointed out.

"The wet nurse sleeps with her. Louella, too, maybe."

"Louella's on my side; don't worry about that."

"We can't trust anyone in that house," Raven muttered.

"Louella won't turn her back on me and my baby," her mother insisted.

"We'd just be putting her in danger," Raven countered. "I say we go in at dinner, when everyone's downstairs eating and Sarita's asleep."

"That's right now."

"That's right." Raven changed back to a bird and hopped onto Hero's back. "Let's go."

"We still don't have a plan."

"We'll figure it out!"

Hero growled.

"What?" Roxaine snapped.

He looked pointedly toward the open back gate of the manor. They could clearly see Liddy Cook and her helpers bustling about in the outdoor summer kitchen.

"They'd spot us," Raven admitted.

"I could fly over the wall," her mother said.

"I'm not letting you go in there alone. It's too chancy."

"I'm not letting you come in there with me. It just doubles the risk. Besides, you haven't healed yet."

Hero gave vent to an irritated snarl and began trotting away.

"Hey!" Raven squawked. "Where do you think you're going?"

His answering growl sounded very much like "Home."

Hero led Roxaine through the shadows to the breeding barn. The workers had gone to their supper; the big building was empty of all but cows. And Mangle. As soon as Roxaine let them in, Hero trotted straight to the big bull's stall. Raven hopped off just in time to avoid getting licked by a huge, wet tongue. Muttering a quiet curse, she fled to the walkway and changed herself to human. Hero rubbed himself against Mangle's legs, purring. The big bull nuzzled him gently. Raven swallowed a sudden lump in her throat.

"Kah!" she muttered. "Right. Let's go, Fur Brain. We need to plan."

Before anyone could reply, the end door slid open. It was

Phillipe. Raven gasped. His hair had gone gray in the short time they'd been gone. His shoulders were hunched. His calves were striped with lash marks that continued out of sight beneath his breeches. His face sagged with sadness.

Hero dashed out of the stall with a wild *yeow* of relief. Almost before Raven could say the words, he was changing. He threw himself into his father's arms. Phillipe lit up with joy.

"Oh, my boy," he mumbled, pressing his face into Hero's mop of hair. "Oh, my happy boy."

Finally, he held Hero at arm's length and looked him up and down. "You're all right, then?" he asked. Hero nodded, smiling through a face full of tears, a small mirror of his father. Phillipe looked past Hero to smile his thanks to Raven and Roxaine. He tried to speak but couldn't. Raven tried to reply, but the lump had come back to her throat and grown. They grinned foolishly at each other.

"Well," Phillipe finally managed. "Well, I didn't expect . . . ever." He wiped his eyes and held Hero out again, studying his face as if it were a forgotten treasure. "Did I just see you a wildcat?" he asked. He turned to Raven. "How did you manage that?"

"Don't look at me," she said. "He's the beast mage."

"A beast mage?"

"Pigheaded about it, too," she said. "But he has real talent."

Phillipe turned back to Hero, shaking his head in amazement. "You always were good with the animals—better than me, surely—but . . . a mage? You're truly a mage?"

Hero seemed to grow three inches. He started telling Phillipe about their adventures.

"Slow down, Son," Phillipe said. He eased himself onto a keg.

"You're hurt!" Hero exclaimed, finally noticing. "What happened?"

"They caught me," Phillipe said softly.

"Who did?" Roxaine demanded.

"Steward's men, lady."

"Steward did that to you?" Roxaine's eyes blazed. "That over-stuffed, swine-bred—"

Phillipe held up a hand. "What's done is done, lady. The important thing is they didn't catch these two." He pulled Hero to him in a fierce hug. "You shouldn't have come back," he whispered, "but I am so glad you did."

Hero squirmed awkwardly in his father's embrace. Raven glanced at her mother. The pesky lump kept coming back to her throat.

"He'll be safe here soon enough," Roxaine said. "I promise you that. As soon as we have my Sarita out of Steward's reach, I'll raise such a cry, his ears will wilt. When the Council of Barons hears what that child-thieving would-be baron has tried to do—"

"Wait a minute," Raven said. "You can't seriously believe the Council is going to listen to you. Have you forgotten how Steward's good friend Baron Stoner had you chained to the wall of his quarry?"

"What do you suggest? Fly away?"

"Yes," Raven said. "After we have Sarita, we can all fly away."

Roxaine sighed. "Haven't you run enough, Daughter? Aren't you sick and tired of that huntsman on your trail? Of bowing and scraping to the likes of Steward and his spawn?"

"I don't bow and scrape to anyone!" Raven snapped.

"No, you just fly away. Never mind the ones you leave behind, who take the lashing for you."

"They could run, too!" Raven cried.

"How?" Roxaine demanded. "They don't have wings."

"They've got feet! They're just too scared!"

"Maybe they're afraid for someone else," Phillipe said quietly.

Raven stared at him, and at Hero, wide-eyed beside him. She
d back to her mother and remembered the fear she had felt
singing pool. They both had felt. She realized how fright-
he felt now, but not for herself. For her mother and her
'er.

202

"You're crazy, Mam," she said. "They'll throw you right back to Stoner."

"They won't," Roxaine replied, "because I'll be there with Cutter's heir."

"You'll still be a bondservant."

"Darvin wrote off my bond!"

"But you can't prove that!"

Roxaine rubbed her eyes wearily. "If only I hadn't lost the receipt."

"I thought you said Steward burned it."

"I did, and he might have—would have if he found it, I'm sure—but it was gone missing before Darvin died. There's a good chance it's still safely lost, right beneath our noses somewhere in that house."

Something stirred in the back of Raven's mind, something about . . . The thought was gone as soon as it had come. She threw up her hands. "We don't have time to search. Even if we did, even if we found it, do you really think that would change anything? These people are in power. They don't need to change. It's the last thing they want."

"Darvin changed. After we fell in love, he listened to me. He raised wages. He stopped the whippings."

"Kah!" Raven muttered. "What about Phillipe here? With Cutter gone, the whippings came right back. Nothing has changed."

"And they never will change, if people keep thinking like you," her mother replied. "Letting things go on like this; not even trying to help the others out of a bondage you can simply fly away from."

"That's not true!" Raven cried. "What about Hero? What about Fireboy?" She turned to Phillipe for support. "I helped them."

It was Hero who answered. "My brother can never come back," he said. "He's as good as banished. Me, too, if I go away now."

"That's right," Roxaine said. "And it's just as true for you and Sarita. I want to live here with my daughters—both of them—

without the constant fear of capture, of a whipping and shackles and being sent off alone to another river. There's only one way I can do that: face down the Council and force them to make me guardian. First we rescue Sarita. Then we spread this tale up and down the middle reach, and all the way to Dunsgow, if you're willing to fly that far. By the time the Council meets, Steward's name won't be worth a handful of dirt." Raven started to protest, but her mother raised a hand. She touched Raven's cheek. "There is no other way, Daughter. I have to try." She looked at Hero and Phillipe. "And the first thing I'll do when Steward's gone is write off every bond on this river."

"First get your little girl back," Phillipe said. "Then worry about changing the world."

"You're crazy, all of you," Raven muttered. She sighed. "Right. What's the plan?"

Hero led them through the back gate of the manor in the deep, tired dark of midnight. He went as a wildcat, their eyes and ears. Raven and her mother followed close behind, treading as lightly as possible. They were dressed in Phillipe's darkest shirts and breeches. Roxaine carried a blanket, ready to enfold Sarita. Raven carried a cudgel. She couldn't fly, but she would fight if she had to.

The first part of the plan was simple: Sneak in, grab Sarita, sneak out. Then it got more complicated: Hurry to the barn and loose the cows. Hero would lead them upriver. Raven would add her own tracks for the hunters to find. Roxaine and Sarita would hide on the estate with Phillipe. The complications grew: Sarita would need feeding; Roxaine needed to get to Dunsgow. There was plenty of milk to be had in the barns, but no easy way to travel downriver. Roxaine could fly, but not with Sarita, and the Council would hardly listen to a parrot. So she would have to stay hidden with Sarita until Raven's shoulder healed. Assuming she and Hero could give their hunters the slip. Assuming they could even rescue Sarita.

Hero led them to the small window at the end of the main hallway, the same window Raven had fled through when she'd run away four years before. She knew it was usually left unlocked, because it had been one of her duties to wash it. The latch was so stiff, none of the chargirls ever bothered to twist it shut.

Raven leaned against the building to be a living ladder. Mam scrambled up, digging a knee into Raven's bad shoulder. Raven fought back a cry. The window squeaked open. Her mother tumbled inside with a dull thud. Hero bounded up Raven's back and into the house. She stifled another cry, mouthed a silent curse instead. Her mother reappeared in the window. Raven handed up the cudgel, then jumped and managed a one-handed grab. Mam clutched her shirt and heaved, and they fell through to land in a heap. They both lay rigid, trying to still their panting breath. Raven strained for any sound of alarm. Her hearing was better than most, but not as good as a raven's. As far as she could tell, the house was quiet as a fresh-laid egg. She and her mother untangled themselves and crept down the hallway, Hero in the lead.

Raven winced at every creak in the floorboards. The first step on the stairs groaned as if it were about to collapse. Even the railing peeped an alarm when she leaned on it. She couldn't believe anyone was still asleep. But no one called out, or even snored behind the closed doors that flanked the dark passage. They crept forward until her mother breathed a faint "stop." The door latch clicked open with a sound like a hammer on iron. They froze.

Silence filled the space between breaths. Roxaine pushed open the door. The window was a faint rim of starlight around the edges of the drapes. Beneath it, the nurse was an uneven ridge on the dark slab of the bed. She didn't move. Roxaine hurried to Sarita's crib.

Raven jumped as Hero slipped between her legs. He stopped dead, ears back. He gave a low growl. Raven's heart sped.

"What?" she breathed.

His growl deepened.

"Mam," she whispered. "Hurry."

"This isn't Sarita!" Roxaine hissed.

A figure burst from beneath the nurse's blanket. "Hoi! To me!" It was Hunter's boy.

"Trap!" Raven cried.

The baby came awake with an earsplitting wail. Hero yowled. He sprang at the huntsboy, swiping at his face with both front paws. The lad cried out and reeled back against the bed. Doors banged open in the hall. Footsteps pounded toward them. Raven threw herself against the door and jammed the bolt home. Her shoulder twinged; she ignored it.

"Mam, Hero, the window!" Her mother still held the wailing baby, trying to soothe it. "Put it down, Mam! It's not Sarita!" A body smashed against the door. The wood cracked. "It won't hold! Let me change you!"

"I'm not leaving you to that swine Steward," her mother replied. Her voice was tight with anger.

"You brainless coot, I can glide far enough!" Raven yelled. "It's our only—"

The huntsboy lunged to his feet and charged Raven. Hero swatted his legs. The boy tripped, arms flailing. Raven lurched back, lifting her hands to fend him off. Her forgotten cudgel struck him right between the eyes. He fell with a heavy thud and lay dead silent. Raven stared at him numbly. The door shattered open behind her.

She spun, swinging wildly with her good hand, but someone caught her wrist. She kicked out but only hurt her toe. The hold on her wrist twisted painfully. She kicked again, higher, but her assailant blocked it, then brought the back of his hand across her face in a stinging blow. Spots starred her sight. Someone grabbed her from behind. An arm went around her neck.

"Stop!" her mother commanded. "You'll hurt the child."

The hold on Raven's throat eased. She blinked back tears.

A pair of men faced her mother, standing off as if in respect.

It was Ostler and his head boy. She looked past them to the door.

"There's a mother somewhere who cares what happens to this baby," she said.

Jan Steward filled the opening, a lantern in his hand. He gave Roxaine a thin, cold smile.

"Where is *my* baby?" Roxaine demanded.

"Safe from you," Steward replied.

"Safe from me? From *me?*" Roxaine lost her calm. She thrust the baby into Ostler's arms and strode toward Steward. "You thrice-cursed son of a maggot! You'd drown her in a moment if you thought it would gain you title to half a dram of tallow!" She stood toe to toe with him, a head shorter but towering.

"Grab her!" he barked, holding out the lantern as if it were a shield. "Don't heed her words! She's a mage, a mind thief. She'll charm your will."

The two men fumbled for her arms, almost dropping the baby between them. It set up a renewed wail.

"Get that mewling git to its nurse!" Steward ordered.

One of the men holding Raven let go to grab her mother's arms and drag them behind her. Raven tried to jerk free, but the other man twisted her bad arm again. The pain stopped her cold. Ostler's boy squeezed past Steward, holding the baby as if it might explode.

"Where is my child!" Roxaine cried.

"Safe with young Steward," Ostler mumbled soothingly, as though he were trying to calm an unbroken colt. "They're down-river just a league or so, safe on a boat."

"Quiet!" Steward cuffed Ostler on the ear. "It's none of her business."

There was a moan from the floor. Hunter's boy was trying to sit up. Both his eyes had gone black and blue. Blood dotted the scratches on his face.

"The cat," Steward growled. His eyes searched the room. "Where's the cursed cat?"

Hero darted from beneath the baby's bed and leaped at Steward's face. The big man stumbled backward, catching the lantern against the door frame. Hot oil splashed across the room. A few flames curled up Steward's cloak. Hero circled, snarling.

"Hero, run!" Raven yelled.

"Find Sarita!" her mother called. "Don't let him harm her!"

Hero yowled and fled down the hall.

Steward charged to the window, still beating at the embers on his sleeve. He threw open the sash. "Hunter!" he bellowed. "He's coming! The wildcat! Watch the door!"

"Ay!" came the reply.

"Hero!" Raven cried. "Watch out for Hunter!"

The room fell silent as everyone strained to hear what was happening outside. There was a crash of glass. A shot. A curse. Then came the cry of Hunter's horn and the wild yip and bay of his hounds, on the chase. The sound grew to a mad belling that echoed through the night. It faded, unrelenting, into the distance.

Steward turned from the window and brushed a few strands of smoldering lint from his sleeve. "They'll catch the cursed thing," he said. "They've hunted cats before."

Twenty-six

Loyal stood at the head of the narrow gangplank, staring into the gloom ashore. He could have sworn he'd heard the baying of hounds in the direction of the manor. Blast his father, sending him away on a nursemaid's chore! If it was truly hounds, there was someone on the run. Which meant one of them at least had managed to slip his father's trap. Double blast! He should have been there. He knew how slippery the witch and the bird girl could be. His father had no idea.

Loyal slapped the top of the railing. His palm burned at the impact, just as his spirit burned at the insult. Sent away on this greasy little stinkpot of a steamboat to hide the witch's whelp. His father thought he could raise her to his will, rule the estate as her guardian, Baron in all but name. A ridiculous idea! You only had to look at her mother to see that. Better for all of them if there had been no heir. Better if she died young. Surely his father had thought of that.

There! He heard it again! Whenever the faint breeze shifted, it carried downriver the hunting bell of hounds. Someone had escaped and was still on the run.

Loyal smiled bitterly. "How do you like that, Father Steward?" he muttered. "Not so easy to catch, are they? I warned you. Who was it who chased them all the way over the high reach? Who was it who suffered the taunts of the cursed woman and the tricks of her unnatural daughter? Me, that's who! But did you listen? No, you . . . you fool! You thought you knew better. So righteous. So powerful. Well, now that you've let them slip, don't come crying to me about it! Cry to your precious little heir. Go ahead, adopt her! Learn what herding a witch's git is like."

Loyal's voice rose to a shout. He caught himself, loosened his grip on the railing.

There was a haze of light over the eastern ridge of the river valley, the first hint of dawn. Mist rose around the little boat, swirling in the fluky breezes. Once again Loyal heard the hounds. A chill dew weighted the shoulders of his cloak, but he ignored it, staring ashore, listening to the sounds of the hunt.

A new sound grated behind him: the mewling of the witch's baby. It made a fitful cry, then coughed and smacked and settled. Loyal shuddered in disgust. His father couldn't adopt her, of course; the Council would never allow it. Though he might— The idea splashed into Loyal's thoughts like a cool drink: He might wed her to Loyal. Jan Steward was her guardian, after all; he had to approve her mate. Loyal could become the next Cutter. For a few moments, he savored the thought: to rule the river. To rule even his father. He choked out a laugh.

The dream caught on a snag: She would still be the true Baron of the River Slow. And still Roxaine's daughter. Loyal imagined himself wed to a small version of Roxaine. Remembered the other daughter: dusky, headstrong, razor tongued. Feathered! Mages knew what cursed talents this one would have. He shuddered again. She couldn't rule the river; she couldn't be trusted. She'd ruin everything he and his father had built. He couldn't allow it. Yes, better she die young.

The baby cried again. Loyal spun, glaring at the cabin door. He could just make it out in the gloom. He took a step toward it. The wind shifted, blowing fog across the narrow deck. The hounds bayed. The baby whimpered. Loyal's thoughts churned.

A sudden loud snore distracted him. Loyal ground his teeth. It was the wet nurse, a whiney, tiresome drab from among the workers at the meat house, hardly more than a girl. But we had to feed the little heir, didn't we?

"Why?" Loyal demanded. Again he spoke aloud, and hearing the words made them stronger. "Blast you, Father, why even bother? Why don't you just drop her in the river and be done with it? Could it be you're afraid? Afraid to grab the chance, even with it laid out before you so obviously? So afraid, you'd let a bond-servant rule?"

The hounds were growing closer, directly upriver. The quarry was getting away! "You're letting it slip by, you old fool! I gave you the cursed woman, chased her right into your hands. And what good did it do? What good, if you let the witch escape, let her daughter live? You're missing your chance to be Baron. *My* chance! My *right!*"

Loyal glared at the door to the cabin, cursing the child inside, the snag in his dreams, the unnatural bastard of Baron and witch. The obstacle had to be removed. His father was too afraid to set things right, but he, Loyal, was not.

He strode to the door. The hounds called again, but he hardly noticed. He grabbed the latch and soundlessly eased the door open. The cabin stank of infant. His lip curled. He listened carefully, but the wet nurse's quiet snores didn't falter. Neither did he. He slipped across the dark room to the bunks. The child was on top, hemmed in by rolled blankets. It burbled in its sleep.

Loyal slid his hands under the small lump and lifted. The filthy thing had grown in the past month. He heaved the bundle off the ticking and backed away. It whimpered, squirming slightly in his hands like a giant maggot. Loathing soured his mouth. He tiptoed toward the doorway, holding the wrapped child away from his body as though it were a dripping gobbet of offal. Its weight unbalanced him, and he stumbled against the doorjamb. The drab snorted. Loyal froze.

"Wha—?" The girl sat upright. "Who's there? What do you want?" She cowered against the wall, blanket clutched to her chest.

Loyal sneered. As if he had any interest in her! He went out on deck.

"What are you doing?" the drab cried.

"Nothing that concerns you," Loyal snarled. "Go back to sleep."

The child woke and began to whimper.

The drab leaped out of bed and ran to the doorway. "You've got the baby," she said. "What for?"

"I told you it was no concern of yours!" Loyal snapped. "Now get back inside!"

The git cried and waved its arms.

"You're hurting her!" the drab whined.

"Back inside!" Loyal yelled.

The drab shrank back, hands clutched at her throat.

"What's going on here?" The boatman appeared in the gloom, squinting blearily at Loyal and the wailing bundle in his hands. The old fireboy peered timidly from behind the boatman's squat bulk.

"Go back to sleep!" Loyal shrieked.

Even the child went silent.

Loyal fought to control his breathing. He glared at the boatman, the fireboy, the cringing drab. "You have no idea what this is all about," he growled. "You don't have the wit to begin to comprehend what must be done or why. Get back to your beds. Now!" They just stared, their beady eyes dim and stupid. "Obey me!" Loyal bellowed. "You will obey me, or by the Baron's curse, I will see you off the river. I will banish you! Do you hear me! Go! To bed!"

The boatman held up his hands, patting the air as if to placate an angry child. The drab's mouth drooped in horror. He stared them down, till they turned and fled. Loyal almost laughed. They'd better obey.

He looked down at the child in his hands. It didn't seem heavy at all now. It whimpered again, and he turned quickly to the rail. He would never have to hear that ugly sound again. He twisted the blanket more tightly around the baby and held it out, over the water.

"Goodbye, little nuisance," he said.

An inhuman yowl split the dawn, followed by a chorus of mad howls. Stunned, Loyal looked toward shore. A pack of hounds came charging up the gangplank, belling in full throat. Ahead of them dashed a frantic cat. A huge wildcat. The beast mage! Ears laid back, fangs bared in a desperate grimace, it streaked down the deck toward him.

Loyal forgot the child in his hands. He turned toward the racing wildcat, arms held out as if to block it.

With an earsplitting screech, it launched itself right at his face.

Loyal leaped back. And flipped headfirst over the railing. The baby flew from his hands. He could hear it wailing as he hit the icy water and went under.

He came up sputtering, surrounded by spray and splashing waves. Half a dozen of the hounds had jumped in after him. More leaned over the railing, like spectators at a whipping. Loyal reached for the nearest, but it snapped at him and swam away. He swirled in the water, trying to understand what was happening. Suddenly, there was a gurgling wail. One of the hounds had grabbed the gasping child and was swimming toward shore with it. The others followed, splashing and barking through the shallows.

Loyal gaped. The hounds on the boat raced to meet the swimmers at the shore. The wildcat led them. The wet nurse stumbled in their midst, herded along by the press of sleek bodies. When she saw the baby, she gave a cry and rushed forward to take it from the lead hound. The wildcat touched noses with the hound, then led the whole group along the path upriver, the wet nurse among them, clutching the dripping child to her chest.

The wildcat gave Loyal one last glance. He could have sworn it smiled.

Twenty-seven

Raven studied the faint light seeping under the door. The manor's wine cellar had no windows. The walls were thick and well mortared. There was no way out except through the door, up the stairs, across the kitchen, and through another door. And she knew there was at least one guard outside this door. Steward had made certain they wouldn't escape this time.

She and her mother sat on the cold flagstones, leaning against one of the floor-to-ceiling racks of kegs and bottles. The room was damp and chill, the walls too close. Raven suppressed a shiver. They might as well be back in the nightmare cave in Stoner's quarry. Except for the thin slit of light seeping under the door. And the lack of Hero's warm weight on her lap.

"I hope he's all right," Mam said, as if reading her thoughts.

"He's smart," Raven said. "He'll lose them." But she remembered the dogs in Broadmeet, how he had panicked and climbed her as if she'd been a tree. If he went up a tree now, Hunter would simply shoot him. She could only hope he wouldn't panic. If he kept his wits, the little fur brain just might be able to give them the slip.

She shifted, trying to ease her sore shoulder. "Mages," she muttered.

"What?" Mam asked. "Is your shoulder hurting again?"

"It's nothing. If we'd had just one more day, we could have flown out of there."

"Without Sarita."

"At least we'd have the chance to come back!"

"We?" Mam asked quietly.

"Oh. Right. You're going to stay here and change the world."

Raven could feel her mother stiffen beside her, but Mam said nothing. The silence grew awkward.

"I'm sorry," Raven said finally. "It's not your fault we're locked up in here. If I hadn't made such a mess trying to rescue you, rushing in without a plan, getting myself shot—"

"Stop that!" Mam said. "Without you, I wouldn't have had any chance at all."

"Kah! Some chance."

"I said stop. There was no way you could have known Steward had been warned."

"I could have guessed."

"How? You're not a seer."

Raven shook her head. "No. Just a bird mage."

"*Just* a bird mage?" Mam took her hand. "Don't you ever think like that, Pi— *Raven*. What you can do is so remarkable, so special! And look what you did with it: You freed me from those shackles in the quarry. You turned me into a bird and led me back here. You uncovered Hero's talent and helped him grow. And now you're going to help me figure out a way to save Sarita and put that Steward in his place. We're not done yet, Daughter, not as long as birds can fly."

She squeezed Raven's hand, and Raven squeezed back, hard. "Thanks, Mam," she said. "Do you have a plan?"

"No," her mother admitted. "We're going to have to grab whatever chance we can."

I keep doing that, Raven thought. Have been for four years. She realized she had to ask now, before anything else could happen to them.

"Mam?" she said. "Why didn't you come for me? That night? We had a plan then."

"You didn't wait for me."

"I was waiting. I waited for as long as I could. Steward came for me, not you. He came right toward the cupboard, peering at every shadow, as if he knew I was hiding there somewhere. If he hadn't gone back to look in the hall, he'd have caught me."

Her mother was silent a moment. Then she asked, "Didn't you ever wonder why he went back to the hall?"

"Great mages, no! I just sneaked out as fast as I could. Then I went to find you and—"

"*I* was in the hall," Mam said.

"You . . . what?" Raven struggled to fit the idea into her memories.

"I knocked over a chair to get Steward's attention," Mam said. "I led him to the front of the building, then ducked into Darvin's parlor so I could double back. But Darvin was there. Drinking. His wife had just died. What could I do? I pretended to be sorry for him. Then Steward started shouting. I saw you run by." Her voice faltered a moment. "By the time I could pry myself loose, you were long gone."

"I saw you," Raven whispered. "With Cutter."

"Ah. And all this time you thought—" Mam squeezed Raven's hand again. "I listened at the window for you every night for a week," she went on. "I thought maybe you were hiding nearby. Half of me hoped you weren't, because I knew Hunter was out looking for you, and Steward was watching me like a hawk. He was sure you'd come back for me. Or that I'd try to follow you. I didn't dare do anything. Not then. But I hoped. I did plan to follow you. But Darvin . . . Steward would have had me whipped that night. He might even have sent me to the prison farm. Darvin wouldn't let him. He said I'd been with him all evening, couldn't possibly have known you were planning to run away. Then he kept seeking me out, just to talk, if you can believe it. Despite myself, I began to like him. Eventually, I fell in love. He did, too. I don't think either of us meant to, but there you have it." She sighed. "And all this time, you thought— Oh, Daughter, I am so sorry."

Mam fell silent. Raven could feel her warmth where their shoulders almost touched.

"I'm sorry, too, Mam," she said. "I should have known you wouldn't . . . wouldn't desert me."

"Never! And if nothing else good comes of this, at least I've had the chance to tell you that. Now, promise me something."

"What?"

"If they take us outside, if you see the slightest chance, promise me you'll change and fly away."

"What?"

"Promise me," her mother begged. "That you'll fly away."

"Mam, I—"

The door banged open. Three bulky figures crowded into the cellar. Raven squinted against the sudden light.

"On your feet," said the leader, a baronsman.

"Why?" Roxaine asked.

"Steward's orders," he replied.

"I don't take orders from Steward," she said.

"Then we'll haul you up, witch," another sneered: Hunter's boy, his forehead wrapped in a strip of bandage. He brandished a stout cudgel.

"No need for that kind of talk." The third man was Ostler. "We have orders to bring you to Steward," he said politely. "It would be easier on us if you'd just come, please."

"Where is he?" Roxaine asked coolly.

"In the Baron's parlor."

"Good. I have a few words to say to him." She squeezed Raven's hand, then stood. "Coming, Daughter?" Raven scrambled up beside her. "If you'll excuse us, gentlemen."

Hunter's boy reached for her arm.

"Touch me and I'll curse you with boils for the rest of your days," she told him.

He stopped short, glancing nervously at the baronsman.

"Let 'em be," the baronsman said. "But if they try anything funny, don't be afraid to give 'em a whack."

Roxaine swept by them without a sideways glance. Raven kept

a step behind, one eye on Hunter's boy. He followed, scowling, his fist clenched around his cudgel.

Roxaine strode into the parlor without bothering to knock. She stopped two steps inside the doorway and regarded the changes in the room. Her lip curled.

Steward sat ramrod straight behind the big desk. "Why isn't she bound?" he demanded.

"There was no need for that, sir," Ostler began.

"I told you to bind them. That should be all the 'need' you need."

"Yes, sir," the baronsman answered quickly. He pulled some thongs from his belt and came toward them.

Roxaine stepped up to the desk, ignoring him. She leaned her fists on Steward's papers and glared into his face.

"It will take more than rearranging this room to make yourself Baron here," she said. "My daughter is the heir, and nothing you do can change that, apart from killing her."

Ostler gasped. The baronsman stopped cold. Even Hunter's boy shifted nervously. They all watched Steward from the corners of their eyes. His face purpled.

"I guess I'm not the only one to think of that, am I?" Roxaine remarked. She scanned the walls again. "Which list is it on, Steward? Housekeeping? Daily butchering? Next year's goals?"

"Quiet!" Steward roared, slamming his palms on the desk.

"I will not be stilled!" she countered. "Not by a pig-faced child thief like you!"

"Very good," he said, restraining himself. "How very well said. The perfect speech for a foul-mouthed runaway. Bind her!"

The baronsman jerked into motion, grabbing Roxaine's hands to tie them behind her back. She never took her eyes from Steward's. Raven tried to stop the baronsman, but Hunter's boy smacked her bad arm with his cudgel. Her eyes teared. In a minute, her own wrists were bound.

Roxaine held herself straight and tall. "It will do you no good,

Steward," she said. "When I tell the Council what you've done—"

"Stop your bluffing, witch," Steward replied. "This is not a matter for the Council, even if they cared about the fate of one unruly bondservant. As the heir's guardian, I have complete charge of her affairs, including the disposition of incorrigibles like you two."

"Incorrigibles? Ha! You're the one who's bluffing, Steward, and you know it."

"Am I? Seeker!" Steward called. "Come in here."

Seeker appeared in the doorway. His clothes were torn and filthy, his hair matted. A crusted scab crowded one eye; the other drooped with fatigue. His small mouth turned up in a smile as he took in Raven and her mother, bound and under guard.

"Are these the ones?" Steward demanded.

"So I'd guess," Seeker said.

"What do you mean 'guess'?" Steward demanded. "Do you know them or not?"

"Never saw them human," Seeker replied. He stepped closer and looked at their feet. His nose twitched. "You'd be the raven girl," he said to Raven. "You the green bird," to Roxaine. "Where's the third?"

"We've put the dogs on it," Steward snapped. "You'll swear these are the ones you followed?"

"Them and the wildcat."

"Thank you." Steward turned to Roxaine. "This man has told me all about the merry chase you led him on. How you viciously attacked him and his party."

"Did the drooling cur tell you that he shot me first?" Raven shouted.

Steward regarded her coldly. "He had every right: You're dangerous runaways."

"Dangerous to you," Roxaine agreed. "No matter where you try to lock us up."

"That's true enough," Steward said. "Normal punishment

doesn't penetrate that tough hide of yours; you've shown us that. You require a more permanent solution." He stood. "Bring them!" he ordered, and strode out the door.

The baronsman and huntsboy hustled Raven and Roxaine after him, along the hallway to the foyer. Steward threw open the double front doors and led them out. Raven stopped in the doorway. She looked up. It was just after dawn. Deep blue stretched overhead, dotted with fading stars. She reached with her talent, searching for birds to call to their aid. Hunter's boy shoved her onto the porch and down the steps. She kept searching, kept calling. Birds replied aloud. Wings rustled in the trees and shrubs. She searched for hawks and owls, for flocks of pigeons—anything that could attack or shield or distract while she changed herself and escaped. With her mother, if possible; alone, if not. Free, she could come back to rescue her mother later. Somehow. She called again, and felt the birds respond.

The men herded her after her mother toward the center of the courtyard. There, on the packed ground between the house and the stables, three or four others were working on a stark structure of beams and braces. Carpenter was pounding a peg through a crosspiece with a heavy mallet, the blows thudding dully through the cool air. A baronsman stood on a ladder set against the ridge beam. He was tying a rope to it. The rope ended in a noose.

Twenty-eight

aven stopped dead, all thought of birds gone. It was a gibbet. She couldn't leave. Not without Mam.

"So," her mother said bitterly to Steward. "The first hanging in the Slow valley in what? Two generations? You think you can bury your crimes with us?"

"Not my crimes," Steward replied. "I'm not the runaway."

"And I'm no bondservant. You know it. Everyone here knows it."

"Prove it," he replied. "Show me the receipt and I will let you go."

"It's in the house somewhere. I can find it."

"I've searched the entire manor. It's not there."

"Because you burned it!"

Steward reddened. "Because there wasn't one."

Raven studied his face, and something stirred in her memory. An image formed: an angry man, red-faced, but cold in his anger, surrounded by exotic faces. The image was vague, as though it had been a dream, or a story someone had told her. Or . . . was it something she saw in that cursed pool? Was that it?

She shook her head angrily. She had no time now for idiot memory games. She had to think about escaping. Her mother and Steward were arguing loudly, trading insults. Everyone was watching. Raven flexed her hands against the thong binding them. Her shoulder hurt, but not all that badly. She ignored it, trying to find some slack in the knot, trying to recall her birds.

"Enough!" Steward barked. "Your curses are empty, witch! I

221

refuse to let them strike me. You can't bemagic me like you did Cutter."

"Magic?" Roxaine exclaimed. "Is that your excuse, now? Another lie to—"

"Gag her!" Steward bellowed. "Stop her voice before she curses us all!"

The baronsman jerked her head back. Twisting and kicking, she fought him. Raven launched herself at the man, butting his stomach. He went down on his knees, but the others jumped in: the huntsboy, Carpenter, baronsmen, stablers—it took all of them to subdue Raven and her mother. And in the press, her mother whispered, "Change! Fly if you can!"

Then they pulled the two of them apart and gagged Roxaine.

When it was finally done, they were no longer alone. A throng of people ringed them, watching in silence. House servants and scullions, workers from barn and wharf. Bondservants and wagehands. Phillipe was at the very front, flanked by Borly and Kurl. Others were still coming, from the cutting house and fields. They spilled through the gate and crowded the edges of the courtyard.

Raven's heart soared. "What now, child thief? You can't gag them all."

Steward smiled meanly, then composed his face and turned to the crowd.

"People!" he called. "I have called you here to see justice done. This woman and her daughter, witch and mage, have used their talents for evil." He pointed to Roxaine. "She to enchant our good, late Baron, to win his affection, only to bring him poison, sickness, and death." He pointed to Raven. "Her daughter, already a runaway, to steal a boy from our barns, turn him to a fanged beast, and use him to help her mother escape from the prison quarry of our neighbor, Baron Stoner."

"Lies!" Raven cried. "The dung-sucking child thief is—"

Hands went over her mouth. Three men grabbed her arms and head. In a moment, she was gagged like her mother.

"You heard how she thinks," Steward said to the crowd. "Child thieving is exactly what they came for: to steal Cutter's heir. To kidnap the young Baron of our river, to take her to their mage cronies on the high reach, to demand who knows what ransom."

The crowd listened in dead silence. Phillipe's eyes blazed. Borly and Kurl gripped his arms tightly.

"They are shape shifters and word witches," Steward went on. "They eluded my son and this man, Stoner's huntsman. They attacked them with beak and claw. They are too slippery to cage, too dangerous to allow to run loose. There is one punishment only that will make us safe and bring justice for the death of our Baron. Watch now, and remember how we deal with incorrigibles such as these." He turned to the guards. "Take them up," he ordered.

There were two ropes now, and a single plank had been set on sawhorses beneath them. Raven and her mother were marched over and lifted onto it. A baronsman went up the ladder, set a noose around Mam's neck, and tightened it.

"Steward." Phillipe pulled free of Borly and Kurl and hobbled forward. "What have you done with my son?"

Steward turned, startled. He glared when he saw who had spoken. "Your son, the runaway? What of him?"

"You said they stole him and turned him to a fanged beast. You said they used him. If that's so, he can't be a runaway."

"Don't bandy words with me, Breeder," Steward growled. "He was their companion and accomplice."

"Where is he, then?" Phillipe demanded. "Have you hanged him already? A mere child?"

"That mere child is a beast mage! A wildcat, and who knows what else!"

"You said the girl changed him to a beast. Is he the mage, or she?"

As Steward sputtered an answer, Raven blessed Phillipe and focused her thoughts on her hands. She had to get them free. She began the words to her spell, slowly, silently, visualizing the gestures while holding herself completely still. She concentrated on her hands and wrists alone. On wings, slender wings. She felt the change start throughout her body: the prickling in her skin, the stretching in her face, the contraction in her bones. She fought it, all but her shrinking wrists and hands. It hurt. The bones ground. The muscles pulled, protesting as she held them back from changing. She bit down on the gag.

The thong loosened. She felt blood pulse into her hands. The skin burned. Feathers began to form—she could feel them, smooth and slippery.

"Where is my son?" Phillipe demanded, his quiet voice lifting above Steward's bluster.

As if in answer, the belling of hounds sounded in the distance.

"There!" Steward replied, with a broad wave. "He came as a beast, so we set the beasts on him. Hunter and his hounds have harried him all night, and now that they've returned, he can join his witches on the gibbet. If he's still alive!"

Phillipe blanched. He turned to stare out the gate, leaning weakly on his cane. Everyone's eyes followed his.

The hounds belled again; then in they came, a fluid mass of brown, black, and tan, sleek fur glistening. At their head ran a giant wildcat, and in their midst lumbered the huge bull Mangle, bearing a rider. The crowd pulled back as the pack moved to the center of the courtyard. Mangle glared around him. The wet nurse slid from his back and stood frozen in the midst of the milling hounds, clutching a bundle to her chest. From the bundle came the cry of a child.

Raven bit down harder, whispering the spell around her gag. The thong slid lower. She let more feathers form on her wrists. Her scalp burned. With a sudden jerk, she wrenched her hands free and stopped the spell. She yanked at the knot on her gag, but her hands were half wingtips. The baronsman, still on his ladder, gave a shout and grabbed at her. She kicked the ladder, and it slid along the beam. The baronsman clutched the rungs. She kicked again, and the ladder toppled sideways with a crash.

"Stop her!" Steward bellowed.

The baby wailed. Mam cried something through her gag. Raven's hands were finally normal again, and she untied the cloth from her mother's mouth.

"Sarita!" Mam cried. "That's my baby!"

"What are you doing here?" Steward yelled at the wet nurse. "Grab her!"

The girl cowered against Mangle's flank. The big bull snorted and pawed the ground. His eyes blazed. He took a step toward Steward.

"Shoot it!" Steward cried. The crowd scrambled away.

Seeker raised his firearm and aimed at Mangle. Hero leaped to the bull's back and yowled a challenge.

"Not the bull!" Steward cried. "Shoot the cat!"

Seeker raised his aim.

"No!" Phillipe lurched through the pack to stand between Seeker and his son.

Raven tore the gag from her mouth. With hands and voice together, she reversed the spell on Hero. Before the eyes of the startled crowd, the wildcat became a boy.

"Don't shoot!" a woman cried. "He's just a child!"

Hero glared at Raven; then he stood tall on Mangle's broad shoulders and pointed at Steward.

"He tried to drown her!" he cried, his young voice clear above the babbling crowd. Everyone stilled, even Sarita. Seeker reluctantly lowered his weapon. "We got to the boat just in time! His son threw her into the river!"

Steward went pale as ice. Then his color returned in a red flush. "That's preposterous!" he bellowed. "The boy is their accomplice. You can't believe him."

"What about her?" Roxaine yelled. "You, nurse! What did they do to my daughter?"

The woman clutched Sarita even more tightly, as though the baby could shield her from all the staring eyes. "It—it's true," she stammered, so low Raven could hardly hear her. "Young Steward was about to throw her in." She glanced at Hero. "He . . . the wildcat . . . he and the dogs came and saved her."

The courtyard filled with hubbub. In the midst of it, Loyal Steward stumbled through the gate at a broken trot. The people pushed back as if he were another bull. He slowed as he noticed the crowd. His eyes fell on Roxaine and Raven up on the plank. He took in the ropes and lurched to a stop, panting. Then he saw his father. His face went dead white.

"Father." He gasped for breath. "Father, I—"

"You worthless idiot!" Jan Steward shouted. "I sent you to guard the child. A baby! A helpless infant! You couldn't even keep her safe from a wild beast. A dumb animal has more sense than you!"

Loyal stared at him, still panting. His mouth drew back, as if he were about to cry. Then he bared his teeth in a snarl. His face went as red as his father's. With a single stride, he reached Seeker and wrenched the firearm from his hands. Spinning on his heel, he aimed the weapon at Hero.

Raven cried out. A dozen others did, too. People threw themselves back. Seeker grabbed for the barrel. Loyal clubbed him with the butt and took a new aim. At Roxaine.

Raven jumped in front; Roxaine dove sideways. They collided, and the plank tipped from the sawhorses. They tumbled. Raven hit the ground hard. Her mother jerked short, legs kicking the air. The noose was still around her neck.

Raven staggered to her feet and grabbed at Mam's legs. A foot struck her nose. She fell back, scrambled up again, forced her shoulders under her mother's flailing feet, taking the weight off the noose. Mam swayed. Raven stumbled right and left. With a hoarse growl of rage, Jan Steward charged her and tried to knock her down. Her bad shoulder tore. She kicked out blindly and drove her knee into Steward's groin. He bent double with a shrill cough. She heard Mangle bellow, voices cry. She blinked the tears from her eyes.

Loyal Steward was staring right at her. He took aim toward her mother, then down at Raven, then back up, as though not sure which target gave him more pleasure. He settled on Raven. He smiled.

Not again, Raven thought.

Her mother kicked at her, choking out two words: "Fly, Daughter!"

Raven gripped her ankles, refusing to move.

Jan Steward tried to straighten. He pawed at her legs, hauling himself erect. "Shoot, you sniveling dolt!" he gasped. "Shoot her!"

At the edge of her vision, Raven saw Mangle lumber toward Loyal, but too slowly. Hero launched himself from the bull's back, changing as he moved. In midair he went from boy to cat. And bigger, flowing in the instant of his arc to a long, muscled panther. His paws swept at Loyal. Loyal shifted his aim a last time.

Raven heard the shot.

Twenty-nine

Raven woke. Everything was silent, the room dark. She sat up. Faint light glowed through the window. Outside, a warbler began to sing, its simple trill lifting through the dawn. Another bird joined in, and soon a chorus sang to her.

Not a bad way to go, she thought.

Moving quietly, she slipped from the bed and went to the window. The eastern sky was a haze of spun gold. The air was cool but fresh. As she turned back toward the room, she noticed her reflection in the windowpane. She touched the pebbled scars on her cheek.

Thank the mages it was birdshot, she thought, not for the first time. And thank them again for Hero. Her scars were nothing compared to the claw marks Loyal Steward bore, from just one blow from Hero's broad paw. She frowned, remembering her last glimpse of young Steward's finger tightening on the trigger. At just that moment, he had shifted his aim. At his father. Jan Steward had taken the brunt of the shot. He was blind in one eye now, his jaw shattered, an ear gone.

Raven studied her marked face. She flexed her hand. The shot had also broken her wrist, along with her mother's ankle, which she'd been holding. Mam would probably limp a bit for the rest of her life. And speak in a husky voice. It would have been much worse if Borly and Kurl hadn't cut her down so quickly. As for Raven . . .

She stretched her arm, from shoulder to hand. She was completely healed. It was time to leave.

She took off her nightshirt and put on a shift. She had practiced changing many times while she healed, but she still couldn't transform more cloth than this. Well, it had always been enough before. When it was cold, she'd stay a raven. She went to the window, pushed it wide, and drew in a deep breath. She glanced down. She fought the urge to change right now and launch herself from the sill. Her arm was healed but still weak.

Raven grinned wryly. I must have picked up a little caution along with the birdshot, she thought. Besides, she wanted—needed—to say goodbye. She closed the window and went out the door.

Sarita's room was just across the hall. Raven crossed to her sister's bed and studied her fondly. "Goodbye, chick," she said. "Take care of Mam for me."

Sarita studied her back.

"Mages save us," Raven said. "Don't frown like that! It's not like I want to go. It's for Hero: He needs to get to the high reach. He's got so much to learn, much more than I can teach him here." She smiled wryly. "And I've got a lot to learn, myself." Sarita's brow wrinkled. Her lip quivered. "None of that, grub," Raven said. "You know I'd stay if I could. Come here. Give me a kiss."

She lifted Sarita from the bed and hugged her close. Sarita made a pleased little gurgle. Raven's arm went warm and wet.

"You little . . ."

At that moment, Louella walked in. "Oh, dear," she said. She reached for Sarita.

"No, I'll do it," Raven told her.

She laid Sarita on the changing table and began untying the soaked diaper. Her sister smiled.

"That's better," Raven said. "Now you don't look so much like your father."

When Raven got downstairs, she heard the faint clatter of pots and pans from the manor kitchen. There were no other sounds. The entire estate seemed calmer since the Council had formally named her mother as Sarita's guardian. Steward had tried to fight it, of course, despite the wet nurse's testimony. That was all the doing of my worthless son, he'd said. But Raven had finally remembered Squint's vision, and the fat seer had testified. More, he'd remembered a phrase from his vision: "It lurks outside your notice, hidden from sight . . . beside the spread of dark reckonings." They had searched the parlor again, and then Cutter's bedroom. The bond receipt was there, neatly folded between the pages of a book in a small bookcase beside the bed. Roxaine herself remembered putting the book away when he'd fallen ill so suddenly. It was a book of poetry; the receipt was tucked in beside a sonnet about marriage. It was signed by Cutter, of course, so the Council had to acknowledge that Roxaine was no longer a bondservant.

Even then, they might have refused to grant her guardianship but for one more thing: Loyal Steward testified against his father. The story of the burned will and the bargain with Stoner spread quickly all along the middle reach. The Council had no choice then. This was an out-and-out crime. They couldn't possibly hand Sarita over to Steward. Grudgingly, they named Roxaine the guardian of the River Slow. And the first thing Mam had done as guardian was forgive the bond on every servant in the Slow valley. Steward had gone purple.

Raven frowned. The Barons hadn't liked it either. Perhaps to rebuke her mother, their punishment for Steward had been banishment rather than prison. Even Loyal Steward had gone free. In her opinion, the whole poxy family deserved a year or two in Stoner's quarry. Instead, they were Stoner's guests. Stoner had claimed that Steward had lied to him, that he'd had no idea Roxaine was the heir's mother, and so on and so forth, each word more coated with crud than the next, but he still gave them haven on his river. Where father and son had to live with each other, and perhaps that was the worst punishment either could imagine.

Still, Raven thought, if I were on the Council . . .

Kah! She had no desire to be on the Council. Mam was welcome to it.

She found her mother in the steward's office. She had chosen to work there instead of Cutter's parlor. "That will be Sarita's room," she'd said.

Mam looked up from the ledger she'd been studying and eyed Raven's shift. "You're not going out in that, are you?" she asked.

"It's all I'll need," Raven replied.

Mam sighed. "So today's really the day."

Raven shrugged. "Hero would shred the curtains if we put it off any longer."

Mam smiled. "I doubt that, but you're right that he'd set up a howl."

She rose and came forward, arms outstretched. Raven returned her tight embrace.

"I almost wish I could go with you," Mam said.

"I wish you could, too," Raven replied. "You'd have to fly, though."

Mam stepped back and studied Raven closely. "And how about you? Is that arm really ready for flying? Wrist and shoulder?"

"I was just going out to test it, worrywart. Would you like to come?"

"Pah! You don't want your bossy old mother along."

"No, Mam, I do. I really do."

Mam glanced at the perch in the corner of her office. Cutter's parrot was watching them, head cocked, one beady red eye gleaming. It winked.

"All right," Mam said. "Since you asked. But make me a raven."

"Pet her! Hug her! That's a pretty girl!" the parrot squawked.

The change was quick and easy, for both of them. Raven stretched her wings, feeling for any pain. There was none. With a happy croak, she leaped into the air. Harder and harder she stroked, pushing her way aloft. Over the wall, the cedars, the manor. Feeling the air stir as the sun burst above the horizon and began to warm the land. She found a faint updraft and arched her wings, letting the current lift her. Up and up she went, with Mam right behind, till the estate was laid out like a map far below. Raven was no warbler, but she chortled a song to flying, and it was beautiful.

They flew together for an hour at least, swooping and soaring and playing tag with swallows over the river. Finally, they returned to the manor, landing by the little bench in the side yard. Raven changed herself, then Mam. They smiled at each other.

"I actually think I could learn to like that," Mam said.

"I'll be back," Raven said.

"Just don't make it four years."

"Not this time. I have to keep watch on my little sister."

Mam made a mock frown. "Are you questioning my abilities as a mother?"

Raven frowned back. "Look what you did with the first one."

"Just awful," Mam agreed. Then her frown broke, and she took Raven in her arms again. "You come back soon, Raven," she said. Her tears wet Raven's cheek.

Raven nodded, blinking back a few tears of her own.

Finally, they stepped apart.

"Be safe," Mam said.

"I will," Raven replied. "Take care of Sarita. And remember: Don't you ever call her Pigeon. They're so stupid."

"Never!" Mam promised.

They laughed.

Raven changed then and launched herself into the air. Her mother waved. Raven dipped her wings and soared toward the farm.

Hero and Phillipe were waiting outside the breeding barn. Raven landed beside them.

"Ready?" she croaked.

"In a minute," Hero said. He stood awkwardly, then grabbed his father in a fierce hug, pressing his face into Phillipe's chest. Phillipe looked surprised.

"Are you sure about this?" Raven asked.

Hero nodded, but he kept his face pressed against his father.

"Because you don't have to come," Raven said. "It's all right. I'm used to being on my own." Even as she said it, Raven felt a tight knot of disappointment squeeze her heart. She was dismayed by how lonely she felt at the mere possibility that he might not come.

Hero turned toward her. "Don't you want me to?" he asked.

"Of course I do!" she croaked. "How else are you going to learn anything about being a mage? Besides," she added, "I'm not happy if I don't have someone to complain to."

He grinned. "Or about."

"You're good for that, at least."

Hero gave his father a last, quick hug and slipped off his outer clothes. Phillipe took them solemnly. Raven noticed the tears sheening his eyes, but he held them in. She turned her attention to Hero, now waiting impatiently. Closing her eyes, she concentrated on the spell, moving her wings through the gestures.

This was something else she had been practicing—speaking spells while in her raven form—and she still had to be very careful. But it worked. Hero's dark fur shone. His amber eyes gleamed. He rumbled a deep growl of pleasure; he loved being a panther. He had been able to change himself only the one time, just as Raven had never been able to repeat her change from one bird directly to another. Neither of them could remember what they had done in the heat of the moment. But they knew it could be done and were determined to learn how, even though it meant leaving home for the high reach, where magic was stronger.

Phillipe knelt and placed a hand on Hero's shoulder. "Walk in strength, Son."

Hero rumbled a reply and pressed his nose to his father's.

Phillipe pushed himself up with his cane. "Take care of him," he said to Raven.

"I'll do my best," she promised, "but he has a mind of his own."

Phillipe smiled. "Don't I know it."

Hero growled and turned toward the open fields.

"Right, right," Raven croaked. "I'm coming."

She flapped to Phillipe's shoulder and brushed his cheek, then leaped into the air. Winging hard, she swooped past Hero's head.

"Let's go, Fur Brain!"

He let out a happy roar and broke into a smooth lope beneath her. A-wing and a-foot, they left the barns behind, slipped through the windbreak, and raced upriver through the brightening day.